THE MIDWIFE'S REMEDY

AMELIA FROST

BLACK SWAN
DIGITAL

FOREWORD

This novel is a work of fiction, but its roots are buried in truth.

Between 1914 and 1929, in the small Hungarian village of Nagyrev, a series of mysterious deaths occurred. Deaths that would later be uncovered as one of the most shocking cases in European history.

The perpetrators were not criminals in the traditional sense. They were not soldiers, bandits, or men of war. They were something else entirely.

And they would come to be known as the Angel Makers of Nagyrev ...

PROLOGUE

I had seen death before, but never like this.

Never so deliberate. Never so quiet.

They had built the gallows in the prison courtyard, just beyond the stone archway where the condemned were led one by one. The wooden beams loomed against the gray sky, weathered and unremarkable, like they had stood there for centuries, waiting.

The executioner moved with the slow patience of someone who had done this many, many times before. He adjusted the rope, tested the knot, checked the drop beneath the platform. It was all routine. Precise. Empty of emotion.

The condemned woman stood with her hands bound in front of her, her wrists chafed raw from the iron cuffs that had been removed only moments ago. Her hair had come loose from its braid, strands falling over her face. The hem of her dress was dirt-streaked and stiff with dried blood.

She was calm. That was the worst part. The guards had expected screaming. Crying. Pleading. But she gave them nothing. No struggle. No words. She simply stood there, waiting.

A priest murmured a final blessing beside her, but she did not bow her head. Her eyes were on me. She smiled. I could not move. The cold air clawed at my skin, but I barely felt it. I had not meant to come here. I had not meant to watch. But some endings are owed witnesses.

She had asked for me. The request had arrived in the form of a small, folded letter, slipped between the bars of my window in the night. No name. No signature. Just one line, written in a hand I knew too well:

Come. I want you to see.

So, I had come. And I was seeing.

She stood upon the gallows, her hands as steady as they had always been. I thought of those hands, how many lives they had brought into the world. How many they had taken away. The noose was fitted around her throat. The wood beneath her feet creaked. Still, she smiled.

I should not have been here. I should have left Nagyrev long ago. I should have taken the train far from the village, far from the river that had swallowed so many secrets. I should have buried the past with the bodies in the churchyard.

But here I was. Because no one leaves Nagyrev. Not really.

The judge had called her a monster. The newspapers called her, "The Angel Maker."

They wrote about men who had died coughing blood, their breath rattling wetly in their lungs, their skin yellowing with poison. They counted the dead. At least fifty, perhaps more. They called it a mass execution, carried out by women with steady hands and empty hearts. But they did not know the truth. They did not know how it began.

The first man had deserved it. That is what we told ourselves, at least. That is what we whispered to each other when the nights were long and our hands still smelled of vinegar and lye, when the bodies were newly buried and the air had not yet cleared of the scent of sickness.

He had beaten his wife so badly she lost three children before they ever took a breath. And so, she had been given something. A gift. A cure. A way out. He died coughing blood into his hands. And after that, the others came.

A woman whose husband locked her in the cellar for days at a time. A girl whose father left bruises on her throat. A mother whose son had turned into the same kind of man as his father.

One by one, they came. And one by one, they died.

At first, it was justice. Then it was mercy. Then it was something else entirely. They thought I was one of them. Perhaps I had been. Perhaps I still was.

When the magistrate came, when the bodies were exhumed, lined up, studied for poison, I stayed silent. When the arrests began, when she was dragged from her house in the dead of night, I did not speak. When they fitted the rope around her throat and waited for someone to weep for her, I did nothing.

The executioner pulled the lever. The floor beneath her feet vanished. For a moment, she did not fall. She hung there, suspended between life and death, between the world she had created and the one that would erase her. There was only the sound of the wind threading through the leafless trees, whistling through the stone archways.

I had seen it. And now, I could never unsee it.

Years from now, when the last of us are gone, when the village has been swallowed by dust and history, when the bodies in the churchyard are nothing but bone and dirt, what will they say about us?

They will say that we were monsters. They will say that we were killers, that we did not weep for the men who died in their beds. They will write books about us. They will use words like:

"unnatural", "vile", "inhuman". They will remember our names not as wives or daughters or healers, but as poisoners.

But they will not remember the men who made us this way. They never do.

1

THE GIRL FROM NAGYREV

I was born in Nagyrev, and I will die in Nagyrev.

Our family has always been here. Our name is stitched into the history of this village, buried beneath the roots of the trees, carved into the headstones in the churchyard, whispered in prayers and curses alike.

My mother used to say that there is no world beyond the river. Not for people like us. And for a long time, I believed her.

I do not remember my father. Not really.

I remember the shape of him, the way he stood tall in the doorway when he came in from the fields, the scent of earth and sweat and tobacco clinging to his clothes. I remember the scratch of his stubble against my cheek when he kissed me goodnight, the low rumble of his voice as he spoke to my mother across the table after I had gone to bed.

And I remember the day he left.

The war had already begun, though I had not understood what it meant. The village had been filled with soldiers that summer: men on horseback, uniforms stiff with sweat, boots caked in mud from places far beyond our quiet fields. They had gone from house to house, reading names from a list, calling men forward with no more ceremony than if they were cattle being sent to slaughter.

My father packed his things. My mother did not cry. I think even then, she knew he was never coming back.

He wrote for the first year. Short letters, simple words, sentences stripped of warmth. My mother kept them folded beneath the mattress, pulling them out at night when she thought I was sleeping. Then the letters stopped. And that was the end of it.

There was no grave for us to visit. No body to mourn. Just an absence that grew larger every year. My mother never remarried. I think she knew better than to place herself under the rule of another man.

She was a woman of few words and quick hands. She knew how to knead dough, how to set a broken bone, how to wring a chicken's neck in a single twist. She was the kind of woman who could survive any hardship, but never without a cost.

She never spoke about love. She spoke about work, about duty, about survival.

"The world does not give to women," she told me once. "It only takes. And so, you must learn how to take, too."

I never knew if she was speaking from experience or warning. Maybe both.

I had a younger brother once. His name was István. He was small and sickly, born in the middle of a cruel winter, when the river was coated with ice and the ground was too hard to dig graves. He did not survive his second year.

I do not remember much about him, but I remember the way my mother held him, the way she pressed his tiny body against her breast even after he had gone still. We never spoke of him after that. My mother carried on as if he had never existed.

But on cold nights, I would sometimes hear her whispering his name.

Our house was small. One room, one table, one bed. The roof sagged; the walls leaned with the wind. The fire never fully died, but the cold still found ways to creep in through the cracks.

The shelves were lined with jars of dried herbs, bundles of garlic hanging from the rafters to ward off sickness and bad spirits. My mother kept a crucifix above the doorway, though she never prayed out loud. We were not godless, but we were not devoted either.

"Faith does not keep a body warm," my mother would say when the priest came knocking, asking why we had not been to Mass. "Faith does not feed an empty belly."

Still, I was baptized. Still, I wore a rosary around my neck.

One must be careful with God. It was better to keep Him close, just in case.

There was little to do in the village, so I learned to pass the time in other ways. I spent my days at the well, listening to the whispers of the women, their stories folded into the sound of splashing water. I learned which men drank too much, which women flinched when their husbands spoke, how to watch without being seen. And I learned how to listen without being noticed.

The war ended when I was thirteen. The men came home in pieces. Some with missing limbs, some with eyes that looked straight through you, as if they had left something behind on the battlefield that they could never get back.

Not all of them returned. Some had died far away, buried in places we would never see, their names written in ink on telegrams that arrived months too late. Others simply disappeared. My father being one of them.

The village was not the same after the war. The women had

been in charge for too long. They had learned how to live without their husbands, and some of them had no interest in going back. But the men wanted everything to be as it was before. They drank more. They hit harder. And when the bruises reappeared, the whispers at the well changed.

No more stories of hunger. No more stories of waiting. Only words spoken in careful, measured tones:

"She can help."

"Go to her."

"Zsuzsanna knows how to fix any problem."

I was fourteen the first time I heard my mother say her name in that way. A name that was not a person, but a solution. A name that was not a woman, but a force.

Zsuzsanna Sárkány. The midwife of Nagyrev. And soon to be my teacher.

Nagyrev was a small place. A village too small for maps, too unimportant for kings, too distant for wars to touch directly. It sat in the heart of the Great Hungarian Plain, where the land stretched flat and endless, a sea of wheat and barley swaying beneath the wind. The river Tisza moved close by, its dark waters winding through marshes and reed beds, slow-moving, treacherous beneath its calm surface.

There were no stone buildings, no grand estates, no cobbled streets. Just houses made of wood and clay, their roofs thatched with straw, their doors worn smooth by years of use. The village had one church, one tavern, one square where the men gathered. A place where people were born, lived, and died without ever setting foot beyond the horizon.

"The world does not need us," my mother had once said. "And we do not need the world."

There were fewer than three hundred of us in Nagyrev. Everyone knew everyone. There were no strangers, only people you had known since birth. The same faces, the same voices, the same routines repeated every day, every season, every year.

Children played in the fields, chasing one another between rows of wheat taller than they were. Women worked the ovens, kneading dough with strong hands, stirring stews that filled the air with the scent of paprika and smoke.

The men—the ones who still lived—worked the land, their backs bent, their skin leathered from the sun.

It was a place of simplicity: of work, of tradition. And of secrets.

The land was both kind and cruel. The summers were hot and dry, the sky stretched vast and pale, so open it felt like it might swallow you whole. The winters were brutal, the wind cutting through the houses, slipping through the cracks in the walls, creeping beneath the blankets at night.

I had watched livestock freeze to death in the fields. I had seen men fall through the ice of the river, their bodies swallowed by the black water, never found again. I had felt the hunger of a poor harvest, when the bread grew thinner, when the stews had more water than meat, when the priest's prayers for mercy went unanswered.

It was a place that did not forgive weakness. And yet, it was home.

Beyond Nagyrev, there were other villages, but none that mattered to us.

To the west was Tiszafüred, larger, wealthier, where people wore coats with buttons that shone in the sun and boots that did not leak in the rain. To the north was Szolnok, a place of markets and trains, where the world felt bigger, where the war had been felt more keenly, where soldiers passed through on their way to the front and never returned.

But Nagyrev remained the same. Unchanged. Forgotten.

Except by those who knew its secrets and those who buried them.

I had always thought I would die in Nagyrev. That I would marry one of the village boys, bear children, tend a home that looked like the one I had been raised in. But now my path had changed and I would not die the way I had imagined.

2

THE ORPHAN OF NAGYREV

I was not born yet when Zsuzsanna Sárkány came to live in Nagyrev, but there was no part of her story I had not heard by the time I was old enough to understand whispers.

Some of the old women claimed she had been left in the woods as a baby, found swaddled in a bloodstained blanket beneath the twisted roots of an elm tree. Others said she was the bastard child of a nobleman's affair, abandoned to die but rescued by the hands of fate.

But the truth was simpler.

She had been born like all of us, into dirt and struggle, her mother a healer-woman who knew too much: who gathered roots and crushed them into pastes, who whispered charms over women's bellies to make sure they would not quicken with child.

And that, I think, is where it all began. With a woman who knew things she should not have known.

Zsuzsanna's mother, by all accounts, was a fearsome woman. She did not kneel in church, did not speak sweetly to men, did not turn her eyes downward when the village priest passed by. She carried herself with the sharp confidence of someone who had no need to apologize for her existence.

And for a while, the village tolerated her, because she was useful. She cured fevers. She delivered babies in the dead of night. She set broken bones with hands that were sure and steady. She gave the women what they needed when they could not take it for themselves.

But usefulness only goes so far. It only takes one mistake. One man, too rich, too important, found dead in his bed. They said it was her. They said she had slipped something into his wine, that she had whispered a curse over his name. And one morning, she was gone.

The village did not speak of what had happened to her.

Some said she had fled into the woods, that she had known what was coming and ran before they could tie a rope around her throat. Others swore she had been dragged from her house in the middle of the night, her body dumped into the river, swallowed by the black, endless current of the Tisza.

But the only truth that mattered was that she left a child behind. Zsuzsanna was twelve when her mother disappeared. A girl without a home, without protection, without a name anyone wanted to say out loud.

The midwife, Borbála, took her in, but not out of kindness. Borbála was old, tired, and needed hands that still had strength. She gave Zsuzsanna a corner of the house to sleep in, a thin blanket, and a bowl of soup in exchange for work. So she worked.

She fetched water from the well at dawn, her arms aching from carrying the buckets up the dirt path, the wooden handles rubbing blisters into her palms. She cleaned linens soaked in the blood of childbirth, her hands raw from scrubbing. She ground herbs into powders, her fingertips stained green and brown, the bitter scent clinging to her skin no matter how much she washed.

She learned quickly. She watched Borbála's hands: how they moved, how they soothed, how they commanded.

She saw how the women came to her in secret, how they whispered in hushed voices when the priest was not looking, how they placed coins in her palm for medicines their husbands would never approve of.

She saw what happened when there was no help. She saw women bleed out in the dark, alone. She saw the way men laughed when their wives cried that they could not carry another child. And slowly, the village began to forget who she had been before. She was no longer the daughter of a dead woman. She was something useful. And in Nagyrev, that was the only thing that kept a woman alive.

By the time I was born, Zsuzsanna was already the midwife. She had taken Borbála's place long before the old woman died, had become a figure as fixed in the village as the well, as the church, as the river itself.

She knew every birth. Every death. She had delivered every child in the village, had placed them in their mothers' arms, had whispered to them in their first moments of life. And yet, she had never had children of her own.

Some said she was cursed. That the sins of her mother had carried on, that God had closed her womb as punishment. Others said she had done it to herself. That she had used her own medicines. That she had chosen her freedom.

And if that was true—if Zsuzsanna Sárkány had looked at the world as it was, at the lives women were forced to live, and decided that she would not bring another girl into it—then I think she was the only one of us who was truly free.

The women respected her. The men tolerated her. And the priest, he feared her. He never said it outright, of course. But I remember the way he looked at her when she passed, his lips pressing into a thin, bloodless line, his fingers twitching at his rosary beads.

He knew what we all knew, what we never spoke aloud. That some women are not meant to be tamed. That some women do not kneel. And that Zsuzsanna Sárkány was one of them.

She married once, a butcher's son. His name was László, though no one spoke it anymore. At first, he was merely indifferent. He did not care what she did, so long as there was food on the table, so long as she did not embarrass him in front of the other men. But over time, the resentment grew. She was more respected than he was. She was needed. And men do not like a woman who does not need them.

The first time he hit her, she did not cry. The second time, she did not flinch.

The last time, he died.

Some people in the village said he had been sick. That he had caught a fever from a slaughtered pig, that his insides had rotted away. Others said it had been her. That she had stirred something into his soup, something no one could trace.

But no one asked too many questions. Because in the weeks after he was buried, Zsuzsanna looked brighter. Lighter. And she was still needed. She had learned the most important lesson of all.

That sometimes, a woman must take her life into her own hands. And sometimes, she must do it quietly.

3

THE MAKING OF A MIDWIFE

There were no roads out of Nagyrev.

Not real ones, anyway. There was the dirt path that led to the river, the thin, winding tracks that disappeared into the marshes, the trails that men took when they drove their carts to market. But there were no roads that led to places beyond what we knew, beyond the fields and the forests and the quiet, forgotten corners of the world where women like us lived and died.

Zsuzsanna Sárkány never left Nagyrev. Not once. And yet, she knew more of the world than most of the men who had ridden through the village, claiming to be scholars, soldiers, priests.

She had seen everything. She had seen life enter the world in the darkest corners of houses lit only by soft candlelight. She had seen women arch their backs in pain, their fingers clawing at the sheets, teeth gritted against the unbearable force tearing through their bodies. She had seen them cry out for mercy, for death, for salvation––and she had seen them go quiet when they realized there was nothing left to do but bear it.

She had watched death creep into the room without a

sound, cold and patient. The kind of death that waited until the screams had stopped, until the sweat on a woman's brow turned clammy, until her breath came in shallow gasps, until her grip went limp, until the child, bloody and mewling, was placed in another woman's arms while the mother lay still, unmoving.

She had witness women survive labor only to die days later, taken by fevers that no prayers could cure. She had seen men pace outside their homes while their wives suffered inside, pretending to care, pretending to worry, even as they drank and joked among themselves, as though their wives were nothing more than cattle waiting to calve.

She had seen what men never saw. What they never cared to see. The pain. The blood. The sheer will of survival.

She learned from Borbála which herbs could coax a stubborn child from the womb and which ones could end a pregnancy before it ever took root. She learned to place her ear against a woman's belly and listen; for life, or no life. She learned when to speak softly, when to be firm, when to tell the truth, and when to lie.

She learned something else too. Something more important. She learned that the world was not kind to women.

It did not care for their suffering, their sacrifice, the ways they bent themselves into unnatural shapes to survive. It did not care when they bore child after child, bleeding and breaking beneath the weight of it. It did not care if they lived or died. And so, Zsuzsanna decided she would not care for it either.

By the time she was fifteen, she had seen more births than most women would in their lifetime. She had seen children slip from the womb too early, their tiny fingers twisted like dried flowers, their skin blue and cold before their mothers ever got to hold them. She had seen babies born healthy, their cries loud and strong, only to be buried weeks later after a cough took them in the night.

She knew what happened when there was no midwife, no healer, no hands that knew how to stop the bleeding, how to stitch a torn body back together. And she had seen what happened when there was no help at all.

She had heard the whispers, the ones about the women who drowned their newborns in the river, the ones who left their infants in the woods when no one was looking. She had watched as mothers with too many mouths to feed wept into their hands, cursing the lives they had been given, cursing the God who had made them into nothing more than vessels for suffering.

And for all the life she had delivered into the world, there was something else she had learned.

How to stop it before it began.

She took over from Borbála before the old woman was even dead. Borbála had grown weak with age, her hands stiff, her eyes blurred, her movements slow. It was Zsuzsanna who did the real work, who the women trusted. It was her they called for in the middle of the night, when the pains came too soon, when the bleeding wouldn't stop, when the prayers they whispered into the dark went unanswered.

And when Borbála finally died, no one questioned who would take her place. She had earned it. Even the men did not argue because they needed her too.

When their sons were born, when their wives fell ill, when their bones broke from accidents in the fields, it was her hands that kept them alive. But usefulness was not the same as acceptance.

They tolerated her. They watched her. The priest warned her not to overstep. She never answered him, she only smiled. And that, I think, was the moment he began to fear her.

The women relied on her for more than just childbirth. She set broken bones, pulled rotting teeth, boiled willow bark to ease fevers. She carried a pouch of dried herbs at all times, tied at her hip, the scent of lavender and wormwood clinging to her clothes. But she was more than a healer. She was a keeper of secrets.

She knew which men drank away the money meant for their families. She knew which women were bruised beneath their clothes, which ones flinched when their husbands raised a hand too quickly. She knew which girls had been forced into dark corners, which ones had wept into their pillows at night, praying they would not feel the first sickness of a growing child.

She knew who had tried to drown their newborns in the river when no one was watching. She knew whose sons weren't really their husbands'. She knew everything. Because the village whispered to her. And Zsuzsanna Sárkány listened.

For years, she was simply the midwife. She did not yet hold the kind of power that would come later. But she was watching. And she was learning. She was waiting. And one day, when the time was right, she would decide how to use what she knew.

~

Zsuzsanna was twenty-three when they told her she had to marry. It was not a suggestion. By then, she had been the village midwife for two years. She had taken over Borbála's place with quiet certainty, had built something of a life for herself: a life she did not have to share, a life that was hers alone.

But women were not meant to live alone. Not for long.

At first, it was whispered: why hadn't she married? She was not ugly, not crippled, not poor. She was clever, steady-handed, respected, a woman who had earned her place among them.

But she had no father, no brothers, no man to speak for her. And that, the village decided, was unnatural.

She refused the first offers.

The older women came to her, smiling, coaxing, telling her she needed a husband to protect her. The priest took her aside after Sunday mass, his voice revealing feigned patience as he told her it was not proper for a woman to live without a man. She ignored them all.

For a while, it seemed as though she might win. But the village did not like women who refused to be controlled. The pressure grew. The men began to watch her differently. Not with curiosity, but with suspicion.

And when a cow was found dead in its pasture one morning, its mouth foaming, its eyes black and bulging, they muttered her name. When a fever spread through the village that winter, taking three children with it, they looked at her hands. When a woman miscarried in the dead of night, the child still and blue before it ever drew breath, they whispered: perhaps the midwife willed it so.

She understood, then, what her mother must have felt. The slow turning of the tide. The moment when usefulness was no longer enough. She would not give them a reason to cast her out. She would not make the same mistake. And so, when they told her she would marry László Barta, the butcher's son, she said yes.

The wedding was held in the church at the center of the village. It was a gray, stone thing, hunched against the wind, its walls coated with mold and soot. Inside, the air smelled of melted tallow, moldy wood, and stale incense. The pews, carved long ago by hands that were long since buried, were darkened from generations of bodies pressing against them.

The altar was bare except for a single iron cross, rust blooming in its corners. A handful of candles moved against the gloom, their wax dripping in uneven streams.

It was winter. The ground outside was frozen, the river solid enough to hold a horse's load. The trees stood stark and bare, their branches brittle against the sky.

Zsuzsanna's dress was plain, a simple white linen, borrowed from a widow whose husband had died the spring before. She had stitched fresh lace to the sleeves to hide where the fabric had thinned, and the hem had been let down to suit her height, though it still fell just shy of the floor.

The women had woven dried rosemary and lavender into her hair; not for beauty, but for protection. To ward off bad luck, bad omens, bad men. But there was no protection for her here.

The church was full, as was expected. The whole village had come to witness the wedding, not out of affection, but because it was an event, a spectacle.

The priest stood before them in his black cassock, his eyes sunken deep into his skull, his thin lips pressed into something that was meant to resemble a smile but did not.

László stood beside her, his shoulders square, his expression set, his jaw tight. He had shaved that morning, but a smear of dried blood marred the edge of his chin where the blade had caught him. He did not smile at her. He did not take her hand. He only stared ahead, waiting.

The service was short. It was not a day for indulgence. There was no music, no songs sung in praise of love. The priest spoke the words quickly, his voice dry and brittle, as if he could not be troubled to make them sound like a blessing.

"Do you take this man?"

"I do."

"Do you take this woman?"

"I do."

No poetry. No softness. Only obligation.

Afterward, the village gathered in the barn behind László's family's butcher shop.

It smelled of hay, of smoke, of blood. The tables were rough-hewn, set with wooden bowls and loaves of bread hard enough to break a man's teeth. The butcher had spared a pig for the occasion, and its roasted body was laid out for them to carve.

Wine was poured. Too much of it. The men drank fast and spoke loudly, their voices filling the rafters. Their faces were already red, already shining with sweat, already careless in the way their hands touched their wives. The women ate without speaking. Zsuzsanna said nothing at all.

She sat beside László, watching the room, watching the way the women looked at their husbands, the way their eyes turned toward her and then away just as quickly. The first dance was expected. László took her hand, his grip too tight, his breath hot with drink, and led her to the center of the room. The fiddler played a slow, reedy tune, and they turned once, twice, three times before he let her go.

The evening went on. László drank more. He laughed louder. And by the time they left, the stars had begun to fade against the dawn.

Their house was small, but it was hers. Or at least, it had been. She had lived there alone before she married him. Now, there were two cups on the table, two sets of boots by the door, two pillows on the bed.

László shut the door behind them with a thud. He did not speak. He did not have to. She already knew how this night would end.

She stood there for a moment, listening to the wind against the shutters, her hands resting at her sides, her body still. László took off his boots, his coat, the belt he wore at his waist. He did not ask her to undress. He simply reached for her, pulling at the laces of her dress with hands that had never been gentle.

She let him. She let it happen. She let the night take her, as it had taken so many others before her.

The first time he hit her, she did not cry. The second time, she did not flinch. The third time, she began to plan. She knew he would die before her.

She did not know how yet, or when, but she knew it the way she knew when a woman's womb would not open, the way she knew when a child would not cry.

And one day, when she was ready, she would act.

4

THE WAR CHANGES EVERYTHING

László was gone before the first frost.

The war had come suddenly, spreading across Europe like a sickness with no cure. It had begun in the summer of 1914, when a man far from Nagyrev, a Serbian nationalist, fired a single bullet into an archduke and sent all of Europe tumbling into war.

Hungary, bound to Austria in an uneasy empire, had no choice but to fight. The King and the generals in Budapest swore it would be over quickly. A victory for the glory of the nation.

But war does not care for glory. It devours.

By the time the Hungarian Royal Army came through Nagyrev, the war was already a ravenous, growing thing, swallowing up young men like grain at the harvest. Soldiers marched through the village with boots caked in the mud of foreign battlefields, their faces drawn, their uniforms stiff with the stink of blood and sweat.

They carried lists, names of every able-bodied man required to fight.

László had tried to protest.

"I have a business," he had told them, arms crossed over his broad torso. "Who will run it if I go?"

The officer had barely looked up.

"It does not matter."

And that was that. Within days, he was gone, along with most of the other men in the village.

Nagyrev became a town of women. And for the first time in her life, Zsuzsanna could breathe.

At first, the village mourned its missing men. The women gathered at the well, wringing their hands, speaking in low, urgent voices. They worried for their husbands, their sons, their brothers, picturing them in trenches filled with mud and rats, in fields littered with bodies, in hospitals where the wounds outnumbered the doctors.

The newspapers spoke of heroism, of battles won, of territories gained. But the letters that arrived told a different story.

Hungary was losing. Thousands of men dead, thousands more wounded, dying in places they could not even pronounce.

Some women lit candles at the church, praying for their husbands' safe return. Others prayed for the war to last forever. Time passed and with time, the fear faded. The village changed. Without men, there was less to fear.

No fists slamming against tables, no drunken shouts echoing through the night. No eyes watching too closely, expecting obedience. The women did not waste away in grief. They thrived.

They worked the fields themselves, tending the crops with hands that had always known labor. They sold what they could at market, kept what they needed, shared what was left. For the first time, the money they earned belonged to them. They sat at their tables without waiting to be served last. They could speak freely, without men's ears listening, without men's tempers dictating which words were acceptable.

And for the first time in her life, Zsuzsanna did not have to answer to anyone.

The doctor had gone to war, leaving only her. She set broken bones, stitched wounds, kept the village alive. Her home became a gathering place, not just for births, but for meetings, for whispers, for plans.

Women came to her with their stories. Not of war, but of relief.

"It is better without them," one woman said, rolling bread dough between her hands. "I eat more now than I ever did before."

"There is no one to raise a hand to me," another added, tilting her chin up for the first time in years. "No one to drink away my earnings."

"What if they never come back?"

The words were a whisper, but they settled deep in the room.

No one spoke against them.

Because they had all thought it. Because they had all hoped it.

And Zsuzsanna simply listened. And she remembered. Because when the war ended, and the men returned, they would expect everything to go back to how it was before. And that could not be allowed.

~

The war did not end all at once.

The newspapers called it a victory, but it did not feel like one.

It ended in fragments: a rumor, a letter, a soldier limping back home with half a leg and a blank stare. The war had stretched on for four long years, long enough for the world to change, and when the men finally returned, they expected to come home to what they had left behind.

But they didn't. The war had been lost long before the officials admitted it.

By the autumn of 1918, Austria-Hungary was collapsing. The empire was fracturing at the seams, its soldiers deserting in droves, its food supplies dwindling, its people rioting in the streets. The war had swallowed a generation whole, and what was left behind was not strong enough to hold the empire any longer.

The newspapers still spoke of honor, of sacrifice, of duty to the king. But those who had been to the front knew the truth.

They had seen the trenches filled with bodies that would never be buried. They had walked through towns turned to rubble, cities stripped bare by bombs and fire. They had watched as their fellow soldiers, boys barely old enough to shave, collapsed from hunger, from sickness, from the kind of exhaustion that made even dying seem like relief.

And in November, it was over. Hungary pulled away from Austria. The monarchy crumbled. The new government signed the armistice. The war had ended. But for the men who had fought in it, there was no victory. There was only returning.

The first men arrived in the autumn of 1918, just as the trees were beginning to turn. They came thin and broken, their uniforms in tatters, their boots held together with scraps of leather and wire. Some had been wounded, their arms missing, their legs crushed beneath the burden of collapsed trenches. Some had been prisoners of war, returning not as victors, but as ghosts.

Some had seen things they could never forget. Some had done things they could never admit. But they all had one thing in common. They were angry.

Not all of them came home. Some were buried in unmarked graves, in fields far from Nagyrev, far from anywhere that remembered their names. Some had died in battle, their bodies never recovered. Others had wasted away in the cold of Russian prison camps, their letters ceasing without explanation, their wives waiting for news that never came.

For these women, there was no closure. No body to bury. No funeral to attend. No certainty. Some clung to hope.

"Maybe he will still come home," they said. "Maybe he is walking back to me now."

Others knew better. They were the ones who did not light candles for their husbands at church. The ones who did not weep. The ones who stood a little taller. For them, the war had given them something else. Freedom.

The men had suffered. But so had the women.

Only their suffering had not come from battlefields or bullets. It had come from hunger, from hardship, from learning how to live without the men who had ruled over them for so long. And that, more than anything, was what the men could not accept. Because the women had not been waiting. They had not been praying for their husbands to return and take up the burden of their lives again. They had been living. And they had been fine.

Zsuzsanna knew the first night that nothing would ever be the same again.

She had watched the first men come down the road, limping, bitter, their eyes scanning the village as if it had betrayed them. They had expected to return home as kings. Instead, they returned to a place where they were no longer needed.

They saw it in their wives. The way they no longer flinched, the way their hands were strong from work, the way they did not shrink beneath them as they had before. They saw it in their homes. How the furniture had been rearranged, how the children no longer sought them first, how the women moved as if they were capable of making decisions on their own. They saw it in Zsuzsanna. And they hated her for it.

László came home in December. Zsuzsanna had known it would happen eventually. She had hoped he would die, of course. She had hoped that war would do what she had not yet dared to. But László had always been too stubborn to die easily. When he stepped through the door of their home, he did not greet her.

He looked around first. At the kitchen, at the shelves, at the table that had been hers alone for years. He looked at the empty space where his boots should have been, the clothes she had burned long ago, the bed that had only ever been warm with her own body. And then, he looked at her.

"Did you miss me?" he asked.

She did not answer. Because they both already knew the truth.

The men resented their absence. But they resented the women's survival more. And so, they began to take back what they believed was theirs. They drank more. They hit harder. They forced their wives to bend beneath them, as if that would make them forget the years they had spent without them.

Zsuzsanna saw the bruises return. She saw the women walk with their eyes downcast once again. She saw the freedom slipping away. And she knew, deep in her bones that something needed to change.

5

THE FIRST DEATH

László lasted six months. Six months of drinking. Six months of anger. Six months of reminding her, over and over, that she was his.

He had come home from the war a man who had lost everything: his strength, his confidence, his control over the world. He had expected to return to Nagyrev and find it untouched, waiting for him, unchanged. But he had found her. Still standing. Still whole. Still Zsuzsanna. And he could not bear it.

The beatings started small. A slap when she did not answer quickly enough. A shove when she refused to give him the last of the bread. Then, the fists.

He hit her when he was drunk. And he was always drunk.

The men had nothing now; no jobs, no purpose, no war to fight. They spent their days in the village square, drinking, cursing the new world they had returned to, spitting on the women who had learned how to live without them. And at night, they went home and took their bitterness out on their wives. László was no different.

Zsuzsanna had healed bruises before. She had seen broken

bones, split lips, women barely able to stand from the damage their husbands had done to them. But she had never been the one bleeding. She had never been the one standing at the well with a swollen cheek, the other women looking at her with pity. And she would not be.

She waited. She was patient. She knew how to bide her time, how to let things run their course. She had learned that from watching women labor. Some pains must be endured. Some struggles must be seen through to the end. And some things must be done slowly.

She fed him well that spring. She kept his cup full of warm broth, his plate filled with rich stews. She spoke softly. She let him believe that he had won. And then, one evening, she prepared something special.

A hearty meal. A cut of pork, stewed for hours, seasoned just the way he liked it. A cup of wine to wash it down.

And in that wine, something else. Something clear. Something odorless that would not act quickly, that would not make him suspicious. Something that would settle in his blood like a slow-moving curse.

It took a week. At first, he only seemed tired. His limbs felt cumbersome and his appetite waned. Then the nausea came. Then the sweating. Then the fever. He grew weaker with each passing day. And she watched as his skin turned sallow, as his breath became labored, as his once-strong body crumpled in on itself like a rotted fruit.

The village doctor had not yet returned from the war. There was no one to ask questions, no one to suspect her. And no one mourned. Because when László Barta died, the village did not grieve.

His body was buried quickly. The earth took him without protest. And Zsuzsanna, she did not cry. She did not flinch. She did not look back. Because for the first time in her life she was free.

~

László's death did not change the village. Not in any way that mattered.

The men drank just as much, hit just as hard. One less of them made no difference. If they spoke of him at all, it was in passing, muttered over mugs of beer, as if he had simply ceased to exist rather than died.

"He was never the same after the war."

"Some men just don't come back right."

"A fever took him. Happens."

No one asked questions. Because questions meant answers and answers meant acknowledging something that no one wanted to say out loud. The village was better off without him.

I was just a child when László Barta died, but I still remember the day they buried him. The funeral was small, rushed, as if the village itself did not want to dwell on him for too long. The priest gave his blessing with the same tired voice he used for everything, his fingers twitching at his rosary beads, his breath fogging in the cold morning air.

I had kept quiet. Because even then, I had begun to notice things. I had grown up watching.

I watched how the women stood a little straighter when their husbands were not home; how they lingered at the well, talking in low voices, their fingers twisting their skirts, a careful excitement in their words. Watching how some of them—the ones with bruises, the ones who had always been quiet, always shrinking, always apologizing—started to change.

They laughed more. They moved differently. Lighter. Freer.

And their husbands, they were the ones who were changing too. Because one by one, the men of Nagyrev began to die.

The women, however, understood. They came to Zsuzsanna quietly at first. Not speaking directly, but with their eyes, with their hands trembling as they reached for hers.

A widow with a bruise hidden beneath her sleeve. A mother with a child clinging to her, whispering that she could not survive another one. A wife whose husband had been cruel before the war, and worse after it. They did not beg. They did not cry. They only sat in her kitchen, their hands wrapped around warm cups of tea, and waited. And when she handed them a small bottle, clear, delicate, its contents shimmering in the candlelight, they took it without a word.

And one by one, the men of Nagyrev began to die. It was not all at once. Not enough to alarm anyone. Not enough to be noticed by those who did not know where to look. But the women knew.

Zsuzsanna never asked why. She never asked what their husbands had done, what final cruelty had driven them to her door. She already knew. Because she had lived it. She had bled under it. She had killed for it. And she would do it again.

It was not murder. It was mercy. It was a kindness. It was justice in the only form that the world allowed women to take. And Zsuzsanna was not alone anymore. Because now, the women of Nagyrev were learning, too. And soon they would not need her at all.

6

THE UNSTOPPABLE FORCE

At first, the poison was a whisper. A secret passed from woman to woman in dark kitchens, at the well, in the narrow paths between houses where men never lingered.

"Go to her."

"She will help."

"It will be painless."

It was only used in the most desperate of cases. For the men who came home worse than before, for the ones who drank too much, hit too hard, took too much from their wives and left them with nothing.

But desperation has a way of spreading. And soon, so did the poison.

I was fourteen the first time I heard a woman whisper Zsuzsanna's name like a prayer. I had been at the well, balancing a bucket between my knees, listening as the village women spoke in their careful, measured tones. I was not meant to be listening, but I always listened.

"It happened quickly," one woman was saying. She had a shawl pulled tight around her shoulders, her fingers clutching the fabric as if afraid someone might pry it away. "One day, he was strong. The next, he was nothing."

"God works in strange ways," another murmured.

The first woman did not look at her.

"Maybe, it was not God."

I had lowered my gaze then, pretending not to hear, pretending not to know what they were saying. Because I had already started to understand.

I was not like Zsuzsanna. I had been born into an ordinary life, to a mother who baked bread every morning and a father who worked in the fields. Our house was small but clean. A single room where the fire never fully died, where the scent of dried herbs clung to the walls, where my mother sang softly to herself while she kneaded dough.

My father was a quiet man. He was not cruel. Not like the others. He drank, but not too much. He shouted sometimes, but he never struck.

I knew, even as a child, that I was lucky. I also knew that luck does not last forever. Some of the girls I had grown up with were already married. They had been given to men twice their age, men who stank of sweat and ale, men who pressed their wives' hands to their bellies after every bleeding, whispering that they would give them sons.

I had seen what marriage could do to a woman. I had seen how quickly it took away the light in her eyes, the laughter in her mouth, the freedom in her step. And I had seen what happened when a wife failed to please her husband. I had seen the bruises. Had heard unspoken things that sat between them like stones.

And I had started to wonder, would that be me one day? Would I be like my mother, kneading bread with red hands and bitten lips? Or would I be like the others, the ones who whispered in secret? The ones who went to Zsuzsanna.

At first, Zsuzsanna kept track. She knew every woman who came to her. She knew every bottle she gave. She knew every man who died. But then, something changed. Women stopped coming to her for help. They already knew what to do. She would pass through the village and hear them speaking in low voices, not in fear, but in understanding. They had learned. They had taught each other. And now, they did not need her at all.

Some used it as a last resort. Some for convenience. A bad husband, a cruel father, or a sick relative who had lived too long, taking too much, needing too much.

It was easy. So easy. The men of Nagyrev began dying in numbers too great to ignore. And for a while, the village was better. Quieter. The scars faded. The fear lessened.

The women walked without hunching their shoulders, without pressing their mouths into thin lines, without waiting for the inevitable blow. For a while, it was good. For a while, it was peace. But peace never lasts. Not forever.

The first to ask questions was the doctor. He had returned to Nagyrev a year after the war ended, expecting to find the village as he left it. Instead, he found too many graves. Too many widows who did not seem to grieve. Too many men who had been healthy one week, sick the next, dead by the time he was summoned. He spoke to the priest, the magistrate. He wrote letters. And then, the magistrate began to suspect.

Zsuzsanna knew before anyone else. She could feel it in the air, the slow shift, the way the whispers turned from victory to fear. She saw the way the women moved differently, as if they knew something was coming. She heard the way the men spoke about the deaths now. Not as tragic misfortunes, but as something unnatural. She knew her time was running out.

This is how it began. This is how the Angel Makers of Nagyrev were born.

7

THE NEW APPRENTICE

I knew something was wrong the moment my mother sat me down.

She had been kneading bread at the table, her hands pressing into the dough with a force that was not entirely necessary. Her sleeves were pushed up past her elbows, her fingers dusted with flour, but her eyes were on me. Watching. Waiting.

It was early morning, and the light coming through the small kitchen window was still soft, spilling in across the rough wooden table, making everything seem gentler than it was. But nothing about my mother was gentle. Not today.

When she finally spoke, her voice was quiet.

"You're to go work with Zsuzsanna."

I blinked. The words did not make sense at first.

"The midwife?"

"Who else?"

The words should have filled me with excitement. I knew other girls who would have envied me, who would have given anything to be taken under the midwife's wing. But my mother's voice did not hold the kind of pride I would have expected. It was flat. Distant. And her hands kneaded the dough too hard, her fingers pressing in deep, twisting, as if she were wringing the neck of a chicken rather than shaping bread. Something about it made my stomach turn.

"Why?" I asked.

She didn't answer right away. She only worked the dough harder.

"Because it's good work," she said finally. A lie.

"Because you'll learn a trade." Another lie.

"Because she asked for you." That was the truth.

I should have felt honored. Zsuzsanna Sárkány had not taken an apprentice before. She did not need to.

"You'll do as she says," my mother continued, not looking at me. "You'll be respectful. You'll listen. And you won't ask questions."

"I don't want to."

I had meant to sound firm, but the words came out too small, too uncertain.

"It's not about what you want."

She finally looked at me then, and there was something in her face that made my stomach tighten. Fear. My mother was afraid. My mother had always been afraid of Zsuzsanna. She would not say it outright—no one would—but I had noticed it in small ways. The way she lowered her gaze when the midwife passed in the street. The way she crossed herself after speaking her name. The way she never let me linger too long near her house.

"You stay away from her," she had warned me once, years ago, when I was still a child. But now she was delivering me to her.

And I did not understand why.

"You're afraid of her," I said before I could stop myself.

My mother flinched.

Her hands stilled, fingers still pressing into the dough, holding it too tight.

"I am sensible," she corrected.

I stared at her.

My mother had always been practical. She was a woman who survived by keeping her head down, by never making trouble. But this was something different.

"Tell me the truth."

She was silent for a long time.

Then, finally, she spoke.

"Do you remember Anna?"

I hesitated.

"The widow?"

My mother nodded.

"She spoke against Zsuzsanna, once. She said the midwife was too powerful. That women should not trust her. That she meddled in things she had no right to."

I swallowed. I had not known this.

"She died, not long after." My mother's voice was careful. Measured. "Some said it was illness. Some said it was God's will."

She finally looked at me, and in her face, I saw what she would not say aloud.

Some said it was Zsuzsanna.

"I do not want you against her," my mother continued. "It is better to be close to her. To be useful. To be on the right side of things."

"But why me?"

"Because she asked for you," my mother said, and this time, her voice was tired. "And when Zsuzsanna asks for something, you don't say no."

I did not argue again. I knew it would do no good. Because my mother had already decided. Or rather, she had accepted. Because she knew.

She knew what happened to people who went against the midwife. She knew that Zsuzsanna did not forgive insults. And more than anything she knew that it was better to be on her side rather than go against her.

Even if it meant giving up her daughter. Even if it meant giving me to her. For my own safety. For hers.

My mother walked me to Zsuzsanna's house the next morning. She did not speak on the way.

The air was still cool from the night, the sky just beginning to pale. The village was quiet, but I could hear the distant sounds of chickens rustling in their coops, of doors creaking open, of water sloshing into wooden buckets at the well.

I carried a small bundle: a change of clothes, a comb, a knife that had once belonged to my grandfather. My mother had pressed it into my hands before we left.

"A girl should always carry a blade," she had said. Not as a warning, but as a fact.

Zsuzsanna's house stood at the edge of the village, set apart from the others. The path leading to it was worn but narrow, as if few feet had ever needed to find their way there.

The house itself was old and crooked, the roof sagging slightly under the burden of years. Moss crawled over the thatching, and the wooden beams were darkened by rain, streaked with lichen and soot. A small garden grew wild along the side of the house, tall stalks of lavender and rosemary twisting together, vines creeping over the fence. Bundles of dried herbs hung from the eaves: sage, wormwood, yarrow. I had been here before, but never inside. Never as someone who belonged.

My mother knocked once, quick and firm. Zsuzsanna

answered almost immediately. She was not old. Not the way I had imagined a midwife should be. She was strong, her back straight, her hands steady. She wore a simple gray dress, the sleeves rolled up past her elbows, her dark hair pulled back, streaked with only a little silver.

Her eyes were the color of iron. Cold. Unshaken. She did not look at my mother. Only at me.

"She is yours now," my mother said, her voice careful. Respectful.

Zsuzsanna nodded. And just like that, I belonged to her.

Inside, the house was warm. A fire burned low in the hearth, filling the room with a steady glow. The scent of clove and mint, of earth and blood, hung in the air.

The walls were lined with shelves, covered with jars and bottles. Some contained dried herbs, their leaves pale and brittle, carefully labeled in ink. Others held dark liquids, preserved roots, strange things suspended in cloudy brine.

A wooden table stood in the center of the room, scarred with knife marks, its surface dusted with a fine layer of crushed herbs. A mortar and pestle rested beside a pile of dried nettles, and several bundles of freshly cut lavender lay tied together with twine.

In the far corner of the room, a small bed had been pushed against the wall, the blankets folded neatly, the pillow thin. Beside it sat a wooden chest, its lid slightly ajar, revealing more bottles, more tools, more secrets.

There was no softness here. No clutter, no indulgence. Only what was needed.

"You will wake before the sun," Zsuzsanna said, without looking at me. "You will keep the house in order. You will boil water, fetch fresh linens, grind herbs. You will listen. And you will learn."

I nodded.

"You will not complain. You will not ask foolish questions."

Another nod.

"And if you prove yourself," she added, finally meeting my eyes, "one day, you will do what I do."

Her gaze was steady. Unblinking. As if she were measuring something in me.

I swallowed. My throat felt dry.

"Do you understand?"

"Yes."

Zsuzsanna nodded.

"Good."

And just like that my lessons began.

8

THE DEPTHS

The house was warm, suffused in the scent of dried herbs and burning wood. Zsuzsanna had set out chairs by the hearth, each pulled close enough to feel the lingering heat from the embers. The floor had been swept clean, and the table was bare except for a single clay pot filled with hot water and a bundle of cloth.

I had seen her prepare for births, for deaths, for sickness, for secrets but never for something like this. This was not an emergency. No one had come knocking in the dead of night, breathless and pleading. This was something else entirely. A lesson.

The women arrived together; one young, one old.

The first, Katalin, barely in her twenties, round with her first child, moved cautiously, as if afraid of breaking herself before she even had the chance to be a mother. Her skin was smooth and unlined, her hands resting constantly on her belly, protective, uncertain.

The second, Éva, was exhausted before she had even taken her seat. Her body had known childbirth seven times before, and it showed; her belly stretched, her feet swollen, her movements slow, the burden of motherhood already pressing on her before this child had even arrived. She lowered herself onto the wooden chair with a deep sigh, pushing wet hair from her forehead.

"I barely have time to eat, let alone sit for a lesson," she muttered.

"Then it is good that you are here," Zsuzsanna said simply. "Because if you do not care for yourself, you will not care for the child."

Éva let out a quiet snort but said nothing.

The lesson began.

"The first thing you must remember," Zsuzsanna said, rolling up her sleeves, "is cleanliness."

She picked up the pot of steaming water, poured a small amount into a bowl.

"You wash your hands before you eat. You wash them before you touch the baby. You wash the baby when it is born, but not too much, not with strong soaps, only warm water and oil. The child must keep its mother's scent, or it will not latch properly."

"Latch?" Katalin repeated hesitantly.

"For feeding."

Zsuzsanna reached for a bundle of cloth, unraveling it until it became clear. A doll. A teaching tool. She cradled it in one arm, showing how to position it against her breast, adjusting it carefully.

"The baby must be placed here, the mouth against the breast, so that it drinks not only from the tip, but from the flesh. If it does not latch properly, it will not take enough milk. You will blister. You will bleed. The child will not grow strong."

Katalin swallowed hard. She looked pale.

"Will it hurt?" she asked.

"At first," Zsuzsanna said. "Then it will not."

Éva let out a dry laugh.

"It always hurts," she muttered.

"Not if done correctly," Zsuzsanna countered. "And not if the mother is strong."

Éva scoffed.

"Strong? I have been bearing children since I was fifteen. I have birthed them in the fields, in the kitchen, in the dark when my husband was too drunk to hear me calling for him. I have bled for them, broken for them. And when this one is born, I will do it all again."

She spread her hands, calloused; worn from years of raising children, of bending, of lifting, of holding.

"What more strength do I need?"

For the first time, Zsuzsanna hesitated. Just for a breath. Then she set the doll down.

"The strength to keep yourself alive," she said.

Éva blinked.

"You have had seven children," Zsuzsanna continued. "And yet you sit here with me today. That is rare. That is luck. Do not mistake it for invincibility."

Éva's face darkened.

"Are you saying I won't survive this one?"

"I am saying that if you do not take care, you will make it harder for yourself."

The room was tense. Katalin fidgeted with the edge of her sleeve, glancing nervously between them. Then, after a long pause, she cleared her throat.

"How do I know when it's time?" she asked, her voice small. "To give birth?"

Zsuzsanna turned to her, her expression softer now.

"You will know," she said simply. "But when the time comes, do not fight it. The child must come, and your body will know how."

"And if something goes wrong?"

"Then you call for me."

Katalin nodded, as if that alone was enough to quiet her fear. It wouldn't be. Not yet. But maybe, when the time came, it would be enough.

The lesson moved on. Zsuzsanna spoke of labor: how to breathe, how to bear down, how to save strength instead of wasting it in screaming. She spoke of fever, of bleeding, of what to do if the child did not cry at first. She spoke of signs that meant danger, of things that could not be helped, of how to know when to call the priest and when to call for her instead.

"Some children are not meant for this world," she said, her voice quiet. "That is not your fault."

Katalin swallowed. Éva only looked away.

By the time the lesson ended, the sun had risen high in the sky, the fire in the hearth nothing but soft embers. Éva stretched, groaning as she rose to her feet.

"If I die," she muttered, "at least I will know I was well-educated."

Zsuzsanna smirked.

"If you listen, you will not die."

Éva sighed, pressing a hand to her aching back.

"We'll see."

Katalin stayed a moment longer, still fidgeting with her sleeves.

"Thank you," she said quietly.

Zsuzsanna only nodded.

The women left, stepping into the bright afternoon. And I sat in my chair, watching Zsuzsanna as she cleaned the table, as she folded the cloths, as she straightened the empty chairs.

"You didn't have to do this," I said.

"Yes, I did."

"Most midwives don't."

"Most midwives do not watch their own mothers die in childbirth."

Her voice was calm. Steady. Matter-of-fact.

I stared at her, but she didn't look up. She only gathered her things, wiping her hands on her apron, already moving forward, already stepping into the next task: the next lesson, the next birth, the next death.

I thought, for the first time, I truly understood her. And I knew then that her mother had not been forced from the village. The rumors were wrong.

9

FIRST LESSONS

I woke to the sound of knocking. Not the sharp, insistent pounding of a fist, but something quieter. Measured. Three taps. A pause. Three more.

I opened my eyes to darkness. The fire had burned low in the hearth, nothing but a dull orange glow beneath the blackened logs. There was something metallic lingering in the air.

Zsuzsanna was already moving. I heard the rustle of fabric as she swung her shawl over her shoulders, the scrape of wood as she pulled a small case from beneath the table. She didn't look at me as she opened the door.

The woman outside was shivering, her hair coated in sweat, her face pinched and pale. She clutched the doorframe, one hand pressed to the small of her back.

"It's time," she whispered.

Zsuzsanna nodded once, then turned to me. "Up," she said. "You're coming."

The village was colder than I expected at night. The mist from the river had settled over the streets, moving around doorways and pressing up against the houses like a living thing.

The stars were sharp and distant above us, the moon no more than a sliver of bone.

I followed Zsuzsanna down the road, her footsteps sure and steady. The woman led us to a small house near the edge of the village, its windows glowing faintly. Inside, a fire crackled in the hearth, throwing shadows against the walls. The smell hit me first. Sweat. Blood. Something earthy and raw.

A woman lay on a straw-stuffed mattress in the corner of the room, her dark hair plastered to her forehead, her breaths coming in low, shuddering gasps. She was young, younger than I had expected.

Her husband stood near the doorway, shifting from foot to foot. He was not old, but already broad around the middle, his face ruddy from drink. He looked at me, then at Zsuzsanna.

"Is she ready?" he asked.

Zsuzsanna didn't answer him. She moved past him without a word, kneeling beside the woman and pressing a hand to her stomach. I hovered at the edge of the room, unsure of where to stand. The man cleared his throat.

"I said—"

Zsuzsanna cut him off with a look.

He fell silent. The woman on the bed let out a soft, guttural moan, her body tensing.

Zsuzsanna turned to me. "Come here."

I hesitated, then stepped closer.

She gestured toward the basin of water beside her. "Wash your hands."

The water was warm, steeped in something that smelled sharp and clean. I scrubbed my hands, my skin tingling from the mixture.

"Good." Zsuzsanna reached for a folded cloth, pressing it into my hands. "Now listen carefully."

I nodded.

She turned back to the laboring woman, her voice calm, steady. "The baby is coming fast," she said. "That's good, but it means she'll need to push soon. Your job is to be ready. When I tell you, you'll support her."

I swallowed hard. My heart pounded. I had seen births before. Once, when I was a child, peering through the cracks in a wooden fence as a neighbor's cow delivered a calf. But this was different. This was a person. A woman. And women, I was beginning to realize, were not like cows.

They did not cry out in the same way. They did not let the pain roll over them like waves on the shore. They fought it. They endured it. And they survived.

The next hour blurred together. I watched, I listened, I learned.

Zsuzsanna was not gentle, but she was not cruel. When the woman cried out, she did not hush her. When she whimpered that she could not push any longer, Zsuzsanna did not offer soft words of comfort. She gripped the woman's chin, forced her to meet her gaze, and said, "You can. You will."

And she did.

The baby came fast and slick, sliding into Zsuzsanna's hands in a rush of blood and fluid. For a moment, everything was still. Then a cry. Thin, piercing, alive.

The woman sagged back against the mattress, tears streaking her face.

Zsuzsanna handed me a cloth. "Wipe the child's face."

I obeyed, my hands surprisingly steady. The baby was small, red, wrinkled, fists clenched tight, a new thing in an old world. I pressed the cloth gently against its face, clearing its mouth, wiping the sticky film from its skin.

Zsuzsanna cut the cord with a swift, practiced motion, then bundled the baby in a clean linen wrap before placing it in the mother's arms. For the first time that night, Zsuzsanna smiled.

The mother wept softly, pressing her lips to the baby's clammy forehead.

The husband, who had been silent the entire time, finally spoke. "A boy?" he asked.

Zsuzsanna didn't turn to him. The woman answered instead, her voice hoarse. "A girl."

The man exhaled, a sharp hiss of breath. "Another useless mouth to feed."

I stiffened. The mother didn't react. She only stared down at the baby, her hands tightening around the small bundle. A quiet moment passed.

Then, Zsuzsanna stood and turned to the man. "You have a daughter," she said. Her voice was mild. Too mild.

He met her gaze. A flicker of something passed between them. A look I didn't understand but could feel. The air shifted. The man lowered his eyes first. Zsuzsanna turned away, already gathering her things. The man hesitated for a moment longer, then grunted and left the house without another word.

I let out a slow breath I hadn't realized I was holding. Zsuzsanna wiped her hands on a clean cloth, then turned to me.

"Well?" she asked.

I swallowed. "She's strong," I said, glancing at the mother.

Zsuzsanna arched a brow. "The mother or the daughter?"

I looked at them, both of them. The mother's fingers clutched protectively at the tiny bundle in her arms. The baby had stopped crying, her face turned against her mother's breast, eyes dark, unfathomable.

"Both," I said.

Zsuzsanna smiled. "Yes."

She handed me the cloth stained with birth, with blood, with the first moments of a life. "Take this outside," she said. "Bury it deep."

I hesitated. "Why?"

She met my gaze. "Because there are things men should never see."

I did as I was told.

Outside, the wind had died and the mist hung low over the village. The world was quiet. I found a place near the tree line and dug a small hole with my hands.

I placed the cloth inside and covered it with dirt. When I stood, I wiped my palms against my dress, breathing in the night air. A light shone in one of the houses nearby. A shadow passed behind the window.

I turned and walked back toward Zsuzsanna's house, my hands still tingling from the warmth of the blood. The village lay silent behind me, but I could feel it watching. Even in the darkness, even in the stillness, something unseen was moving beneath the surface. I didn't know it yet, but I had taken my first step into something that could never be undone.

10

THE MEN OF NAGYREV

The war had come and gone, leaving its mark on the village in ways that would never fade. It was in the empty spaces between houses, where men had once stood but no longer did. It was in the fine cracks in the well's stone, where a woman had once carved her husband's name, only to scratch it out when he failed to return. It was in the quiet of the church on Sundays, where fewer and fewer voices joined the hymns.

I hadn't been in Nagyrev during the war, but I had grown up hearing stories of it. How the fighting had dragged on for years, how men had been marched away in uniform, some never to return. Hungary had been part of the great Austro-Hungarian Empire then, a vast, crumbling thing tied together by the old ways, by rulers in cities far removed from villages like this one. The war had taken everything from that empire: land, power, men. When it ended, the old world had fallen apart.

Here in Nagyrev, the war had taken the men. And for a time, the women had been left alone.

I first heard them speak of it late one evening, when we were gathered outside Ilona Boros's home, husking corn by the firelight. The summer air was scented with the sharp bite of burning wood. The women worked steadily, peeling back husk after husk, their hands moving without thought. I listened as they talked, their voices low, threaded with something almost wistful.

"It was better then," one of them said.

A pause. Then another woman nodded. "It was."

I glanced up.

They were speaking of the war, of the years without men.

"We managed everything just fine," Ilona murmured, tossing a stripped cob into the pile at her feet. "The land. The livestock. The houses. Even the tavern."

A woman across from her chuckled. "Better, even. No one drinking away the profits. No one coming home reeking of pálinka, demanding dinner like a child."

"No one locking their wives out in the cold," another muttered.

"No one leaving bruises," someone else added.

The words drifted through the air like embers, glowing, then fading just as quickly. I said nothing. But I watched.

I saw the way their hands stilled slightly as they spoke. How their shoulders tensed, as if they were waiting for someone to disagree, for someone to remind them that it wasn't right to think such things. No one did. The only sound was the crackling of the fire, the steady rustle of husks being peeled away.

"They never should have come back."

It was Kata who said it. Her voice was quiet, but the words spoke volumes.

No one answered her. No one needed to. We all knew the truth. For those few years, Nagyrev had belonged to the women. They had run the farms. They had tilled the fields. They had mended roofs and slaughtered pigs and repaired fences. They had gathered in the evenings to drink and talk, without fear of a man's hand landing on their arm, their cheek, their throat.

That night, after the husking was done and the fire had burned low, I sat outside Zsuzsanna's house, watching the stars. She came out after a while, standing beside me in the dark. For a long time, neither of us spoke.

Then, she said, "You heard them."

It wasn't a question.

I nodded.

"They're not wrong," she murmured. "It was easier then."

I swallowed. "But the war couldn't last forever."

"No," she agreed. "But some things should have."

I turned to look at her, but she was already walking away, back toward the house. I sat there for a long time, staring out at the village, listening to the quiet drone of the insects, the distant bark of a dog.

The war had ended years ago but here in Nagyrev, something else had begun. And it was still going on.

The men of Nagyrev could be heard before they were seen. It was their voices that carried first, loud, slurred with drink, drifting from the tavern in waves, rolling through the narrow streets, breaking against the closed doors of the houses where their wives waited. I heard them every evening as the sun dipped below the horizon, their shouts and laughter growing rougher, sharper, meaner. Some nights, I heard the crack of glass shattering against the tavern walls. Some nights, I heard screams.

By morning, the streets were littered with evidence of the night before. A broken clay jug, its contents dried to a dark stain in the dust. A wooden stool overturned in the road, kicked or thrown. A smear of something, blood or wine, it was hard to tell, on the tavern's doorframe.

And the women, always the women, merging from their homes at dawn to sweep the steps, scrub the walls, patch the bruises. Their eyes downcast, their shoulders squared. They were not weak, not fragile, not even particularly afraid. If anything, they were patient.

It did not take me long to understand what kind of place this was. The men of Nagyrev were not gentle.

I first saw Kata's husband when I went to the well one morning. The village had only one well, a deep stone pit on the eastern side of the square, near the old church. The women gathered there just after sunrise, buckets swinging at their hips, voices low, words swallowed quickly when footsteps approached. The air held the scent of wet stone, and the wooden beams creaked as the rope was pulled, the water sloshing below.

Kata was already there when I arrived, one hand gripping the rope, the other pressing gingerly against the side of her face.

The cuts and bruises were still fresh, a deep purple shadow spreading from her cheekbone to the corner of her mouth. She was trying to hide it, but not very well. Her fingers twitched slightly where they rested against the well's edge, her eyes flicking toward the road every few seconds, as if expecting something—or someone. The other women did not ask.

They only exchanged a look. One I didn't yet understand. I know now that it wasn't pity. It wasn't outrage. It was acknowledgment. As if that was simply the way of things.

A few feet away, I heard loud footsteps approaching. A man, broad-shouldered, thick-fingered, with a belly that strained against the buttons of his shirt. He smelled of sweat and old beer, his face unshaven, his boots caked in dried mud. His presence filled the air, strong and oppressive, his breath slow and steady. He reached past Kata to grab the rope, yanking the bucket up with a force that sent water sloshing over the sides. Not a single woman moved.

I stood frozen as he turned to Kata. "You're late," he said, voice low, measured.

She bowed her head. "I ... I woke up feeling unwell."

The corner of his mouth twitched, as if deciding whether or not to be amused. "Maybe you'll wake up feeling better next time." Kata gave the smallest nod. She did not look up. The bucket in her hands trembled slightly.

The man let the stillness stretch a moment longer, then turned and walked away. Not a single woman spoke until he was out of sight. Then, someone muttered, "He won't live long."

Then there was laughter.

I spent the next few weeks watching. I saw the way Lajos Barta grabbed his wife's arm outside their home, squeezing hard enough to leave prints in her skin. I saw the way Miklós Csepely's wife carried herself, shoulders hunched, always flinching before he even raised his voice. I saw Péter Fazekas strike his wife across the face in the middle of the road, knocking her to the ground, then step over her like she was nothing but a stray dog in his path. And I saw how no one stopped him.

Not the men. Certainly not the men. Not the women, either.

I asked Zsuzsanna about it once, late one evening, when we sat at the table, drying herbs by the fire. She glanced at me, then back at her hands, rubbing the leaves between her fingers, releasing their bitter scent into the air.

"This is the way of things," she said. It was not an answer. But it was the only one I would get.

The first time I heard the joke, it came from Ilona Boros. She was older than most of the women in the village: widowed, childless, sharp-eyed. She walked with a limp, a wound left behind from the husband she had before. We were sitting outside her home, our hands deep in a pile of beans, snapping off the ends, stripping them of their strings. The other women talked in low voices, eyes darting to the road every now and then.

Ilona sat beside me, her fingers moving slowly, carefully.

"Zsuzsanna knows how to fix any problem," she said.

There was a pause and then chuckles. Low, knowing. The kind of laughter that made my stomach twist.

I glanced up. The other women were nodding. Agreeing. And for the first time, I understood. They were not afraid of their husbands. Not anymore. Not really. Because they knew something the men didn't. Something final. Something absolute.

The women spoke in half-sentences. Little fragments of things, buried under laughter and soft smiles.

"He used to be mean, but he's so much easier now."

"She never did get used to the sound of his coughing."

"His mother is still mourning. We told her it was a sickness. What else could we say?"

Their words had edges. Blades, hidden in cloth. I sat there, listening, trying to make sense of what they weren't saying. Trying to piece together what, exactly, Zsuzsanna could fix.

One evening, I followed her to the river. She hadn't told me where we were going, just motioned for me to come. We walked along the bank, past the narrow boats, past the wooden posts where fishing nets were hung to dry. Then, she stopped and crouched low, reaching into the water.

When she pulled her hand back, she held a small strip of flypaper.

I frowned. "What's that for?"

She smiled. "A cure."

That night, I lay awake, listening to the wind rattle the shutters, thinking about the men in the village, thinking about their wives. Thinking about how quickly laughter could turn to something else.

A few weeks ago, I had thought Nagyrev was like any other village. Now, I wasn't so sure.

11

THE GLASS BOTTLE

It had rained that morning, a slow, steady downpour that had darkened the earth to a deep, sodden black. The fields were steeped in mud, the roads slick and glistening in the weak light of afternoon. The air smelled of moist hay and churned-up soil, with the sharp, metallic scent of wet iron lingering from the horseshoes that had clattered through the square earlier that day. A dark fog had rolled in from the river at dawn and never fully lifted, turning the village into something dim and shapeless, as though the world itself was holding its breath.

I sat at the wooden table, grinding dried herbs between my fingers, inhaling their bitter scent as I worked them into a fine powder. The fire burned low in the hearth, its glow shining across the stone walls, casting long, dancing shadows. Outside, the last remnants of rain dripped from the thatched roof in rhythmic, patient taps, pooling in the hollows of the uneven ground.

Zsuzsanna stood at the counter, her back to me, mixing something in a small wooden bowl. Her movements were steady, practiced. An exact amount of pressure, a precise stir, a measured pause before adding another ingredient. Watching her work was like watching the river move; inevitable, effortless, unstoppable.

Then came a knock. Three short raps against the wood. A hesitation. Three more. I looked up.

Zsuzsanna didn't turn immediately. She set down the bowl, wiped her hands on her apron, and exhaled. The knock came again. It was soft, but insistent. Zsuzsanna pulled open the door.

Kata stood on the threshold, wrapped tightly in a threadbare shawl. Her hair was wet from the rain, sticking to her temples, her skin pale and drawn too tight over her cheekbones. There was a faint tremor in her hands, though she held them stiffly at her sides, as if willing them to be still.

But my eyes were drawn to the bruise beneath her left eye. It was old, yellowed at the edges, fading, but still there. And she was trying to hide it, turning her face slightly, keeping to the shadows of the doorway.

For a long moment, no one spoke.

Then, Kata whispered, "Please."

Her voice was barely audible, more breath than sound.

Zsuzsanna stepped aside.

Kata entered quickly, moving as though she expected someone to come running after her, someone who might drag her back. She stood near the fire but did not warm her hands, did not shiver, did not move at all except for the slight, unconscious clenching of her fingers against the rough fabric of her skirt.

I did not speak. Neither did Zsuzsanna.

She simply walked to the far wall, where the wooden shelves stood, stacked with glass jars and vials, each filled with something different: dried leaves, oils, powders, and other things I had not yet learned the names of.

She ran a finger along the bottles, stopping at one in particular. A small, clear bottle. She lifted it carefully, almost reverently, and turned back toward the table. The liquid inside was thin, colorless, unremarkable. It could have been water. It wasn't.

Zsuzsanna set the bottle down. The faintest clink of glass against wood filled the quiet. She looked at Kata and said nothing. Kata's breath was uneven, though she was trying to steady it. She reached for the bottle, her fingers hesitating just above the glass, hovering there for the briefest of moments; like a moth before a flame, knowing the danger but unable to resist the pull of it.

Then she took it and tucked it into the folds of her shawl. Still, Zsuzsanna said nothing. Neither did I. But the air was different now. Loaded.

Kata pressed her lips together, her jaw tight, her shoulders squared. She nodded, just once. Not in thanks, not in gratitude. But in understanding. Then she turned. Pulled the door open just enough to slip out, vanishing into the rainy evening. The door clicked shut behind her.

Zsuzsanna returned to the counter, picked up the wooden bowl she had been mixing, and resumed her work.

The air in the room did not change. The fire crackled. The rain dripped from the roof. The herbs in my hands still smelled bitter. But something had shifted. A quiet, unspoken thing had passed between them. Between all of us.

I looked at the spot where the bottle had been. The wood beneath it was still wet, a faint, circular mark left behind. Zsuzsanna did not look at me. But she must have felt my stare.

"Say it," she murmured, crushing the herbs between her fingers, releasing their scent into the warm air.

I swallowed. "Say what?"

"That you have questions."

I hesitated.

The truth was, I did. I had too many. I had known that

Zsuzsanna provided medicines, that she helped women with things they could not ask for at the apothecary in town. I had even begun to suspect there was more to it than that. Whispers exchanged at the well, women laughing too softly, speaking in half-sentences.

But I had never seen it so plainly. I had never seen a bottle passed into a woman's hand, silent and final. I opened my mouth. Then closed it.

Zsuzsanna's lips twisted slightly, something amused, something dark. "Good."

She reached for another jar, shaking out a small handful of dried leaves.

"People like to believe there's only one way for a woman to be free," she said. "That she must wait for a man to die of his own accord. That she must endure until fate grants her mercy."

She looked at me then, her gaze steady, unreadable.

"But fate is slow," she murmured. "And men live longer than they deserve."

I felt something twisting in my stomach.

The fire popped in the hearth, spitting embers onto the stone floor. Outside, the village stretched dark and still beneath the clouded sky.

Kata would be home by now. She would set the bottle somewhere safe, where no child could reach it, where no wandering eye might notice it. And then, one evening, she would open it. She would stir a single drop into soup, into pálinka, another into the cool well water that always tasted faintly of iron. She would not watch him drink it. She would not need to. She would wait.

And then, one morning, her husband would wake with his stomach burning. He would stumble from their bed, his skin slick with sweat, his breath coming in short, shallow gasps. His hands would clutch at his throat, his chest, his gut. He would collapse to the floor, his body convulsing, foam gathering at the corners of his mouth.

By the time the sun rose, he would be gone. And Kata would be free.

I could see it now, as clearly as if it had already happened. I turned back to Zsuzsanna. She was watching me. She said nothing. Because there was nothing left to say.

12

A DEATH

I heard about the death before I saw the body. News moved strangely in Nagyrev, sometimes as fast as wildfire, spreading before the first whispers had even settled; other times slow, crawling through the village like a low fog, waiting to be acknowledged. This was the second kind. The kind that was known before it was spoken.

I had woken early that morning, the air moist and cool, the scent of wet earth from the storm the night before. Zsuzsanna had already left the house, though she hadn't said where she was going. That wasn't unusual. People came for her at all hours: for births, for sickness, for things that weren't spoken aloud.

I dressed quickly, wrapped a shawl around my shoulders, and made my way toward the well. The village was quiet, but not in the way it usually was. Even the dogs that normally lurked near the tavern were nowhere to be seen, as if they, too, sensed something had changed.

The first sign that something had happened was the gathering.

Women stood clustered near the well, their heads bent close, voices low. Not hurried or frantic. Not the kind of whispers that followed an accident or a fire. This was something else.

I slowed my steps. Kata was not among them and that, more than anything, told me what I needed to know.

I reached Ilona first. She was peeling a potato with slow, steady strokes, the blade whispering against the skin in long, unbroken curls. The knife was sharp. I could hear it, feel it in the way the skin split effortlessly under the blade. She didn't look up when she spoke.

"He's dead."

I didn't ask who. I didn't need to.

"When?" I murmured.

"Last night."

She tossed the peel into the basket at her feet. The other women kept talking, but it was not the talk of grief. There were no wails, no shaking heads, no murmured prayers for his soul.

I looked toward Kata's house. The door was open, but the inside was dark, shadowed. The breeze carried the scent of wet earth and something else. Something sour.

Ilona followed my gaze.

"The magistrate will come, if he hasn't already," she said. "They always do, when a man dies too soon."

I nodded. The women around us continued their hushed conversation. Someone laughed, not loud, not crass, but soft, a breath of sound that sent something cold through me. No one mourned him. No one even pretended to. I felt the significance of their indifference.

I should have turned away. I should have gone back to Zsuzsanna's house and waited for her return. But my feet moved of their own accord, carrying me past the well, past the watchful eyes of the women, toward Kata's home.

The door was still ajar. Inside, the house was stifling. The air held the scent of unwashed linens, dank wood, something else beneath it. Something acrid, like metal, like sweat. The kind of smell that clung to the walls, to the furniture, to the skin.

Kata stood near the hearth, staring at nothing. Her hands were folded in front of her, her shawl wrapped tight around her body. She did not move, did not blink. And then I saw him.

Her husband lay on the floor near the foot of their bed, his body twisted at an unnatural angle. His eyes were open, staring at the ceiling, his mouth slack. His skin was pale, but there was something off about it; a yellowish tint, a dullness that did not belong to the dead.

He looked ... shrunken. As if something had drained him from the inside out.

My breath caught in my throat. Kata's voice, when she finally spoke, was flat.

"He came home from the tavern and said his stomach hurt," she said. "Thought it was something he ate."

She inhaled sharply.

"Then he started sweating. Shaking."

I glanced at the bed. The sheets were crumpled, dark with something that looked too much like bile. A metal basin sat nearby, filled with water tinged pink at the edges, a rag floating in it like a discarded petal.

Kata's voice lowered.

"He couldn't breathe, by the end. His hands ..." She paused. "They clawed at his throat, like he thought he could pull the sickness out."

I swallowed, my mouth suddenly dry.

A fly buzzed near his face, landing on his parted lips.

She didn't shoo it away.

I turned to her. "Kata ..."

She finally looked at me. Something unreadable passed over her face.

Then, she said, "He was a bad man."

I had no answer for that. Because I had seen the evidence of abuse. I had seen the way he gripped her at the well, the way his voice sent a shudder through her shoulders. I had heard the way the other women spoke about men like him. And I had seen the bottle.

She tilted her head slightly, watching me. There was something steady in her gaze, something too calm, too knowing.

My heart thudded painfully. I stepped back, suddenly needing air. Outside, the women were still gathered. They saw me. I knew they did.

But none of them called out. None of them asked what I had seen. Because they already knew. Zsuzsanna had known, too.

That was why she had said nothing when she passed the bottle into Kata's hands. That was why there had been no warnings, no hesitations. Because this had happened before. Because this would happen again. And no one—not the magistrate, not the priest, not even the village itself—would stop it.

I turned and walked away, my pulse roaring in my ears. I did not look back. But I could still feel their eyes on me.

The magistrate would come. He would ask questions. He would kneel beside the body, lift an eyelid, turn the wrist in his hands, examine the dark veins beneath the surface. He would frown and mutter about the sickness, about the damp, about something in the water. And the women would watch him, their expressions neutral, their hands still, their words measured.

The death would be recorded. A name written in a ledger. A sickness. A sudden, tragic thing. And that would be the end of it.

A week from now, the bruises on Kata's arms would fade. She would walk through the village with her shoulders a little straighter, her head held a little higher. The other women would pass her in the square, nodding, their eyes saying everything their mouths would not.

And the world would move on. Because in Nagyrev, men died. And no one ever asked why.

13

THE QUIET WIDOW

Kata returned to the world quietly.

Three days after her husband was buried in the churchyard, she came to the well at sunrise, just as she had always done. Her shawl was wrapped tightly around her shoulders, her hands empty save for the bucket swinging lightly at her side. The hem of her dress was wet from the morning mist, her hair combed neatly beneath her scarf. She looked the same as she always had.

But she moved differently, like a woman who had spent years walking with a load on her back, only to wake up one morning and find it gone.

The other women were already there, standing in a loose cluster around the well, their breath visible in the cool air. The morning light was dim and silvered, the world still half-asleep, the only sounds the steady creak of the pulley as someone drew up water, the rustle of skirts shifting, the occasional murmur of conversation.

When they saw Kata, they did not gasp. They did not whisper behind their hands.

They did not rush forward, clutching her hands and offering

words of pity, as they might have done in other villages, in other lives. Instead, they made space. A small shift in their stance, a slight step to the left, the kind of movement that could mean nothing but meant everything.

Kata stepped into the space without a word. She set down her bucket, gripped the rope, and pulled. The well groaned softly, the pulley creaking as she drew up the water, the morning hush unbroken save for the rhythmic splash as the bucket hit the surface below.

No one asked her how she was. No one spoke her husband's name. The only voice that spoke was Ilona Boros's.

"Will you be needing bread today?"

It was such a normal question, asked as if nothing at all had happened.

Kata exhaled slowly, as if adjusting to a new load on her shoulders, or the absence of an old one.

She shook her head. "No," she said simply. "I have enough."

No tears. No prayers. No mourning.

She left with the bucket in one hand and her shawl drawn snugly around her, walking down the path toward home. I watched her go, the sound of her footsteps fading into the hush of the village. No one followed her. No one asked if she was alright. Because she was. She was free.

I stood there, uneasy. Where I had grown up, widows dressed in black for a year. They wept in church, whispered of their losses, walked with heads bowed, shrouded in grief as if it were a second skin.

Here, the widows of Nagyrev walked taller. Their eyes did not shine with sorrow, but with something clearer, sharper. The more I watched, the more I saw it.

Kata was not the only one. There were other widows in the village, too many, I realized, for a place this small. Women who had once moved cautiously, carefully, their bodies bent inward like dried leaves, as if trying to make themselves small enough to escape notice.

But now they stood straighter. Now they laughed more freely. Now they spoke without fear.

I felt it again, that shifting sense of something just beyond my reach. Something unspoken but known.

I found Zsuzsanna in the garden behind the house, crouched low among the rows of herbs, pulling weeds with quick, practiced motions. The morning mist clung to the plants, beading on the leaves, catching in the fine threads of spiderwebs that stretched between the wooden stakes marking the rows.

She didn't look up when I approached.

"Say what you want to say," she murmured.

I hesitated. "No one mourns him."

Zsuzsanna plucked a weed from the soil, tossed it into a small wicker basket beside her. "No."

I swallowed. "Not even Kata."

That made her pause. She sat back on her heels, brushing dirt from her palms. "Would you?"

I didn't answer.

She turned her head slightly, studying me. "You think it strange."

"I think it's ..." I struggled for the right word. "Unnatural."

She smiled, just a little. "You think grief is a duty."

"In most places, it is," I said carefully. "A wife loses a husband. A mother loses a son. She wears black. She weeps. The village mourns with her."

Zsuzsanna nodded, as if considering this. "And then what?"

I frowned.

"What happens when the black dress comes off?" she asked. "When the tears dry?"

I didn't know how to answer that.

Zsuzsanna exhaled softly, turning back to the plants. "Some

men die when it is their time," she murmured, more to herself than to me. "And some women have already grieved them long before they are gone."

Her voice was quiet. Steady. But I couldn't shake the feeling that, here in Nagyrev, it was the women who decided when that time had come.

Later that evening, as I sat at the table, I thought about the way the women had made space for Kata at the well. The way Ilona had asked if she needed bread; not with concern, not with pity, but with acceptance.

I thought about how quickly the world had moved on. A man had died. His absence barely caused a ripple. And something about that frightened me.

The fire burned low in the hearth, throwing shadows against the stone walls. Outside, the night air was buzzing with the sound of insects, the occasional rustle of wind through the trees. Somewhere in the village, a dog barked once, then fell silent.

Zsuzsanna sat across from me, her fingers working deftly as she tied a bundle of dried lavender, securing it with twine. She did not speak.

But she didn't have to. I knew she had seen the same thing I had.

I wanted to ask her, had this happened before? Had she given other women the same bottle, the same quiet permission? But I did not ask because a part of me—a part I did not want to look at too closely—wasn't sure I wanted to hear it.

I turned my gaze to the window. The village lay quiet. And somewhere, in the dark, another woman was waiting for her time to come.

14

THE DOUBTING MAN

The knock came just as the sky was beginning to lighten, the first thin streaks of pale blue creeping over the horizon.

I was still half-asleep, blinking against the dim glow of the fire, when the sound of hurried footsteps echoed outside.

Then, a voice. Frantic, breathless.

"Please come quick! It's the goat, she's struggling!"

The door swung open, and a woman stood there, her cheeks flushed from running, her shawl slipping from her shoulders, her hands clutched tightly in front of her.

Her face was weathered but kind, lined from years spent working in the sun. She was a farmer's wife, that much was clear. The scent of hay and earth clung to her clothes, and her hands were calloused, the nails edged with dirt. Not a woman afraid of hard labor, but now she was shaking, her dark eyes wide with fear.

Zsuzsanna barely hesitated.

"Where?"

"Our farm, the old Szabó place, just beyond the field."

"How long has she been laboring?"

"Since before dusk." The woman swallowed, her throat

working as she tried to steady herself. "She should have birthed by now. My husband says to leave her, he thinks it's no use."

A shadow passed over Zsuzsanna's face.

"Your husband is wrong."

She reached for her basket, gathering the things she would need: cloths, a sharp knife, a small bottle of oil, a length of cord. I hurried after her, my pulse quickening, relieved to be going toward something that was meant to bring life, not death.

We stepped out into the cool morning, and the woman led us quickly across the fields. I did not look back. I did not need to. Zsuzsanna was already beside me, moving with the kind of certainty that made men afraid.

The farm was old but well kept. A wooden fence ran along the perimeter, though parts of it were beginning to lean, the posts softened by years of rain and wind. A few chickens stirred restlessly in the yard, pecking at the ground, their feathers ruffled as if unsettled by the night's events.

The barn loomed ahead, its doors slightly ajar, the dim light of a lantern spilling onto the dirt path. The scent of sodden straw, warm animal musk, and something sour--the unmistakable smell of labor and fear—hung in the air.

Inside, the barn was dim, the wooden beams stretching high overhead, their surfaces darkened with age and soot from old lamps. A row of stalls lined the walls, each filled with slumbering creatures: sheep huddled together in piles of wool, cows shifting in their sleep, the occasional restless shuffle of hooves against packed earth. But all attention was on the farthest stall.

The goat lay on her side, flanks shuddering, her swollen belly rippling with contractions. Her fur was slick with sweat, her breathing ragged. The ground beneath her was wet with fluid, the first signs of a birth that had started but had not finished.

A man stood nearby, his arms crossed over his body, his jaw set tight. He was broad-shouldered, his beard unkempt, his clothes smelling of tobacco and wet wool. I knew his kind. Men who did not trust women like Zsuzsanna. Men who believed a woman's hands were meant for soft things, not for the work of gods.

"You shouldn't have brought them," he muttered, his voice dripping with dismissal. "There's nothing to be done."

Zsuzsanna ignored him.

She knelt beside the goat, her hands already moving, pressing gently but firmly along the mother's belly, feeling for the position of the kid inside.

And then, her face darkened.

"The cord is wrapped," she murmured.

The man scoffed.

"And what do you think you'll do about that?"

Zsuzsanna finally looked up. Her eyes, sharp as a blade in the dim light, met his.

"Save her."

The man shifted uncomfortably but said nothing.

Zsuzsanna was already working. She reached for the oil, warming it between her palms before slipping her hands inside the mother.

The goat bleated weakly, her body convulsing, her hooves scraping at the straw.

"Easy," Zsuzsanna murmured, her voice low, soothing, as if speaking to a child.

The kid's muzzle appeared first. It was blue.

"Breathe, little one," Zsuzsanna muttered under her breath, her fingers working carefully, loosening the umbilical cord from around its fragile neck.

I held my breath as she shifted it, turning the tiny body ever so slightly, making sure its passage would not be blocked.

"Push," she said softly.

The goat did. And the first kid slid free. Limp. Lifeless. The barn was silent.

I felt something cold settle inside me, the same creeping horror I had felt before. The same understanding that sometimes, no matter what we did, death won. But Zsuzsanna did not hesitate. She took the kid by its hind legs, turning it upside down, swinging it gently in an arc.

"Come on," she muttered.

Nothing.

She massaged its tiny ribs, pressing firm but careful fingers against its chest.

"Breathe."

Still nothing.

The farmer shifted beside me, scoffing. "It's dead ..."

And then a gasp. A tiny, wet, shuddering gasp.

The kid jerked, coughed, sputtered and then, finally, let out a thin, weak cry.

Alive. It was alive.

The farmer's wife clapped a hand over her mouth, a choked sob escaping her. The man, silent now, stared at Zsuzsanna as if seeing her for the first time. Zsuzsanna, unfazed, handed the kid to me.

"Clean it," she said, already turning back to the mother. "She's not done yet."

Because there was still another. Another set of tiny hooves emerging, another life waiting to be pulled into this world.

And when the second kid took its first breath—a stronger one this time, a healthier one—the farmer finally spoke.

"I was wrong."

Zsuzsanna wiped her hands on a cloth, standing slowly, meeting his gaze with something unreadable in her own.

"Yes."

And that was all.

We walked back as the sun crept over the hills, the sky streaked with pink and gold, the air alive with the smell of dewy grass, of morning, of life. I glanced at Zsuzsanna as we walked, at the way she carried herself. Not proud, not smug, but simply certain, as if she had never once questioned whether the goat would live or die.

"You knew you'd save them," I said.

"No," she admitted.

I frowned.

"Then why did you act like you could?"

She shrugged.

"Because someone had to."

I thought about that as we walked. And for the first time, I thought that maybe, just maybe I wanted to be like her.

As we walked away, the fields stretched wide before us, painted gold in the first light of morning. The sky had shifted from the deep, endless black of night into something softer; a pale, hazy blue, tinged at the edges with streaks of rose and amber. The earth smelled fresh, moist with the lingering breath of the night, the air holding the scent of dew-covered grass and the last remnants of burning wood from the farmhouses in the distance.

We said nothing at first, the only sound being our steps crunching over the frost-kissed ground. Zsuzsanna moved steadily beside me, her basket swinging lightly in her hand, her shoulders squared as if she had already put the night's work behind her.

But I hadn't. I kept thinking of the kid. Its limp body, its blue-tinged face, the way it had gasped back into the world under Zsuzsanna's hands.

I had been ready to mourn it. She had not and I needed to understand why.

"How do you do it?" I asked finally, breaking the quiet.

She did not look at me.

"Do what?"

"Stay so calm."

She exhaled, a slow breath showing in the cold morning air.

"Because there is no other choice."

"That's not true," I pressed. "Most people would panic. Most people would doubt themselves. But you ..." I shook my head. "You don't hesitate. Not ever. I've never seen you afraid."

"Then you haven't been looking hard enough."

That surprised me. I turned to her, studying her face in the early light. She looked the same as always; unshaken, unreadable, her expression as solid and immovable as the ground beneath our feet.

"You're afraid?" I asked cautiously.

"Of course," she said simply.

"Of what?"

"Of the same things you are."

That answer unsettled me. Because I had never once believed Zsuzsanna feared anything at all.

She did not fear the work. She did not fear men. She did not fear death.

But now, I wasn't sure.

"Then why do you never show it?"

She was quiet for a long moment, as if deciding how much of herself she was willing to give away.

Then, at last, she said, "Because fear is useless to me."

"Useless?" I echoed.

"Fear will not bring a baby into the world. Fear will not stop a woman from bleeding. Fear will not bring a dead thing back to life."

Her voice was even, matter-of-fact, as if she were listing ingredients for a recipe rather than speaking of life and death.

"So, I do not waste my time on it."

"That's not how fear works," I muttered.

"No," she agreed. "But it is how I work."

I frowned, trying to understand.

"And the times when you don't know if you'll succeed?" I asked. "What then?"

"Then I pretend I do."

"Why?"

"Because if I believe it, sometimes the world does too."

We walked a little farther, the sun creeping higher, chasing away the last of the morning chill.

I tried to imagine what it must be like, to move through life with such certainty, even in the face of impossible odds.

"You saved the kid," I said after a while. "When I saw it, I thought it was already gone. But you didn't."

She glanced at me, a small, knowing smile tugging at the corner of her lips.

"I have seen things come back when they had no right to," she said simply. "I have seen a woman labor for three days and survive. I have seen a child born blue and gasping take its first breath and live to be an old man. I have seen a girl who thought she had no future become something stronger than she ever dreamed of."

Something in her voice shifted slightly on that last sentence, but I did not press.

"And I have seen the opposite," she continued, her voice softer now. "I have seen men healthy one day and dead the next. I have seen mothers hold stillborn babes in their arms and beg God to take them instead. I have seen lungs stop, hearts fail, bodies betray themselves. I have seen death come too soon. And sometimes, I have brought it myself."

The words settled into my skin, into the spaces between my ribs, sinking deeper than I wanted them to.

I knew what she meant. What she was talking about was not just nature.

Not just fate. It was a choice. And I wondered how often she had made it.

"Does it ever weigh on you?" I asked carefully. "The ones you couldn't save?"

She was silent. Then, she finally spoke:

"They are not the ones who keep me awake at night."

A shiver passed over me. Not from the cold. From her words. Because I understood what she meant. And I did not know if I was ready to know it.

We were nearing home now, the house in sight, its crooked roof barely visible through the trees. The sun had risen fully, bathing the world in gold, and for a moment, it was easy to pretend that this had been just another morning.

Just another walk through the fields. Just another animal brought into the world, just another night's work finished, just another task completed. But I knew better.

And so did she.

Because Zsuzsanna did not just bring life into the world. She had taken it.

And one day, I knew, she would ask me to do the same.

15

A GOOD CAUSE

The poison had other uses. I heard the story from Kata first. It was whispered among the village women, passed from mouth to ear like a ghostly confession. They spoke of Marta, a farmer's daughter, the woman who had been seen slipping into the woods with an Allied prisoner of war. It was her husband's parents who first heard the rumors, and they did not take kindly to the shame she had brought upon their family.

Marta must have known her time was running short. The old ones would not stand in her way.

At dusk, she prepared their evening broth, stirring a fine white powder into the pot with deliberate patience. When she placed the bowls before them, she sat watching as they ate, their usual complaints about the cold and the failing crops fading into slow, uncertain quiet.

Her father-in-law blinked first, his spoon slipping from his fingers and clattering against the wooden table. Her mother-in-law followed, a soft groan escaping her lips as her body sagged forward.

Marta did not move. She only exhaled, slow and steady, as the weight of their judgment dissolved into the night.

The hours that followed, I can only recount from those who claimed to know. Marta sat in eerie silence, her pulse slow and measured, staring at the old couple's still bodies. The candlelight flickered, casting grotesque shadows across their faces. It was done. But there were still matters to attend to.

She collected the bowls, emptied their contents into the embers of the hearth, watching as the fire hissed and swallowed the evidence. She wiped the rims of the bowls, scrubbed them clean, her hands working methodically. The rhythmic sound of water lapping against porcelain was the only noise that filled the room.

A knock at the door shattered the stillness. Marta hesitated. The knock came again, harder this time, more insistent. Wiping her hands against her apron, she crossed the room and opened the door just enough to see the shadowed figure beyond it.

It was Kata, wrapped in a dark shawl, her face partially obscured by the night.

"Are they here?" Kata's voice was low, urgent.

Marta hesitated, gripping the edge of the door. "Who?"

"Your in-laws. I saw no light from the window. It's unlike them to be asleep so early."

Marta forced a chuckle. "They're tired. It's been a long day. You know how they are, always fussing over the smallest things."

Kata's gaze lingered for a moment longer before she nodded. "Let them know I stopped by."

Marta nodded, closing the door before Kata could press further.

Her husband was returning. I imagine she must have felt something like dread settle deep into her bones. He had left weeks ago, saying nothing. An unspoken accusation. He knew. Or at least, he suspected. And now, he was coming back.

Marta turned to the silent figures in the chairs. There was no time to waste. With great effort, she moved them to a wooden chest, wrapping them in blankets, pressing down until she heard the faintest click of the latch. A sound outside made her freeze. Footsteps, muffled but distinct, moving past the cottage.

She held her breath, listening, counting the seconds until they faded into the distance. Only then did she wipe the sweat from her brow. Tomorrow, she would bury them. Tomorrow, her husband would return. And tomorrow, she would look him in the eye and convince him that nothing had changed.

Dawn broke, painting the village in muted tones of gold and gray. Marta sat at the kitchen table, fingers wrapped around a cup of weak tea, the bitter taste grounding her. The chest remained where she had left it, hidden beneath an old woolen cover. Soon, she would load it onto a cart and take it deep into the woods.

But first, she needed to act normal.

When she stepped outside, the chill in the air bit through her shawl. The village was stirring. Farmers led their cattle to pasture, children ran through the muddy lanes, their laughter sharp against the morning hush. Marta forced a smile as she passed Kata, nodding in greeting.

"Heading to market?" Kata asked, her eyes scanning Marta's face, searching.

"Yes," Marta replied smoothly. "The meat won't sell itself."

She turned away quickly, feeling the burden of suspicion press against her back. Time was running out.

By midday, she had fetched the cart, its wooden wheels creaking as she pulled it toward the cottage. The heaviness of the trunk tested her strength, but she heaved it onto the cart, her muscles straining, breath coming fast.

With one last glance at the village, she set off toward the forest, the trees standing sentinel against the secrets she would soon bury deep within their roots.

The deeper she went, the more the isolation crept in. The

crunch of dried leaves under the cart's wheels, the soft chirping of distant birdsong, all seemed unnervingly loud. She kept her head down, eyes fixed on the path ahead.

She reached a clearing, one she had scouted before. The soil was soft here. She pulled the spade from the cart, plunging it into the earth. She dug, sweat pooling at her brow, arms burning from the effort. The sun climbed higher, the gravity of the deed pressing on her, heavier than any burden she had ever known.

A rustling in the distance made her pause. Was it just the wind? Or had someone followed her?

Marta turned slowly, gripping the spade tighter. The forest was vast, empty save for the whispering trees. She could see no one, but she felt it. The pressure of unseen eyes. A branch snapped. She held her breath.

Panic gnawed at the edges of her mind, but she steeled herself. She needed to finish this. Quickly. Digging faster now, the hole deepened, dirt flying. The sun was now overhead, casting sharp beams through the trees. Then, a voice.

"Marta."

She spun around. There, half-shrouded by the trees, stood her husband.

16

THE BOY IN THE WOODS

The knock at the door was frantic. Not the slow, measured kind of someone coming with a question, nor the steady rapping of a woman in labor. This was different. Urgent. Panicked.

Zsuzsanna was already moving before I had even risen from my chair. She pulled the door open, and a woman stumbled inside, breathless and wild-eyed.

"Please!" she gasped. "Please, help me!"

Her shawl had fallen from her shoulders, and her dress was soaked from the knees down, mud caked at the hem. She had been running.

"What is it?" Zsuzsanna asked, her voice even, controlled.

"My boy, he's in the woods! He fell, he's hurt, he's bleeding—"

I sucked in a breath. A child.

Zsuzsanna didn't ask for details. She simply grabbed her basket, slung a woolen cloak over her shoulders, and stepped into the cold.

"Come," she said.

And we followed.

The woods were deep and dark even in daylight. The trees stretched tall and skeletal, their bare branches clawing at the gray sky. The ground was slick with wet leaves, patches of ice still clinging to the roots where the sun had not yet reached.

The mother led the way, half-running, half-stumbling as she pushed through the underbrush, her breath coming in ragged gasps.

"I told him not to go far," she said, more to herself than to us. "I told him to stay near the house, but boys ..."

Her voice broke.

"He fell," she whispered. "And then he didn't get up."

A sick feeling coiled in my stomach.

And then a cry. Weak. Pained.

"Mama!"

The woman let out a sob and sprinted ahead and there, beneath the tangled mess of fallen branches, lying at the base of a gnarled oak was a boy. He was no older than six or seven, his small frame trembling, his skin too pale against the brown of the earth.

His leg was bad. The cut was deep, running jagged from his knee down to his shin, torn open by something sharp; maybe a rock, maybe an old, rusted wire hidden in the brush.

The blood had slowed, but it had pooled beneath him, staining the leaves a dark, wet red. He was breathing fast, too fast, his chest rising and falling in short, uneven gasps. Terrified.

"Mama!" His voice hitched, his hands gripping the dirt.

His mother fell to her knees beside him, stroking his hair, whispering nonsense, pressing frantic kisses to his forehead.

"Hush now," Zsuzsanna murmured, kneeling beside them.

She did not rush, did not panic, did not raise her voice. She simply reached out, steady, gentle, touching the boy's forehead, brushing his sweat-slicked hair from his face.

"What's your name?" she asked.

The boy blinked up at her, dazed.

"Tibor," he whispered.

"Tibor," she repeated. "Good. A strong name."

Her hands moved to his leg.

"I won't lie to you, Tibor. This will hurt."

I swallowed hard as I watched. The wound was worse up close, the edges torn and uneven, dirt and debris already embedded in the skin. If it wasn't cleaned properly, if it festered —I didn't let myself linger on that.

"Girl, hold him down," Zsuzsanna ordered, and I moved before I could hesitate, crouching by his shoulders, bracing him. "Tibor, listen to me," Zsuzsanna said. "You are going to count to ten. Can you do that?"

His lip trembled. His small hands clenched into fists.

"Yes."

"Good boy. Start counting."

"One ..."

And she pressed a wet cloth to the wound. Tibor screamed. His mother sobbed, pressing her forehead to his hair, whispering his name over and over as he writhed under my hands.

"Two," he gasped. "Three ..."

"Almost done," Zsuzsanna murmured. "Keep counting."

She worked quickly, washing the wound with clean water, her hands moving with the ease of someone who had done this a thousand times.

"Four ... five ..."

The rag was red now, soaked through.

"Six ..."

The bleeding was slowing.

"Seven ..."

She reached for a small bottle, pulling the cork free with her teeth, pouring its contents over the cut.

"Eight ..."

His whole body seized.

"Nine ... ten."

And just like that, she was done.

"There." Zsuzsanna leaned back, her fingers stained with his blood, but her expression unreadable. "You are very brave, Tibor."

The boy whimpered, his face streaked with tears.

"It hurts," he hiccupped.

"Of course it does," she said. "But you are alive. That is better than the alternative. Make sure you grow up to be a good man."

His mother let out another choked sob, kissing his cheeks, her fingers brushing against the bandages Zsuzsanna had wrapped tightly around his leg.

"You must keep this clean," Zsuzsanna instructed. "No walking for a few days. No dirt, no mud. If it swells, if the skin turns red, if he gets a fever, send for me."

The woman nodded fiercely, gripping her son's hand.

"Thank you," she whispered. "Thank you, Zsuzsanna."

But Zsuzsanna was already moving, standing, dusting the dirt from her knees.

"Come," she said to me. "Help me carry him."

We carried him together. His mother walked ahead, lighting the way with a lantern, its glow bouncing against the dark trees, casting long, reaching shadows. The boy was small, but he pressed into me, real and solid and warm. Zsuzsanna bore most of it, her grip firm, her pace steady, never faltering.

I stole a glance at her as we walked; at the smudges of dirt on her face, at the faint smear of blood on her wrist, at the way her expression never changed, never wavered. I had seen her save a newborn. I had seen her end the suffering of a dying animal. And now, I had seen her pull a child back from the brink of something dark and dangerous. She had never hesitated. Not once. And I was in awe.

Tibor's mother, Julianna, would remember this night. She

would remember how the midwife saved her son, how the midwife was stronger than the men in the village, how she did not flinch in the face of blood and pain.

And when the time came—when her father-in-law struck her across the face for the last time, when he left bruises on her arms, when he spat at her feet like she was nothing—she would remember what Zsuzsanna had done. She would come to the midwife. She would ask for help.

And Zsuzsanna would give it to her.

17

THE BOILING POT

The house smelled different that morning. It always carried certain familiar scents. Dried lavender hanging from the rafters, crushed herbs steeping in small ceramic bowls, the ever-present smoke from the hearth, clinging to the wooden beams like an old ghost. Some smells lingered longer than others, buried in the walls, in the stone floor, in the very bones of the place. But today, something was different.

I noticed it the moment I stepped through the door. Steam curled in slow tendrils through the dimly lit room. The usual scents—earthy, floral, sharp—had been overtaken by something else. Something pungent, something deep and metallic that clung to the back of my throat.

I stopped in the doorway. Zsuzsanna was standing at the hearth, stirring a iron pot, her back to me. The fire beneath it burned low, but the liquid inside was at a rolling boil, bubbles rising to the surface and bursting with a faint, wet pop. A thin film had formed along the edges of the pot, dark and glossy.

She did not turn when I entered.

"Close the door," she said.

I did. The heat in the room was stifling.

My skin prickled with it, sweat gathering at the base of my neck, soaking into the back of my dress. The steam from the pot twisted around my arms like unseen fingers, warm and cloying.

I took a step closer.

"What is that?" I asked.

She lifted the wooden spoon, letting a stream of the liquid drip back into the pot. It was oily, darker than I had expected. It left a thin residue on the spoon, coating the wood in something slick.

"Medicine," she said simply.

The word sat strangely in the air. Medicine.

It was not a lie. And yet, it did not feel like the truth. I moved closer, drawn forward despite the heat pressing against my skin.

The pot was wider than my arms could stretch, its blackened surface worn from years of use. A deep, steady churning filled the room, the sound of liquid rolling over itself. The smell was stronger here, rising with the steam. It was potent, like the scent of wet soil and bitter roots.

Zsuzsanna stirred again, unhurried, methodical. Her sleeves were rolled up to her elbows, her forearms dusted with flecks of dried herbs. A few loose strands of hair clung to her temple, damp with sweat. She looked calm. Focused.

I swallowed. "For what?"

Finally, she turned. Her dark eyes found mine, unreadable.

"For those who need it," she said.

The words sent a shiver through me. I didn't ask anything else. Because I wasn't sure I wanted to know. She gestured to the small wooden stool near the table, and I sat, watching her as she worked.

Zsuzsanna rarely wasted words. She spoke only when necessary, and even then, only in short, measured phrases. I had spent weeks trying to read her, trying to understand what lay beneath that sharp, knowing gaze.

"Where did you learn?" I asked, nodding toward the pot.

She stirred again, lifting the spoon, inspecting the liquid before letting it drip back into the rolling depths. "From my mother. And hers before her."

Her voice was even, steady, but there was something in the way she said it. It was edged with finality.

I hesitated. "Were they—"

"Midwives?" she finished for me, a wry smile tugging at her lips. "Yes."

I nodded. "And was that what you wanted? Or was it just ... expected?"

She tilted her head slightly, as if considering my question. "Expectation is a heavy thing, but it is not always a cage. Some things are in the blood. Whether we choose them or not."

I thought about that for a moment.

"Did you choose this?" I asked.

Zsuzsanna looked at me then, truly looked. I saw something in her eyes, something I couldn't name.

"I chose not to be powerless," she said finally.

The words settled between us, filling the space with something unspoken.

I let my gaze drift over the room: the bundles of dried herbs hanging from the rafters, the rows of carefully labeled jars stacked against the wall, the wooden table where she mixed her tonics and tinctures. This was more than a house. It was a place of quiet power, built from knowledge passed through generations, from whispered secrets and careful hands.

She had chosen not to be powerless. And yet, I couldn't help but wonder, how many others had made that same choice?

"You think you don't belong here," Zsuzsanna said suddenly.

I glanced at her, startled. "No."

She smirked. "I can tell."

"How?"

She gave a slow, knowing nod toward the window, where the village lay quiet beneath the light of the afternoon sun. "You still look at them like you're waiting for something. Like you expect people to behave a certain way."

I hesitated. "And they don't?"

Her smirk deepened. "No. And they never will."

I exhaled, shifting slightly on the stool. She wasn't wrong. The women of Nagyrev were not like the women I had known before. They did not whisper apologies to their husbands. They did not bow their heads. They moved through the world as if they carried a secret. One they did not care to share.

"Where do you want to go?" she asked, stirring again.

"Somewhere north," I said. "Somewhere different to here."

She arched a brow. "And yet, here you are."

I hesitated, then smiled slightly. "I chose not to be powerless, too. And to follow my mother's wishes."

Something shifted in her expression. Amusement, maybe. Understanding.

She dipped the spoon back into the pot, lifting a dark, glistening drop to her lips. She tasted it, nodded in approval, and then, without looking at me, said,

"Then you will do just fine here."

The afternoon stretched long, the scent of the boiling pot filling every corner of the house. I watched Zsuzsanna work, learning from her the way I had since the day I arrived. Not through instructions, but through observation; through the careful unraveling of secrets she never spoke aloud.

I didn't ask what was in the pot. I didn't ask who would come for it, or what they would do with it. Because here, in Nagyrev, those questions had no answers. Or rather, they had answers I wasn't yet ready to hear.

I didn't ask what had happened to Martha in the woods. I also knew the answer to that. And I knew this was one of the reasons she was busy with her remedy.

18

THE STRANGER

The day was already warm when I went to the well. The air smelled of wet earth and wheat, the last breath of spring fading into the heat of summer. My dress clung to my back as I walked, the morning sun pressing against my skin. The well stood at the heart of the village, its stone worn smooth by years of hands pressing against it, its wooden bucket creaking as it was lowered and pulled back up.

I had gone to fetch water, as I did every morning. But that day, I was not alone.

A young man stood at the well, his back to me, shirt rolled up to his elbows, lifting a bucket with strong, steady hands. His skin was sun-darkened, the muscles in his arms taut as he hoisted the water up in one smooth motion.

I slowed my steps. I did not know him. And in Nagyrev, everyone knew everyone. He turned as I approached and I saw him clearly for the first time.

He was handsome, but not in the way of noblemen or city men. His features were rough, his nose slightly crooked as if it had been broken once, his jaw sharp, his brow strong. His hair was dark and unruly, waving slightly at his temples.

His eyes, a deep, rich brown, fixed on me. And something stirred inside me.

I had seen many men in Nagyrev. I had watched them grow crueler with age, their kindness worn away by drink and disappointment. I had learned that men's tempers were unpredictable, their affections fleeting, their kindness a thing that could vanish with the turn of a mood. But this man, he was not like them.

Not yet. Not now. He held himself with a quiet confidence, but not arrogance. And when he spoke, his voice was low and even, without the rough edge of impatience I was used to.

"I haven't seen you before," he said.

"I live here," I replied.

A flicker of amusement passed through his expression.

"Then I suppose it is I who am the stranger."

I had never felt shy before. Not even when speaking to Zsuzsanna. But as he stood there, watching me, I felt the intensity of his gaze, the way it lingered. Not rudely, not hungrily, but as if he were simply taking me in, as if he were trying to place me in the landscape of the village.

"Who are you?" I asked, my fingers tightening around the handle of my empty bucket.

"Ádám," he said. "My family is from a village near Szolnok."

A newcomer. It was rare for people to come to Nagyrev unless they were born here. The land was not wealthy, the village not prosperous. It was a place of inheritance, not ambition.

"And you?" he asked.

"You already know," I said.

"I know you live here. That is not the same as knowing who you are."

A small smile touched his lips. Not mocking. Not unkind.

I did not know what to say to him. Because who was I? A girl without a father. A daughter given to the midwife. A girl who carried secrets that she could never speak aloud.

"I am no one," I said at last.

"I don't believe that."

His voice was quiet, but firm. And for the first time in a long time, I wanted to be seen.

We stood there for a moment, neither of us speaking. The bucket of water in his hands dripped slowly onto the dirt, pooling in dark spots between his boots.

The village was waking around us; women stepping out of their houses, the sound of a rooster crowing, the clang of metal as a farmer hitched a horse to a cart.

I should have left. But I lingered.

"Will I see you again?" he asked.

I hesitated.

"Yes."

And when I walked away, I could feel his eyes on me. I did not turn around. But I was smiling.

19

A WALK THROUGH THE WHEAT

The fields stretched golden beneath the setting sun, the stalks of wheat tall and swaying, whispering secrets to the wind. The air smelled of earth, of ripening grain, of the last breath of summer before autumn claimed the land.

I had not expected to see him again and yet, there he was. Ádám.

Standing at the edge of the field, his sleeves rolled to his elbows, the scent of cut wheat clinging to his skin. He must have been working since dawn, yet he did not carry himself like a man exhausted.

He carried himself like a man who had something left to say.

"You again," he said, as if amused by fate itself.

"I could say the same."

"I told you we would see each other again."

"That was not a promise."

"It was a certainty."

The corner of his mouth lifted slightly. Not a smirk, but something softer. Something almost hopeful. And that was what unsettled me the most. Because I did not know what to do with hope.

"Walk with me."

It was not a question.

I hesitated.

The village was still distant enough that no one would see. No watchful eyes, no whispers waiting to be born. The fields stretched long, the path leading toward the river, where the land dipped into the marsh, where the world felt wider.

I should have said no. But instead, I nodded. And we walked. The earth was soft beneath our feet, our steps muted by the hush of the fields. The wind played with my hair, catching loose strands and twisting them in the dying light.

"You never told me your name," he said after a while.

"You never asked."

"I'm asking now."

I glanced at him. His gaze was steady, patient.

"Eszter."

"Eszter," he repeated, as if tasting it on his tongue.

There was something in the way he said it. Careful, deliberate.

"You are not from here."

"No," he admitted. "But I am trying to make it my home."

"And?"

"And it is a strange place."

I stopped walking.

He turned to face me, waiting.

"You don't belong here," I said, before I could stop myself.

"And you do?"

"I was born here."

"That is not the same thing."

I looked away because he was right. Because Nagyrev was not a place that one simply belonged to. It was a place that held you, that buried you, that turned your body into soil long before you were dead.

"I grew up in Szolnok," he said after a while. "But it was never home."

I glanced at him, waiting for him to go on.

"My father was a merchant. He traded grain, flour, things that people always needed. He wanted me to do the same, to marry well, to be the kind of man who shakes hands in taverns and makes his money in whispers."

"And you didn't want that?"

"I wanted something real."

He ran a hand through his dark curls, his fingers dusted with dirt from the fields.

"I like working with my hands. I like feeling the land under me. I like planting something and knowing it will grow."

He said it simply, like a man who knew what he wanted. Like a man who had already chosen his path.

"So, you came here?" I asked.

"My uncle died in the war. The land passed to my father. My father passed it to me." He glanced at me then, a flicker of curiosity in his gaze. "And what about you?"

"What about me?"

"What is it that you want?"

I hesitated.

Because I had never been asked that before. Because wanting was dangerous. Because I already knew there were things I could never have.

"I don't know," I lied.

"Tell me something." His voice was low, careful.

"What?"

"What is it that no one says?"

I felt my stomach tighten.

"What do you mean?"

"I have lived in other villages," he said. "I know what a place feels like when it is hiding something."

I kept my expression still.

"Nagyrev is like that."

The wind rustled through the wheat. A sound like sighing.

"I don't know what you mean." My voice was even.

"I think you do."

I turned to leave.

"Eszter—"

"Go home, Ádám."

I did not look back because if I had, I was afraid I might let him follow.

20

A VISIT TO THE SICK

The knock came just after midday, a hesitant tapping against the wooden door, light enough that I barely heard it over the wind rattling the shutters. I had been sitting at the table, rolling dried mint leaves between my fingers, reducing them to dust, breathing in their sharp, cool scent. Across the room, Zsuzsanna was wiping down the shelves, moving in slow, deliberate motions, rearranging jars filled with powders, leaves, and things I had not yet learned the names of.

She stopped when she heard the knock. She turned her head slightly but did not rush to answer. Instead, she wiped her hands on her apron, exhaled through her nose, and walked to the door with the same unhurried certainty with which she did everything.

The girl standing on the threshold was too young to have eyes that held such sorrow.

She was wrapped in a thin, threadbare shawl, the fabric worn at the edges, patched in places where it had frayed beyond repair. The skin beneath her eyes was hollowed, dark with exhaustion, her lips chapped from the cold. She smelled of sodden wool and desperation.

She looked at Zsuzsanna. Then at me. Then back again.

"My husband," she said softly. "He's sick."

Zsuzsanna studied her for a long moment, her expression unreadable.

"How sick?"

The girl swallowed. "Fever. Coughing. He can barely sit up."

Her voice was thin, barely above a whisper. There was something in the way she held herself. Not just exhaustion, but something deeper. Was it hope?

Zsuzsanna tilted her head slightly, gaze steady. "And what do you want me to do?"

The girl hesitated. Her fingers tightened around the fabric of her shawl.

"I need help," she said finally. "Please."

Zsuzsanna considered this. Then, without a word, she turned, walked to the far shelf, and reached for something. A glass bottle. The same kind I had seen before. My stomach clenched. She handed it to me.

"Go with her," she said.

I hesitated. "What am I supposed to do?"

Zsuzsanna met my gaze, steady and calm. "Give her two drops in his broth," she said. "That will help him rest."

The girl did not react. She did not ask what was in the bottle, or what it would do. She simply nodded.

I gripped the bottle carefully in my palm. And then I followed her out into the bitter afternoon.

The village was still, the streets nearly empty. The girl's home was small, tucked away at the edge of the village near the forest. It was a simple structure; one room, a sagging roof, smoke drifting from the chimney in slow, lazy tendrils. A small garden sat beside it, mostly bare now that winter was settling in, a few stubborn herbs clinging to life in the frozen soil.

She led me inside without a word. The warmth hit me first.

The fire in the hearth was burning low and the smell of sickness clung to the walls. Sweat. Stale breath. The sour tang of fever.

The man was in the bed against the far wall, barely more than a shape beneath the blankets. I stepped closer. He was young, no more than twenty-five, I guessed, but already looked worn. His face was slick with sweat, his hair matted, his breathing shallow and uneven. His lips were cracked, his hands twitching slightly against the sheets.

The girl moved past me, dipping a wooden ladle into a pot that hung over the fire. The broth inside was thin, watery. Not enough meat. Not enough strength. She poured it into a small clay bowl, then turned to me. I hesitated. The glass bottle was still in my hand, the liquid inside sloshing gently as I turned it between my fingers. Two drops. That was what Zsuzsanna had said.

I looked down at the man. His eyes fluttered slightly, his lips parting, though no words came. He looked so small like this, his body bent in on itself, sinking into the mattress as if it were trying to swallow him whole.

I looked back at the girl. Her face was unreadable. She was not afraid.

I opened the bottle. Two drops. The liquid hit the surface of the broth and vanished instantly, dissolving into the golden depths without a trace.

I handed her the bowl. She took it without hesitation, moved to the bed, and knelt beside him.

"Drink," she murmured, pressing the rim to his lips.

He swallowed.

I watched his throat bob, watched his fingers twitch against the sheets. The girl pulled back, setting the bowl aside. Then, finally, she looked at me.

"Thank you," she said.

And for the first time, I wasn't sure she was talking about the medicine at all.

The walk back to Zsuzsanna's house felt longer than before.

The air was crisp, the sky stretched wide and gray above me. In the distance, I could see smoke wafting from chimneys, the scent of burning wood carried on the wind.

I felt the heaviness of the empty bottle in my pocket. It had been so easy. Two drops. That was all it took. Zsuzsanna was still at the table when I returned. She did not look up as I closed the door behind me.

"Did you give it to her?" she asked.

I hesitated. Then nodded. "Yes."

She nodded once, as if this was the only answer that mattered.

She reached for a bundle of dried thyme, plucked a few sprigs, and began tying them together with twine. Calm. Unbothered. As if what I had just done was no different from delivering herbs, from fetching water from the well.

I swallowed. "Will it help him?"

Zsuzsanna's hands did not pause in their work.

"It will do what it is meant to do," she said simply.

And that was all.

Outside, the wind picked up, rustling the bare branches of the trees and I stood there for a long time, listening.

21

A DARK UNDERSTANDING

It was just before dawn when I heard the news. I had barely slept.

The fire had burned down to embers, throwing faint, restless shadows against the walls. Outside, the wind pressed against the shutters in slow, rhythmic gusts, a quiet reminder that winter was not far off. I had stared at the ceiling for hours, my mind circling the same thought over and over.

Two drops. I could still see them falling, vanishing into the broth without a trace. I had told myself it was nothing. That it was just medicine. That it was a coincidence. Then came the knocking. Hard, insistent, shaking the wooden frame of the door.

Zsuzsanna was already moving before I could sit up, throwing a shawl over her shoulders, her bare feet silent against the stone floor. She didn't hesitate, didn't glance at me before pulling the door open.

The cold rushed in, carrying the scent of wet earth and frost-kissed wood. Ilona stood in the doorway, her face unreadable. Not surprised. Not alarmed. Just ... expectant.

"It happened in the night," she said simply.

She didn't say who. She didn't have to.

Zsuzsanna nodded, as if she had already known. "I'll come."

I rose from the bed, my limbs sluggish, my stomach twisting itself into knots. "What happened?"

Ilona turned her sharp gaze on me.

"He's dead."

The house was even smaller than I remembered.

The walls seemed to lean inward, pressing close, the air holding the cloying scent of sickness and sweat, now layered with something else. Something final.

The girl sat by the hearth, her hands folded neatly in her lap. She wasn't crying. She wasn't even looking at him.

The body was still in the bed. I swallowed hard.

The man lay stretched out beneath the thin blankets, his face slack, his mouth slightly open. He didn't look peaceful. There was no grace in his death, no softness. His skin was too pale, almost waxy, his lips tinged with a deep, unnatural blue.

His hands were contorted into stiff, claw-like shapes. His fingernails had dug into his own palms, leaving deep, crescent-shaped marks. His body had not gone easily.

Zsuzsanna moved past me, slow and deliberate, peeling back the blanket, exposing more of him to the dim light filtering through the small window. She studied him for a moment. Then turned to the girl.

"When did he go?"

"Late," the girl said softly. "The fever was bad. He kept gasping, clutching his stomach. And then ..."

She gestured vaguely, as if the rest did not need to be said. And perhaps it didn't.

I felt something cold unfurl inside me. I turned, moving toward the door, my breath coming too fast, too shallow. I needed air.

The village was still waking. Smoke wafted from chimneys, the first voices drifting through the square, slow and easy, untouched by the news of the dead man in the house behind me. A normal day. A normal death.

I pressed a hand to my heart, trying to quiet the hammering beneath my ribs.

It wasn't me. It was the fever. It was chance. It was the war, taking its toll on men who had already been weakened, broken from the inside out. It was not me.

A hand touched my arm. I startled, turning sharply. It was Ilona.

She regarded me carefully. "You're pale."

I forced a tight smile. "It's the morning chill."

Ilona tilted her head, watching me with that knowing look that the women of Nagyrev always seemed to have. Like they had seen this before. Like they had seen everything before.

She glanced back toward the house. "He's not the first, you know."

I knew she wasn't just talking about sickness. Something inside me twisted.

I exhaled sharply. "What do you mean?"

Ilona gave me a small, almost amused smile. And then, in the same casual tone she might use to discuss the price of bread, she said,

"Some men are harder to kill than others."

My stomach dropped. She turned, walking back toward the house, leaving me standing there, my breath sharp in the morning cold.

When we returned to Zsuzsanna's house, she went back to her work as if nothing had happened. She pulled down a bundle of dried chamomile, picking apart the stems, setting the flowers aside for tea. Calm. Unbothered.

I sat at the table, hands folded in my lap, the significance of what I had done pressing into me like wet earth. She didn't look up when she spoke.

"You think it was you," she said.

I stiffened. "I don't know what you mean."

Zsuzsanna let out a short, quiet laugh. "You do."

I said nothing.

She plucked another flower from the bundle. "People like to think of death as something distant," she mused. "Something that only comes for the old, the frail, the ones who have earned it." She paused. "But death has never been fair, has it?"

She set the chamomile aside, finally looking at me. "Did you hold him down? Did you put your hands around his throat?"

I shook my head.

"Then you did not kill him."

The words should have been comforting. They weren't.

I closed my eyes, pressing my palms against the worn wood of the table, grounding myself in the roughness of it.

"You told me to give it to him," I said finally.

Zsuzsanna leaned forward, her expression unreadable. "I told you to help her."

I thought of the girl, sitting by the hearth, her hands folded so neatly in her lap. Not crying. Not grieving.

"She's free now," Zsuzsanna murmured, as if she had plucked the thought straight from my mind. "That is what matters."

I opened my mouth. Then closed it. Because wasn't that the truth?

Hadn't I seen the bruises on Kata's arms, the hollow look in the eyes of other women? Hadn't I heard them laugh when they thought no one was listening? Hadn't I, in some quiet part of myself, already understood?

Zsuzsanna watched me. And for the first time, I wasn't sure if she was waiting for me to accept it or to turn away.

Outside, the wind picked up, rattling the shutters, carrying the sounds of the waking village. Another day had begun. Another man had died. And still, the world kept turning.

22

THE PACT

The first frost of the season came that night. It crept in through the cracks in the shutters, settling over the rooftops like a thin veil of white. The air smelled of wood smoke and wet leaves, and the dirt paths between the houses had turned solid beneath the weight of the cold. The village had grown quieter in recent days. Or perhaps I had simply learned to listen differently.

I was restless. Ádám was there, like an indelible mark on my mind.

Sleep had been fitful, broken by strange dreams that felt like half-remembered warnings. The sickness was also on my mind, or rather, the way it had ended. I had tried to convince myself that it was the fever, the war, the hunger that had weakened him. That the broth had done nothing at all. But I wasn't sure I believed that anymore.

The women of Nagyrev moved through their days the same way they always had: washing clothes at the river, kneading bread, sweeping the dust from their doorsteps. But now, I saw it. The quiet looks they exchanged. The way their conversations turned away when a man passed by. The knowing glances, the nods.

I wasn't supposed to hear them that night. But I did. It had been late when I stepped outside, needing air.

The wind had a bite to it, slipping beneath my shawl as I pulled it tighter around my shoulders. The village lay dark and still, save for the dull glow of a few hearth fires behind shuttered windows. Somewhere in the distance, a dog barked once before falling silent.

I had only meant to walk to the well and back. But then I heard them. Voices low, steady, deliberate. I stopped. They were coming from Ilona's house, just a few steps ahead. The door was slightly ajar, allowing a sliver of golden light to spill onto the cold earth. Shadows moved inside, shifting, leaning in close.

I should have turned away. But I didn't. I stepped carefully, my breath barely rising in the cold air as I pressed myself against the outer wall, close enough to hear.

"She says he drinks more than he used to," a voice murmured. "And that he's been worse since the war."

A pause before another woman spoke. "They're all worse since the war."

A low noise of agreement followed.

"Has he hurt her?"

"Not yet."

"But he will."

"Does she want help?"

A chair creaked. Someone shifted.

"She's afraid."

"Of him?"

"Of being free."

Another voice, older, firmer. "She'll ask, when she's ready."

A pause. Then the first woman again, quieter now.

"And if she doesn't?"

Someone exhaled slowly, as if considering. Then, finally, a voice I recognized. Ilona's.

"Then we decide for her."

I stepped back from the door, my pulse thrumming in my ears. The cold seemed sharper now, the night heavier.

I walked quickly, keeping my head down, my hands clenched inside my shawl. I didn't stop until I was back inside Zsuzsanna's house, the door shut firmly behind me.

The fire had burned low, casting long shadows across the stone floor. Zsuzsanna was at the table, stripping dried thyme from its stalks, her movements slow, methodical.

She didn't look up. But she knew.

"You heard them," she said.

It wasn't a question. I hesitated. Then nodded as she set the thyme aside, finally lifting her gaze to mine.

"Are you afraid?"

I swallowed. "Should I be?"

Zsuzsanna held my stare for a long moment. Then, she smiled.

"No," she murmured. "Not unless you're a man."

I barely slept.

The whispers I had heard in Ilona's house replayed in my mind, circling like birds over a dying thing. The women had spoken so plainly, so easily, their voices never rising, never faltering. They were not plotting. They were deciding.

It had been a conversation like any other. As if they were discussing the harvest. As if they were choosing which dress to mend or which loaf of bread to bake.

Then we decide for her.

I turned onto my side, staring at the dying embers in the hearth, my body stiff from lying awake. The words felt heavier now, pressing against my heart like a stone. I could still hear Ilona's voice, steady, calm, without hesitation.

I had not imagined it. I had not misunderstood. They had spoken of life and death as if the line between them was not a line at all but a door. One that could be opened, quietly, without fuss, whenever they deemed it necessary. And I had helped them do it.

I closed my eyes, inhaling deeply, as if I could rid myself of the knowledge by breathing it out into the cold night air. But I could not unknow what I had heard.

And worse, I could not deny the part of me that understood it.

Morning came slowly.

The house smelled of dank wood and dried chamomile, of the lingering warmth of last night's fire. I rose stiffly, rubbing the sleep from my eyes, but the heaviness inside me did not lift.

Zsuzsanna was already up, standing at the counter, grinding something in a small clay mortar. The rhythmic scrape of pestle against stone filled the room, steady and unhurried.

She didn't look at me as she spoke.

"You didn't sleep."

I pulled my shawl tighter around my shoulders, watching the way her hands moved; precise, practiced, as if she had done this a thousand times before.

"I heard them," I murmured.

She didn't stop grinding. "I know."

The pestle scraped again, crushing whatever was inside into something finer, something more easily swallowed.

I swallowed, my throat dry. "It was ... different, hearing it that way. Out loud."

Zsuzsanna nodded, finally pausing, turning the mortar in her hands. "You're still thinking about it."

"Wouldn't you?" I asked.

At that, she did look at me, her dark eyes sharp, unwavering. "I stopped thinking about it a long time ago."

I exhaled, turning away.

"I don't know what I expected," I admitted. "Maybe that they would speak of it differently. With guilt. With hesitation."

Zsuzsanna let out a quiet laugh, shaking her head.

"You think too much like a girl," she said.

I frowned. "And what does that mean?"

She leaned forward, resting her elbows against the table. "It means you were taught that suffering is a woman's duty. That endurance is the mark of a good wife, a good daughter, a good widow."

She tilted her head slightly, studying me.

"But here, we do not endure. We do not wait for fate to hand us mercy. We make it."

Her words sent a shiver through me, though whether it was from fear or understanding, I did not know. I thought of the way the women had gathered at the well, making space for Kata without a word. I thought of the quiet way the widows carried themselves. Not in mourning, but in relief.

I thought of the laughs I had heard when no men were listening. And I thought of the girl with the sick husband, sitting at the hearth, her hands folded neatly in her lap, her face smooth, untouched by grief.

I closed my eyes, exhaling slowly.

"I never meant to be part of this," I said softly.

Zsuzsanna's voice was gentle, but firm.

"But," the pestle scraped against the mortar again, a slow, deliberate sound, "You are."

23

SUSPICION

The village square was quieter than usual. Not empty, never empty, but there was something missing in the way the men gathered. The usual sounds of raised voices, of beer mugs thudding onto rough wooden tables, of laughter bubbling up through the cold morning air, had thinned into something smaller. Something uncertain.

I did not sit too close. I did not need to.

The well stood at the edge of the square, its stones glistening with morning mist, its wooden beams slick beneath my fingers. I drew up a bucket, slow and careful, letting the weight of the water steady me as I listened.

"They buried Mihály yesterday."

A soft voice. One not meant for my ears.

"Which Mihály?"

"The younger."

A pause. Someone exhaled sharply. "He wasn't sick."

"No. He wasn't."

There was a pause in conversation. I turned my back to them, dipping my ladle into the bucket, letting the cold water run down my throat. It was an old trick. When you drink, no one expects you to speak.

Someone shifted on the wooden benches behind me. A boot scuffed against the dirt. "And Károly?"

Another pause. Then: "Three days ago."

The men were careful with their words. It was not in their nature to acknowledge fear; not in themselves, not in each other. They did not say, *too many*. They did not say, *this is not normal.* But I could hear it, unspoken in the gaps between their sentences.

"They say it was his heart," someone muttered.

"They always say that," another man replied, his voice flat.

I kept my back to them, my hands tight around the bucket's handle.

"József's boy is dead too," a third voice joined in. "Barely twenty. Just ... gone."

A chair scraped against the ground. Someone was shifting, uneasy.

"What do you think it is?"

A cough. A clearing of the throat. Then, softly, cautiously: "Something's moving through the village."

A chill threaded through me, slow and deliberate. Not someone. Something. I swallowed against the lump in my throat. They did not suspect. Not yet. But they were counting.

And once men begin counting their dead, it is only a matter of time before they begin looking for the cause.

I turned from the well, careful not to move too quickly. I gripped my bucket, stepped back toward the road, wove through the morning market with steady, measured steps. But inside my thoughts were tangled, tight, writhing in the space between my ribs.

How many had there been?

I had stopped keeping track. I had thought it better not to know.

At first, it had been easy. A single name. A single man. A single story, whispered low in a dark kitchen, hands twisting in skirts, words slipping out like breath.

But now the names piled like stones in my mind; many and uncounted.

I had told myself it was justice. I had told myself it was mercy. I had told myself it was necessary. But had I ever told myself it was right? Questions twisted inside me like smoke. Ones I did not want to ask.

When had it stopped being about survival? When had it stopped being about them? When had it become about us?

I stepped onto the path leading home, the bucket of water sloshing against my legs, the village still murmuring behind me.

I did not look back because I was afraid of what I might see and returned to the house which stood as it always did; still and in shadow.

Smoke wafted from the chimney, pale against the early morning sky. Bundles of herbs swayed from the rafters, drying in the cold air, their scents sharp and lingering: rosemary, sage, wormwood. The door was closed, but it never needed to be locked.

No one entered Zsuzsanna's house unless they had reason to. I hesitated at the threshold.

The water in my bucket was still cold, my hands wet from carrying it. A small thing, but grounding. It kept me tethered to something simple. Something ordinary. I knocked once, then pushed the door open.

Zsuzsanna was at the table, grinding something to powder using a mortar and pestle. The scent of crushed roots filled the room. She did not look up.

"You're late," she said.

I set the bucket down by the hearth. "I stopped at the well."

She made a soft noise, scraping the powdered herbs into a small glass vial. "Did you hear anything interesting?"

I opened my mouth, then hesitated. Should I tell her? Did I want to?

I had never kept anything from her before. I had never *wanted* to. I forced myself to move, kneeling beside the hearth, taking the kindling in my hands. It gave me something to do. Something to focus on.

"The men are talking," I said finally.

Zsuzsanna did not stop working. "They always talk."

"Not like this."

She lifted her gaze then, eyes steady, sharp. Waiting while I swallowed.

"They're counting," I said. "Not openly, not accusing, but they know. They know something isn't right. Too many of them have died too quickly. And they're starting to feel it."

Zsuzsanna sighed through her nose, wiping her hands on her apron. She leaned back against the table, considering.

"And what do you think?" she asked.

The warmth from the fire did nothing to settle the cold in my stomach.

What did I think?

I thought about József's son. Barely twenty, barely a man. I thought about the way the women whispered in the dark, their hands closing around small glass bottles with trembling fingers.

I thought about how easy it was. How easy it had become. I stared at my hands, at the faint dusting of soot on my skin.

"I don't know," I admitted.

Zsuzsanna tilted her head slightly, watching me in that way she always did, like she was measuring something in me.

"You knew what this was," she said. "From the beginning."

"I did."

"And you believed in it."

"I did."

She waited.

I did not speak the next words aloud. *But do I still?*

Zsuzsanna pushed away from the table, crossing the room, kneeling beside me at the hearth. She took the kindling from my hands, arranging it with practiced efficiency, striking a match against the stone. The flames caught, then spread.

"This world takes from women," she said softly. "It always has. It always will."

I closed my eyes. I thought of Ádám. I hoped she was wrong.

"I know."

"We did not start this," she murmured. "But we will finish it."

The fire burned hotter, stronger, the warmth reaching out, brushing against my skin. I opened my eyes. Zsuzsanna's gaze was steady. Certain. She had never doubted. I envied that certainty. I feared it. I wanted it.

But all I felt was the worry in my soul, the slow, creeping sense that something was shifting inside me. Something uncertain. Something I did not have a name for.

I turned away from the fire, away from her, and whispered, "And if we are wrong?"

The flames cracked and spat their answer. Zsuzsanna said nothing.

24

THE WORLD BEYOND

I found Ádám by the river.

The Tisza had not yet frozen over, though its surface was sluggish, a dark, glassy thing reflecting the dull winter sky. The reeds at the water's edge were stiff and brittle, their tips dusted with frost, the earth beneath them hardened by the creeping cold.

He was sitting on a fallen log, a book balanced in his hands, his head slightly tilted downward as he read. I hesitated. I had never known a man to read the way Ádám did. Not just for prayer, not just for knowledge, but for understanding. He absorbed words the way others absorbed warmth from the sun, leaning into them, letting them settle into his bones.

I almost turned back. Then, without looking up, he spoke.

"You're staring."

I huffed. "I'm not."

He turned a page.

"You are."

I sighed, stepping closer.

"What are you reading?" I asked.

He finally looked up, his sharp, clever eyes studying me, amused. Then he held the book out toward me.

I frowned at the cover.

"*The Collapse of the Dual Monarchy*," I read aloud. "That sounds dreary."

"It is," Ádám said, tucking the book under his arm. "But it's important."

"Why?"

"Because everything we are living through now, everything Hungary has become, started with what happened to the Empire."

I blinked.

"You mean the war?"

He smiled, but not very kindly.

"I mean everything."

I sat beside him, pulling my shawl tighter around my shoulders.

"I don't understand why you care so much about things that don't touch us," I admitted.

Ádám sighed, rubbing a hand over his jaw.

"Eszter, everything touches us."

I frowned. "Not here. Not in Nagyrev."

"Especially in Nagyrev," he corrected.

I crossed my arms. "Go on, then. Educate me."

He exhaled, shaking his head like I was exhausting, but there was something warm in his expression.

"You know we lost the war," he started.

"Of course."

"But do you know what that meant for Hungary?"

"We ... suffered?"

He gave me a look.

"We lost two-thirds of our land," he said. "More than half of our people now live in foreign countries. In Transylvania, in

Slovakia, in Austria, in Yugoslavia. Families have been cut apart. Our army was dismantled. Our economy shattered. And it wasn't just suffering, Eszter. It was humiliation."

I hesitated.

I had heard people whisper about the Treaty of Trianon. I had seen the way the men in the village talked about it, the way their jaws tightened when it was mentioned, the way their fists clenched in their laps. But I had never truly considered what it meant.

Ádám saw the hesitation in my face.

"You don't think about it because you've never had to," he said. "The women of this village, they work. They survive. They do what they must to keep their children from starving. But the men ..."

He glanced at the water.

"The men have lost their pride. And they are angry."

The words settled between us.

I thought of the men in Nagyrev. The ones who came back from the war hollow-eyed and broken. The ones who drank their wages away, who staggered home to their wives with shaking hands and sharp tongues. The ones who still had bruises on their fists from fights they never spoke of. And I thought of the ones who never came back at all.

"It isn't just here," Ádám continued. "Across the country, the government is barely holding together. King Charles tried to take the throne twice last year. He failed both times. Horthy controls everything now."

"Miklós Horthy," I said, carefully.

I had heard the name before, whispered in the marketplace, muttered by the men at the tavern.

"Yes. The Regent. Our king without a crown." Ádám's voice was tinged with something unreadable. "He says he's keeping

Hungary safe. But already, we are slipping into something worse. Do you know what the White Terror is?"

I shook my head. He sighed.

"After the war, after the communists were driven out, men who supported Horthy hunted them down. Executed them. But it wasn't just communists they killed. It was anyone they didn't trust. Leftists. Jews. Intellectuals. Thousands of people. Gone."

I swallowed. I had never heard that.

"And still, people starve," Ádám went on. "We are drowning in debt. The economy is in ruins. Hyperinflation is getting worse. In Budapest, people line the streets begging for food. And it won't get better, Eszter. Not for a long time."

I shifted, uneasy.

"And that means something for us?"

Ádám turned his gaze toward me, searching, careful.

"It means people are desperate."

A sharp gust of wind swept over the river, biting at my cheeks. I pulled my shawl tighter, but it wasn't the cold that made me shiver.

"The men," I murmured. "You said they are angry."

"Of course they are." Ádám leaned forward, resting his elbows on his knees. "Men are raised to believe they are owed something. A good job. A family. Respect. But when the world takes those things from them, they lash out."

I looked away. I knew what he meant. I had seen what angry men could do.

"They will start looking for someone to blame," Ádám said. "And the government will be happy to give them an answer. Horthy already pushes blame on the communists. On the Jews. On outsiders. But what happens when that isn't enough?"

My stomach twisted. I didn't want to think about it.

"We're safe here," I said instead.

Ádám smiled, but it didn't reach his eyes.

"Are we?"

I stood. I didn't want to hear any more.

"Thank you for the history lesson," I muttered.

He sighed. "Eszter—"

"No," I cut in. "I understand. The world is cruel. The men are cruel. The government is cruel. But that isn't new."

"It's getting worse," he said.

I shook my head.

"And what do you expect me to do about it?"

He was silent. The wind howled.

Finally, Ádám stood too, brushing snow from his coat.

"I don't expect you to do anything," he said quietly. "I just wanted you to know."

I hesitated. For a brief moment, I thought about telling him.

About Zsuzsanna. About the women. About the poison.

About the quiet power that had been growing in Nagyrev, spreading through the village like a slow-burning fire.

But I didn't. Because Ádám might have understood the world better than I did but he did not understand women. And he never would.

We parted ways without another word. As I walked home, his questions echoed in my mind. And for the first time, I realized was scared and I didn't have the answers.

25

THE DEAD OF WINTER

The cold had settled deep in the bones of Nagyrev, creeping into the walls, into the earth, into the very breath of the villagers. Winter here was not gentle. It never had been.

The wind howled through the barren fields, slipping through the cracks in the wooden cottages, seeping into the spaces between fingers and toes. The river had frozen over weeks ago, its surface coated with ice, the reeds at its edge stiff and brittle, breaking like glass under the sharpness of the frost.

Smoke rose from every chimney, the only proof of life beneath the hush of the snow. Christmas was coming. And the village prepared.

The way we celebrated Christmas had not changed much over the years. The old women still spoke of the way their mothers and grandmothers had done it before them, long before the war, before the world had cracked and reshaped itself.

The Hungarian countryside was a place where tradition clung to the bones of the people, where customs stretched back farther than memory. Christmas had always been sacred, a time when heaven felt closer, when the veil between the living and the dead was thinner.

For weeks leading up to it, the village observed Advent, a time of fasting, prayer, and quiet preparation. The first candle was lit on the Advent wreath four Sundays before Christmas, marking the slow approach of the holy night. Meat was scarce, but it was not eaten on these days anyway, replaced by simple meals of bread, cabbage, and fish, if it could be spared.

The children were told to be good, lest they anger St. Nicholas, or worse, his dark counterpart, Krampus, who was said to drag wicked children into the forests and leave them for the wolves.

In the evenings, people gathered in homes, telling old stories, whispering superstitions passed down from the days when Hungary was still full of pagans.

"On Christmas Eve," one of the old men had told me once, "the animals speak."

"But you must never listen," his wife had added. "If you do, you will hear your own death foretold."

I had been too afraid to ask more.

The days leading up to it were filled with work. Women scrubbed their homes from top to bottom, washing floors and bleaching linens, as if dirt from the past year could not be carried into the next. They decorated with whatever they had: branches of pine tucked into corners, dried apples strung along the beams, wax candles placed in windows to guide the Christ Child to their homes.

The men, when they weren't repairing fences or cutting more firewood, trudged into the forest to bring back small trees or evergreen boughs. Not everyone could afford a Christmas tree, but a few branches, tied with red ribbon and set near the hearth, were enough.

The church was cleaned as well. I had seen the village priest, a thin and serious man, his hands red and raw from scrubbing the stone steps. Women brought embroidered cloths to drape over the altar, and fresh straw was laid in the nativity scene, though no one dared touch the wooden baby Jesus until Christmas Eve.

And it was always the food that made Christmas feel real.

Women pounded dough on wooden tables, rolling it out for bejgli, the walnut and poppy-seed rolls that would be sliced thin on Christmas Day. Cabbage was boiled, apples were baked, and flour-dusted hands worked tirelessly to prepare what little they had into something worthy of celebration.

For most, Christmas was a time of joy. For others, it was simply a reminder of all that had been lost.

Zsuzsanna did not celebrate. Not really. She did what was expected. She cleaned the house. She tied small dried flowers to the beams. She made her usual soups and breads, adding a handful of nuts to her stores as a gesture toward the season.

But there was no joy in it. No wonder. No warmth.

She spoke little of her childhood, but I had learned enough in my time with her to know that Christmas had meant nothing in the house where she was raised. Her father, a cruel man, long dead now, had seen no reason to mark the birth of Christ. Her mother, a woman worn thin from bearing his children and his temper, had been too exhausted to care. And when she had been old enough to marry, Christmas had only meant more bruises, more broken things, more unspoken words.

Now, Christmas meant work. It meant trudging through the snow to tend to the sick. It meant delivering babies in cold rooms, boiling water in blackened pots, wiping blood from wooden floorboards.

It meant going to Midnight Mass with the rest of the village, standing stiffly in the candlelit church, watching the others bow their heads in prayer while she stared straight ahead.

It was routine. Nothing more. But still, she let me have my own small joy in it.

She let me slice apples for drying, let me arrange walnuts in neat rows on the table, let me braid strips of dough for the sweet bread we would take to the priest on Christmas morning.

She let me pretend, just for a little while, that this season was something sacred. And maybe, in its own way, it was.

Christmas Eve arrived with a sky so black it looked like the earth had been swallowed whole. The village was quiet. The only sound was the distant toll of the church bell, calling the faithful to Midnight Mass.

I walked beside Zsuzsanna, our boots crunching in the snow, our breath coming in soft, silvered clouds.

The village square was alive with soft candlelight, shadows stretching across the white drifts as people shuffled into the church.

Women wrapped in dark shawls. Men with caps pulled low. Children with red cheeks, their hands buried deep in their pockets. A hush fell over the crowd as we stepped inside.

The air was suffused with the scent of beeswax and incense, the warmth of too many unwashed bodies packed into too small a space. We found our place at the back, standing against the stone wall.

The priest raised his arms, and the service began. Latin prayers, chanted in deep, rhythmic tones. The lighting of candles, one by one, until the entire church shone with golden fire. Hymns, sung in voices so soft they felt like whispers.

And then, calm. The moment before the bells rang out. The moment when all was still, when the air held its breath, when time itself seemed to pause.

I turned and saw Zsuzsanna, her face unreadable in the candlelight. She was not praying. She was not singing. She was simply watching. And for the first time, I wondered, what did she see?

By Christmas morning, the fast was over, and the feasting began. Neighbors knocked on doors, bringing apples, walnuts, dried plums, small offerings of hospitality and goodwill. Laughter, louder than usual. A warmth that had little to do with the hearth. And beneath it all, something unspoken.

The women of Nagyrev moved through the streets with knowing glances, small smiles twitching at the corners of their lips. Not all gifts were meant to be shared in daylight. Not all kindnesses were for men to witness.

Christmas was for peace. But the days after were for decisions.

And as I watched Zsuzsanna drink a small cup of pálinka that night, her expression unreadable, I knew happiness did not matter. But power—power lasted.

26

IN LIFE AND DEATH

The first scream tore through the night, splitting the quiet in half.

I had been asleep, or half-asleep, but the sound sent me upright so fast my vision blurred. The wind outside howled against the walls, rattling the shutters, shaking the old wooden beams of the house. The air held the scent of burned-out candles and sodden wool, the fire in the hearth nothing but dying embers.

Another scream.

This one worse. Raw. Ragged. A sound pulled straight from the depths of a woman's suffering. I scrambled to my feet. Zsuzsanna was already at the door, wrapping her shawl around her shoulders, slipping her feet into boots.

"Come," she said.

As always I obeyed.

The house belonged to Anna Varga, a woman not much older than me, but already swollen with her third pregnancy.

Twins, Zsuzsanna had said. Two babies, which meant double the risk. And when we entered the house, I knew something was very wrong.

The room was stifling. A fire raged in the hearth, but the heat was suffocating, smelling of sweat and iron. Candles burned low on every surface, their wax dripping onto the wooden floor, pools of melted light collecting like small, glowing wounds.

Anna was on the bed, her legs spread, her dress bunched around her thighs, her hands twisted into the sheets, her knuckles white with pain. She was drenched in sweat, her hair sticking to her forehead, her face contorted into something barely human.

Her mother stood beside her, clutching a moist rag, murmuring prayers that had long since lost their meaning.

Anna's husband was nowhere to be seen. I had stopped being surprised by that.

"Zsuzsanna," Anna gasped, her voice hoarse.

"I'm here," the midwife said, calm, steady in the face of panic. She set her basket down, rolled up her sleeves. She did not rush. She did not hesitate.

I wished I could say the same for myself.

My hands trembled as I set out the tools: the knife, the cord, the clean rags. Things I had seen before, but never like this. Never with so much blood already on the sheets.

I swallowed. I had expected to bring life into the world. Not to watch it slip away.

"The first one is coming," Zsuzsanna said, pressing her hands against Anna's belly, feeling the contractions. She nodded to me. "Be ready."

Anna let out another scream, her body convulsing with the effort. It was primal, guttural; something that belonged more to beasts than women. I had never heard a sound like it.

And then, a head.

A tiny, wet, dark-haired head.

"Push, Anna," Zsuzsanna commanded.

And Anna did. The first child was born. A boy.

"He's breathing," I whispered, relief flooding through me as I wiped him clean, as he let out his first weak, protesting cry. Alive. He was alive.

But there was no time for celebration because Anna had already started to convulse again. There was still another baby to be born. And something was wrong.

The second child did not come as easily.

Anna's screams grew worse, her body arching, her nails digging into her mother's arm as another contraction wracked her body. The blood was heavier now, soaking through the sheets, pooling beneath her like a tide that would not stop rising.

"It's stuck," Zsuzsanna muttered.

I felt my stomach turn to ice.

"What do we do?"

"We must wait."

"She's bleeding too much."

"I know."

I stared at her, at her calm, unwavering face, at the way her hands remained steady as she reached for the knife.

She had done this before. She had seen this before. But I hadn't. And I didn't know if I could.

"Eszter," Zsuzsanna said suddenly.

I looked at her.

"If the baby does not come, the mother will die."

I swallowed, my throat dry.

"Can we save them both?"

She didn't answer right away. And that told me everything.

Another contraction. Another scream. The baby slipped free. But it did not cry. It did not move.

It was smaller than its brother, its skin pale, its tiny mouth open in a silent scream it had never gotten the chance to make. Dead. The second baby was dead.

Anna was too weak to understand. She was limp now, her head lolling to the side, her lips moving without sound, her skin pallid beneath the candlelight.

Zsuzsanna worked quickly, pressing cloth to the place where the blood would not stop, whispering instructions to the mother, the grandmother, to me.

"She will live," Zsuzsanna said finally, but her voice was quieter now.

We had saved the mother. But not both children. And that was a loss that weighed upon me.

The dead baby was wrapped in linen, placed in the arms of the grandmother, who did not weep, only whispered words that I did not understand.

The living child nursed at its mother's breast, unaware of the blood, of the loss, of the fragile balance that had nearly tipped toward death.

And I stood frozen, staring at the pool of red staining the floorboards, at the pale bundle of cloth in the old woman's hands, at the breathless body that had never even opened its eyes.

"You did well," Zsuzsanna said.

I turned to her. She was washing the blood from her hands, methodical, efficient, as if she had already left the moment behind.

"This is what it means to be a midwife," she said.

I swallowed.

"I don't know if I can do this."

Zsuzsanna looked at me for a long moment.

And then, to my surprise, she sighed.

"I once thought the same."

She dried her hands and wiped them on her blood stained apron. Then she turned away.

And I was left standing there, staring at the blood, at the mother, at the child that would never take a breath.

And for the first time since I had stepped into Zsuzsanna's house, I wondered if I had made a terrible mistake.

27

THE MIDWIFE'S CONFESSION

I had been waiting for her to speak.

Ever since I overheard the women in Ilona's house, since I had seen the man's body stretched stiff beneath the thin blankets, I had been waiting. For days, there had been something unspoken between us. I watched her the way one watches an animal in the woods; half-curious, half-wary, never sure if it will let you near or turn and bite.

But Zsuzsanna never bit. She waited. And then, one evening, when she was ready, she finally spoke.

The fire was low, casting shadows along the walls. The scent of drying herbs clung to the air, lavender and thyme, mingling with the faint, metallic tang of something older, something that lived in the bones of this house.

Zsuzsanna sat at the table, a small blade in her hand, slicing dried roots into thin slivers. Her movements were steady, unhurried, as if this were any other night.

"You have questions," she said.

I looked up from where I sat across from her. She didn't look at me. She simply continued slicing, the thin rasp of metal against wood the only sound between us.

I hesitated. "Do you want me to ask them?"

She set the knife down, brushing the thin curls of root into a small wooden bowl. Then, finally, she met my gaze.

"I want you to know," she said.

"Know what?"

She folded her hands in front of her.

"We are not murderers," she said simply.

Her voice was calm, measured but there was something beneath it. Something unshakable. Something final.

"We are liberators."

I exhaled slowly.

I had expected her to deny it, to dance around the truth as she had before. But this was different.

"You don't hesitate," I said. "Not even for a moment."

Zsuzsanna smiled, but it was a small, knowing thing.

"I stopped hesitating a long time ago."

I swallowed. "But—"

"You want to understand," she interrupted, leaning forward slightly. "You want to make sense of it. But tell me, what is there to understand?"

Her eyes were dark, gleaming in the firelight.

"You have seen them. The men. You have heard the way they speak, the way they touch, the way they take." Her voice was quiet. Steady. "You have seen the bruises."

I clenched my jaw. She wasn't wrong.

Then, softly, she said, "Why should we let them live?"

She stood and crossed the room, reaching for something on the shelf. A small glass jar, its contents pale and fine as sand. She set it on the table between us.

I stared at it. She did not speak right away. She let me look.

"Arsenic."

The word hit the air like a stone dropping into water. I stiffened.

She reached for a small strip of yellowed paper from the windowsill. Flypaper.

"This is where it comes from," she said. "We soak it in water. The poison lifts from the paper, dissolves into the liquid."

She turned the jar slightly. The powder shifted inside.

"When it dries, we scrape it down to this."

I swallowed hard.

She leaned back against her chair, studying me. "Simple, isn't it?"

The room felt smaller. The air heavier.

I had seen her hands mix herbs, grind powders, measure careful drops of medicine into ailing mouths. I had seen her help women bring life into the world.

Now I saw her for what she truly was. And what I might become.

Zsuzsanna tilted her head slightly. "Say what you're thinking."

I exhaled sharply. "I don't know what I'm thinking."

She smiled. "Yes, you do."

She reached for the jar again, twisting the lid open.

Inside, the powder was light, soft, like ground bone.

"You have already given it once," she said.

My stomach tightened. "You told me it was medicine."

"It was."

I shook my head, gripping the edge of the table. "Medicine saves people."

Zsuzsanna's gaze didn't waver.

"And do you not think we are saving them?"

I faltered.

She leaned in, her voice low, steady. "How many women have you seen flinch when their husbands pass by? How many walk with their shoulders hunched, their mouths tight? How many lie awake at night, hoping, praying, that they will wake up and find themselves widowed?"

The fire crackled softly.

"Tell me," she murmured. "Do you think those prayers go unanswered?"

A chill ran through me.

Zsuzsanna closed the jar and pushed it toward me.

I didn't move. I couldn't.

"You are not a child," she said. "You've seen what life is like for women in this village. For women everywhere."

She exhaled, shaking her head slightly.

"And yet you still hesitate."

I swallowed.

She was right. I had seen it. The bruises, the broken skin, the fear written into the lines of their faces. I had seen the way Kata stood taller after her husband was put in the ground, how the other women never mourned.

I had seen it. And I had done nothing to stop it.

She watched me carefully. "You can still leave."

The words landed sharp, cutting through the air between us.

I met her gaze. She was not testing me. She was giving me a choice. I could stand up. Walk out. Pretend none of this had ever touched me. I could leave Nagyrev behind.

And yet, I thought of the women gathered around the well, standing shoulder to shoulder, belonging to something greater than themselves. I thought of the girl with the sick husband, sitting by the hearth, her hands still, unshaking. I thought of the quiet laughter in the marketplace, the space the widows took up, unburdened, unafraid. I thought of Zsuzsanna, sitting across from me, her dark eyes unwavering.

She had given me a choice. But the truth was, I had already made it.

I reached forward and took the jar in my hands. I did not let go.

THE POWER OF POISON

I had expected to feel horror. To wake in the night with the glass jar pressing against my body, to feel my fingers tremble at the thought of what they had touched. But the horror never came.

Instead, something else settled inside me. It was a certain understanding.

The village did not change, but my vision of it did. I saw it now for what it was; a place shaped by women's hands, controlled by them in ways the men would never suspect.

The women of Nagyrev moved through the world as they always had: fetching water, kneading dough, gathering in the square with baskets on their hips, exchanging quiet words over their work. But beneath it all, there was something sharper.

A power that existed in their voices, in their gestures. A power that could end a life as easily as it could bring one into the world.

I first saw it in Kata. She was different now. Lighter, freer. There was something new in the way she carried herself, something I couldn't name but understood all the same. She laughed more. She moved without hesitation. When she sat with the other women, there was no longer that small, wary tilt to her shoulders, that ever-present burden pressing against her spine.

I had seen widows before. True widows, their grief trailing behind them like a funeral shroud, swallowing them whole. But in Nagyrev, widowhood was not a burden. It was freedom. And Kata was not alone.

I saw it in others, too. Women who should have been beaten

down by life, who should have carried sorrow like a yoke across their backs, and yet ... they did not.

They had found another way. Or rather, they had made another way. The power of the poison was simple. It was quiet.

A sickness, a bad meal, a fever in the night. No blood. At least not very much. No struggle. Just a quiet, painless death. And that, I realized, was the real danger. How easy it was. How invisible. How impossible it would be to stop, now that it had begun.

The first time I heard a woman mention it openly, I felt my stomach twist. Not with fear, but with recognition.

I was helping Ilona shell peas by the fire, my fingers working mindlessly through the pile in my lap. The other women were talking, their voices low and unhurried, the kind of conversation that should have been about market prices or a child's fever.

But it wasn't.

"Janos drinks himself stupid every night," a woman murmured, shaking her head.

Ilona chuckled. "At least that keeps him out of trouble."

The first woman exhaled, shaking her head. "Not enough. He still comes home angry. He still leaves marks."

The words settled like dust in the air.

No one gasped. No one wrung their hands. They simply nodded. Acknowledging. Understanding.

The woman sighed, rubbing her hands over her tired face. "Maybe he'll fall into the river one night and save me the trouble."

A soft chuckle rose among them. Not cruel. Not malicious. Just knowing.

A few years ago, I would have dismissed it as idle talk, as nothing more than a tired wife venting her frustrations.

But now, I knew better. The poison was real. And once you

knew it existed, once you knew it was being passed between hands as easily as bread and salt, you could never unknow it.

The women of Nagyrev held more power than any man in this village could have imagined. Some wielded it with care. But others ... others wielded it as easily as a needle through fabric, stitching and unstitching lives at will.

The first time I heard of a man dying who didn't deserve it, the realization struck me like a knife between the ribs.

I was standing outside the apothecary in the next village, waiting while Zsuzsanna traded for supplies. The air was crisp, carrying the scent of dried herbs and cold earth, the street bustling with quiet conversation.

Two women stood nearby, their heads bent close. I wasn't listening at first, until I heard his name.

"Poor Istvan," one of them murmured. "He was a good man."

The other sighed. "He never should have married that one. I knew she'd be trouble."

Something in my stomach clenched. I turned slightly, watching them from the corner of my eye.

"I heard he was healthy one day and gone the next," the first woman continued. "No warning, no sickness. Just like that."

The other woman exhaled, shaking her head. "It happens."

They moved on, their conversation shifting to something else, something unimportant. But I stood there, frozen. I knew Istvan.

He had been kind. He had worked his land without complaint. He had spoken softly to his wife, had touched her gently when they stood together at the market. He had not deserved to die. And yet he had died all the same.

My pulse thrummed in my ears. The poison had been created for men like Kata's husband. For the cruel ones, the brutal ones, the ones who had long since forfeited the right to draw breath.

But now it was something else. Something bigger. Something out of control.

~

That night, I sat across from Zsuzsanna, watching the fire flicker in the dim light. She was tying small bundles of dried sage, her fingers moving with the same practiced ease they always had.

"They're killing men who don't deserve it," I said.

Zsuzsanna did not look up. "Some would say no man deserves to live," she murmured.

Her words sent a chill through me.

I exhaled sharply. "But Istvan, he was a good man."

She looked at me then, tilting her head slightly. "And yet, he's dead."

The words were simple. Final.

I felt something sink inside me. "It wasn't supposed to be like this."

Zsuzsanna smiled, but there was something sharp beneath it.

"And who told you that?"

I had no answer. Because no one had told me. I had assumed. I had believed, foolishly, that justice had rules, that it could be controlled. But now, I was beginning to understand. This was not justice. This was power. And power does not follow rules. It spreads. It grows. It devours.

Zsuzsanna studied me for a long moment, then set down the bundle of sage.

"Now you see," she murmured.

And I did. I saw it all. And I knew it was too late to stop it.

~

The sky had turned the color of dying embers by the time we returned home, the sun bleeding out behind the hills, stretching shadows long across the village. The air smelled of wet earth and wood smoke, the promise of another cold night settling deep in my bones.

Zsuzsanna walked ahead of me, her pace unhurried, her hands tucked neatly into the folds of her shawl. I followed, my thoughts tangled but aware of the significance of what I had learned.

It was not just the cruel ones. The poison was not always given to the men who deserved it. Some women were using it for more. For convenience. I had thought I understood what this was. But I had been wrong. I had been so terribly wrong.

When we stepped inside, the house was warm, the fire casting soft light across the walls. The scent of drying flowers clung to the air, but beneath it, something else lingered. Something sharp, metallic, familiar.

I knew what it was before I saw it. A glass jar sat on the table, lid tightly sealed, the fine white powder inside shifting as the light from the fire danced over it.

I stopped just inside the doorway. Zsuzsanna walked forward, shrugging off her shawl, moving toward the table with the same quiet certainty she always carried. She sat down, turning the jar between her fingers.

Then, she looked at me.

"Come here."

I didn't move.

She sighed, tilting her head slightly. "Are you afraid?"

I wasn't sure how to answer.

I stepped forward, slowly, until I was standing across from her. The jar sat between us, small and unassuming. But I knew better now. Small things could be the deadliest.

Zsuzsanna studied me, then unscrewed the lid, dipping two

fingers inside. When she pulled them back, they were coated in the fine, pale dust.

"Put out your hand," she said.

My breath caught. "Why?"

Her lips twitched slightly, the shadow of a smile.

"Because one day, you will need it."

I stared at her. She held my gaze, patient, expectant. She was not asking me.

This was a test. A choice. I looked down at her fingers, at the powder resting against her skin, soft as flour. My heart pounded.

I thought of Kata. Of Ilona. Of the quiet strength in the women's voices as they discussed who would be next. I thought of the men who had deserved it. And the ones who had not.

I exhaled slowly. And then, I lifted my hand.

Zsuzsanna reached forward, pressing her fingers into my palm. The powder clung to my skin. It was cool, deadly.

I curled my fingers around it, closing my hand into a fist.

Zsuzsanna leaned back, satisfied.

"Keep it," she murmured. "Someday, you'll be glad you did."

The fire crackled softly between us. And I knew that I had just crossed a line that could never be uncrossed.

28

THE THINGS WE CANNOT SAY

The sun hung low in the sky, spilling gold over the fields, stretching long shadows across the dirt path that led toward the river. The heat of the day had softened into something gentler, the scent of cut wheat and distant smoke emanating from kitchen hearths.

Ádám was waiting for me beneath the willow tree. I had known he would be.

I had known because I had seen the way he looked at me in the days since our last meeting. The way his gaze lingered a second too long when I passed him in the square, the way he seemed to always find a reason to be where I was.

And I had let him. I had let myself be near him, even when I knew I shouldn't. Even when I knew it could lead nowhere. Even when I knew I could never be the kind of girl who belonged to a boy like him.

"You came."

"You knew I would."

He smiled, but there was something careful about it. Something hesitant, as if he already knew that I was holding myself back, that something inside me was resisting.

"I'm beginning to think you don't like me very much, Eszter."

"That isn't true."

"Then why do you always seem like you're trying to run away?"

I opened my mouth to answer, but the words wouldn't come.

Because how could I explain it? How could I explain that I had grown up learning to fear men? That I had seen what they did to their wives, their daughters, the women who had no choice but to stay. That I had been taught to look for danger in them, not tenderness. That I had learned to see men as problems to be solved, as burdens to be rid of, as things that could be removed with a few drops of clear liquid in their evening drink.

And yet, Ádám did not feel like a problem and that frightened me more than anything.

"You're different from the men in this village," I said at last.

"Is that a good thing?"

"I don't know."

He exhaled, shaking his head, looking at me the way someone might look at a riddle they couldn't quite solve.

"You always answer like that. Like you don't want to tell me what you really think."

"Maybe I don't."

"Why?"

"Because it wouldn't change anything."

The wind shifted, rustling through the branches above us. The river was just beyond the trees, its surface dark and slow-moving, the reeds bending lazily at its banks.

"You think too much."

"You don't think enough."

"Maybe," he admitted. "But what is there to think about? You and I ..." He paused, rubbing a hand over the back of his neck, searching for the right words. "We could have something, Eszter."

Something. Something like the kind of life I had never dared to picture for myself. Something that made my heart ache, my breath too shallow.

"You don't know me."

"I know enough."

"No, you don't." My voice was sharper than I meant it to be. "You don't know what I've done. You don't know what I know. You don't—"

I stopped myself before I said too much.

Before I ruined whatever fragile thing was hanging between us. Before I gave him reason to pull away.

But he didn't. Instead, he stepped closer. Close enough that I could smell the earth on him, the sweat from his work, the faint trace of wheat that must have come from the fields he had passed through.

"Tell me, then." His voice was softer now. "Tell me what you know."

I swallowed. I couldn't.

Because if I told him, I would lose him. And if I let myself care for him, I would lose myself.

The sounds of the village had long since faded into the distance, leaving only the rustling of the wheat, the soft lapping of the river against the bank, the chirping of cicadas hidden in the reeds.

He was looking at me like he was waiting for something.

Like he wanted me to say something that would make sense of all of this; of why I pulled away, why I was always running from something unseen.

"I never had a choice before," I said finally, my voice quieter than I intended.

"A choice?"

"In what happens to me."

He frowned, tilting his head slightly. His expression was unreadable.

"And now?" he asked.

"Now I don't know if I do or not."

He exhaled through his nose, thoughtful. He ran a hand through his hair, his curls damp with sweat, sticking slightly to his forehead.

"You do," he said. "You just don't believe it yet."

I wanted to believe him. God, I wanted to.

But I had been raised by a mother who taught me that women do not make choices. That life is not something we decide, it is something that happens to us.

And yet here was Ádám, standing before me, telling me I could be different. Telling me I could want. Telling me I could have.

"I should go." I turned, but he caught my wrist. Not roughly. Not forcefully. Just enough to make me stop.

"Eszter," he said, my name like a question, like a plea.

I could feel the warmth of his palm against my skin, the steadiness of him, the quiet patience in the way he held me as if waiting for me to decide.

And for one foolish, fleeting moment, I wanted to give in. I wanted to pretend that there was no midwife, no poison, no whispers in the dark. I wanted to believe that I could have something normal. That I could be someone normal.

His grip was warm, firm but not demanding. A tether to something safe, something solid.

I could almost picture it. A life not dictated by fear, by secrets, by the quiet, knowing glances of the women at the well.

But I knew better. And so, I pulled away.

"Goodnight, Ádám."

I did not look back as I walked away. Because if I had, I knew I would not have had the strength to leave.

29

MERCY

It was well past midnight when the knocking came. Sharp, hurried. A fist against wood, hard enough to rattle the shutters. Zsuzsanna did not flinch.

She was already rising from her chair, already reaching for her shawl before I had even registered the sound. She always knew when someone was coming.

I scrambled to my feet, blinking the sleep from my eyes, my limbs sluggish with exhaustion, but she was faster.

She unlatched the door, and a gust of cold air pushed its way inside, carrying the earthy scent of autumn and something sharper beneath it. Blood.

The girl at the door was shaking. Her face was stark white, her lips blue from the cold, her hair loose and wild around her shoulders. She was young. Perhaps sixteen, perhaps younger, but there was something old in her eyes. Something desperate.

Her dress was torn at the hem, soaked to the knees with mud, and she smelled of the open fields, of sodden straw and rain and animal sweat.

And in her trembling arms the dog. It was barely a dog anymore. More a heap of torn fur and exposed flesh, a ruined thing that should not have still been breathing. But it was. Barely.

Its throat had been ripped open, a deep, gaping wound where something had torn through skin and muscle, where its blood still pulsed weakly, soaking into the girl's dress.

One of its hind legs dangled at an unnatural angle, the bone splintered, a jagged shard of white pushing through the skin like a broken blade.

It had once been a working dog. One of the large, sturdy ones, built for guarding, for herding, for protecting.

Now, it was something else. Something beyond saving.

"He was attacked," the girl gasped. "By wolves. Please, I—"

Zsuzsanna did not ask why she had come here instead of the priest. Instead of her father. Instead of someone who might have cared more for dogs than children. She simply stepped aside, letting the girl inside without a word.

The house was warm, the fire still burning low in the hearth. The dog twitched in the girl's arms, a faint, pained tremor passing through its body. Its breathing was ragged, a thin, wet whistle with every exhale.

I grabbed a blanket, but Zsuzsanna did not take it. She only looked at the dog. Its black eyes, half-lidded, glassy with agony, were still trying to focus, still searching, still seeing.

It would have been easier if they were already empty.

"Can you save him?" the girl whispered.

She was still clutching the animal to her breast, her fingers buried in its fur, as if she could will it back together with her hands alone.

Zsuzsanna took one step forward. Bent down. Ran her fingers gently over the dog's body, pressing along its ribs, feeling the way the bones shifted beneath her touch. Then she sighed.

"No."

The girl inhaled sharply, her grip tightening.

"No, there must be something. There has to be something. You saved my mother when she was sick. You saved my baby brother when he stopped breathing. You—"

"That was different," Zsuzsanna said.

"How?"

"They were not already dead."

The wind rattled against the walls, and for the first time, I realized how eerily silent the dog had become.

It was still breathing. But it did not move. It did not struggle. It simply lay in her arms, its body limp, its eyes dull, unfocused. It had already surrendered. It had already given up.

"The wolves," I murmured. "There aren't many left, are there?"

The girl shook her head.

"No. They were hunted after the war. But sometimes, in the colder months, they come down from the hills. Desperate."

Desperate. That was the word for it.

The dog had been herding when the wolves came. Protecting. Defending. And for his loyalty, he had been ripped apart, left to bleed out in the dirt.

The wolves would be long gone by now. Hungry still. Hunting still. They had taken their share, but they would be back.

"Put him down," Zsuzsanna said.

The girl clutched the dog tighter.

"No. Please. Please, just try!"

"I am trying," Zsuzsanna said, *"to be kind."*

The girl stared at her. Then at me.

Her fingers clenched so tightly in the dog's fur that her knuckles went white.

"I can do it," I found myself saying.

I do not know why. Perhaps to stop the girl from breaking

apart in front of me. Perhaps to stop myself from doing the same.

Zsuzsanna only shook her head.

"No," she said simply. "This is my job."

Then she picked up the spade. The girl screamed. Or maybe I did.

The sound came from somewhere between us, between the moment before the spade came down and the moment after, when the dog was still. Completely still. No breath. No twitch of a paw. Just gone. Like he had never been there at all.

The girl was sobbing, rocking back and forth, her hands still slick with blood that no longer belonged to anything living. I could not move. I could not breathe.

The air smelled of copper and earth and firewood, but all I could taste was iron.

Zsuzsanna was already cleaning the blade. She had turned away.

She had wiped her hands, wiped the spade, as if it had all been inevitable, as if it had never been a choice at all.

"That was kindness," she said.

Her voice was flat. Matter of fact as if she were stating the temperature. As if she were commenting on the season.

I stared at the dog's broken body. The blood pooling beneath it. The girl sobbing into her hands. And I wondered. Was it? Was that kindness? Or was that simply Zsuzsanna? Was there a difference?

I did not know. I still do not know.

But when I closed my eyes that night, I heard the crack of the spade echo in my mind. And I did not sleep.

30

A HUSBAND'S SUSPICION

The wind carried voices through the village that morning.

I heard them before I saw anything. Low, clipped words, like the edge of a blade being sharpened. At first, I thought it was just the usual sounds of the square. Women trading, the occasional bark of a dog, the rattle of a wheel rolling over uneven stones. But then I heard his name.

Janos.

And suddenly, I was listening.

I was at the well, my hands wrapped around the worn wooden bucket, the cold from the water seeping into my skin. The other women were gathered around me, moving through their morning tasks with the same slow, measured rhythm they always did.

But there was suspense in the air. Something unspoken. Something waiting to take shape.

I lifted my head, trying to push away the growing feelings I had for Ádám. This was important. I had to focus. I had to pay attention and stop my daydreaming.

Janos stood in the square, feet planted wide, his face dark with something I had only ever seen in men who were looking for a fight. His coat, made of wool and lined with fur at the collar, was worn but still carried an air of importance; a man who had always considered himself stronger than the others, a man who thought himself untouchable. His boots were scuffed, the leather cracked from years of hard use, and his hands—large and scarred from years of labor—clenched and unclenched at his sides.

But it was his eyes that unsettled me the most. Dark and searching, darting from face to face, as if looking for someone to blame. He wasn't just speaking. He was accusing.

I had never paid much attention to Janos before.

He was a large man, broad-shouldered, with a strong brow and a permanent scowl carved into his face. The kind of man who always smelled faintly of sweat and smoke, whose voice carried even when he wasn't shouting.

He was not the worst of them, but he was not the best, either. A man who drank, who argued loudly in the tavern, who sometimes shoved his wife too hard but never left marks. But today, there was something new in his stance. Something dangerous.

"My brother was a strong man," he said, voice carrying across the square. "He never got sick. And yet, one day, he was fine, and the next ..."

He gestured sharply, his meaty fingers clenched into a fist.

The other men murmured, their faces unreadable. Some shifted, uncomfortable. Others simply watched.

Janos turned in a slow circle, as if daring someone to meet his gaze. "You think I don't see what's happening?" he spat. "First it was Kata's husband, then Istvan, now my brother? How many more?"

I stiffened. Too many.

Janos exhaled sharply, rolling his shoulders. "And all of them left behind a widow who barely shed a tear." He spat onto the ground, the glob landing near the worn leather shoe of a younger man standing nearby. And yet, no one moved. No one challenged him.

Then, finally, a man spoke.

"Be careful what you're saying, Janos."

It was Miklós, the blacksmith.

Miklós was just as big as Janos, but he carried his body differently; a quiet, slow-moving strength rather than something explosive. His arms were bursting with muscle, coated in the soot and burn marks of his trade, his hands calloused from years of swinging a hammer. But it wasn't just his size that made the other men wary of him.

It was the way he never raised his voice, never rushed to anger.

Janos turned to him. "Or what?"

Miklós shrugged, arms crossed over his broad torso. "You think a woman killed your brother? With what?"

Janos hesitated. And that was when I realized. He didn't know.

He suspected. He felt it in his bones, the way a man senses the shift in the wind before a storm. But he didn't know how. Not yet.

Janos clenched his jaw. "Something isn't right," he muttered. "Mark my words. I'll find out."

I forced myself to walk slowly back to Zsuzsanna's house, even as my pulse thrummed beneath my skin, even as my legs ached with the effort of keeping calm. Janos knew. Not everything, but enough. And that was dangerous.

Inside, Zsuzsanna was grinding dried herbs, her hands steady, the scent of sage and wormwood permeating the air. She didn't look up as I entered.

I shut the door behind me.

"Janos is talking," I said, breathless. "He thinks his brother was poisoned."

Zsuzsanna kept working, her pestle scraping rhythmically against the stone mortar.

I swallowed hard. "You don't seem surprised."

She exhaled, shaking her head. "I'm not."

I hesitated. "Do you think—"

"He doesn't know anything," she interrupted smoothly. "He's guessing. And men guess at things they don't understand all the time."

I wasn't sure if that was reassuring or terrifying.

I crossed my arms, trying to steady myself. "What if he finds out?"

Zsuzsanna finally looked at me. Really looked. Her dark eyes were unreadable. Then, she smiled.

"Then," she said, "Janos will need to be helped, too."

I stared at her. Her meaning was clear. I felt my stomach drop. Janos was strong. A fighter. And he would not go down quietly.

Zsuzsanna turned back to her work, her fingers precise, unshaken.

Outside, the village carried on and inside I wondered if Janos had just signed his own death.

~

The river had always moved slowly this time of year.

In the colder months, the Tisza ran sluggishly, snaking through the land like a dark ribbon, its surface often shrouded in mist at dawn. The reeds stood tall along the banks, brittle now, bending beneath the frost. It was a river that had swallowed many things over the years: lost boats, the bodies of livestock that had wandered too far, and, sometimes, men.

That morning, it gave one back.

The first to see him were the fisherman, out before the sun had fully risen, pushing their small wooden boats through the icy waters. They had set out expecting the usual haul: pike, perch, maybe a fattened catfish if luck was on their side. But instead, they found Janos.

He had drifted near the bend, face-down, his coat waterlogged, the fur collar stiff with ice. The reeds had tangled around his legs, as if the river itself had tried to hold onto him, reluctant to return what it had taken.

The men pulled him to shore without speaking, their breath visible in the cold air, their boots sinking deep into the mud. His skin had gone pale, almost waxy, his lips tinged blue from the night's chill. His hands, once strong, had softened in the water, his fingers half-curled, as if reaching for something he would never grasp.

He looked nothing like the man who had stood in the square just yesterday, chest puffed, voice full of anger. He looked like something forgotten.

The news spread fast, though not in the way true tragedy spreads.

There was no wailing, no urgent footsteps rushing through the village. Instead, it passed in quiet murmurs, in the way glances were exchanged at the well, in the way voices lowered when men entered the room.

I had been in the square when I first heard. Two men stood near the apothecary, speaking in hushed tones, their breath misting in the cold air.

"He washed up near the bend," one of them muttered, shifting uneasily. "Face down. Been in the water all night, by the looks of him."

The other man grunted. "Too much drink, I suppose."

"Maybe." A pause. A slow glance toward the women at the well. "Or maybe something else."

The second man did not ask what that *something else* was. I did not go to see him. I did not need to.

I already knew what I would find. Janos, bloated from the water, his skin pale and swollen, his once-powerful hands limp and useless. The river had taken the fight out of him. Or rather, the women had.

That was the truth of it, wasn't it?

It had happened quickly. Quicker than I had expected.

The day before, he had stood in the square, his voice sharp, his threats hanging in the cold morning air. And now, he was gone. And no one was surprised.

The men muttered, shook their heads, cursed the bad luck of it. Some even played their part, feigning concern, wondering if it had been an accident or something worse.

But the women... The women did not speak of him at all.

No one asked what had happened. No one questioned how a man as strong as Janos had suddenly drowned, when only yesterday, he had been standing tall, his chest heaving with anger, his fists clenched at his sides.

I watched them carefully, trying to see if any of them would flinch, if any of them would let the secret slip between their teeth.

But they didn't.

Not Ilona, who hummed softly as she plucked a chicken for the evening's meal. Not Kata, who stood at the well, passing a bucket to another woman without so much as a glance toward the square. And not Zsuzsanna.

They moved through the day as if nothing had changed, as if Janos had never existed at all.

And perhaps, in their eyes, he never had.

That night, I sat across from Zsuzsanna at the table.

She was tying bundles of dried herbs, her hands moving with the same slow precision they always did. The room smelled of lavender and crushed chamomile, of smoke curling in soft tendrils from the dying fire.

I watched her fingers work, wrapping twine carefully around the dried stems, securing them in neat, tight knots. She did not look shaken. She did not look different at all.

But something had changed. Something in *me.*

I exhaled slowly. "You knew."

She did not look up. "Knew what?"

"That they would take care of him."

A pause.

"He wasn't careful. He wasn't good."

The words were simple. Final.

"And that's all it takes?"

Zsuzsanna finally met my gaze.

"Sometimes, yes."

Her voice was soft, but there was steel beneath it.

The fire crackled softly.

I thought of Janos, of the way he had stood in the square, of the certainty in his voice. He had thought himself powerful. He had thought himself safe. But no man was safe in Nagyrev. Not if the women decided otherwise. And I worried for Ádám.

Zsuzsanna set down the bundle of herbs, brushing stray flecks from her lap.

"You still don't understand," she murmured, tilting her head slightly.

I swallowed hard. "Then explain it to me."

She exhaled, folding her hands in her lap.

"There is nothing more dangerous than a man who thinks he is untouchable."

I stiffened.

She continued, her voice smooth, unhurried. "Janos believed he could ask questions. He believed he could threaten. And that we would cower, that we would let him."

She leaned forward slightly.

"We do not cower," she said simply.

The words sent a chill through me.

I thought of the gathering at Ilona's house, the low, steady voices, the way they had spoken of life and death as if it were nothing more than choosing which bread to bake. I thought of the quiet understanding between them, the way no one had questioned Janos's death, the way they had already moved past it. I thought of the river, the way it had swallowed him whole, only to give him back.

Janos had been right about one thing. Something *was* happening in this village. And now, it would never stop.

31

THE DOCTOR

The doctor came on a cold morning.

The air was brittle, sharp with the promise of winter. A thin mist drifted over the fields, clinging to the trees like a second skin. The wind cut through the village in small, creeping gusts, rattling loose shutters, sending stray leaves scraping against the frozen dirt.

It was the kind of morning that carried sound strangely. Voices seemed sharper, footsteps heavier, the rustling of fabric too loud. And so, when the first creak of a cart's wheels sounded from the road leading into the village, people noticed.

I had been at the well, my hands raw from the cold, the metal handle slick with frost. Around me, the other women worked, breath rising in soft plumes, scarves drawn tight over their mouths.

Then came the sound of hooves. Slow, deliberate. Not the hurried clip of a farmer returning from the fields, nor the swaying roll of a merchant's cart. Something more measured. Something that did not belong.

I looked up. The doctor's cart was simple; black wood, well-kept, but not ostentatious. The horse pulling it was dark-coated, its mane neatly trimmed, its harness without fray.

But it was the man himself who unsettled me. He was not like the men of Nagyrev.

His coat was formal, buttoned to the throat, the leather of his gloves creaking as he pulled them tighter. He sat straight-backed, his shoulders stiff against the cold. Beneath the wide brim of his hat, his face was pale, angular; sharp lines and cold eyes, the kind of man who saw everything, even what was not meant to be seen.

A foreigner, in every sense of the word. And foreign men did not come to Nagyrev without reason.

He went first to the priest. I followed at a distance, keeping to the edges of the square, watching as he dismounted from the cart and stepped up toward the church steps.

The priest, Father Lázár, was a man of soft features and softer words. He was not like the priests in the cities. No stern, booming voice, no sharp lectures on sin. He understood what life was like for the people here. Which meant he understood what went on in the dark. And he did not speak of it.

The doctor stood before him, hands tucked neatly behind his back, his expression unreadable.

They spoke in hushed voices, but sound carried easily in the cold.

"Three in the past month alone ..." the doctor was saying. "That is ... unusual, wouldn't you say?"

Father Lázár exhaled slowly. His fingers twitched over the rosary beads in his hands. "The war took many men," he muttered.

The doctor nodded, but his gaze did not soften. "Yes. But the war ended two years ago."

The priest hesitated. "It left wounds that have not healed."

"Poison leaves wounds too," the doctor said softly.

The priest's face did not change, but I saw the way his grip on the rosary tightened. A small, involuntary movement. A tell. The doctor noticed it, too.

"You have been here a long time," the doctor continued, his voice smooth, conversational. "You have buried these men. Have you noticed anything ... unusual?"

Father Lázár looked at him for a long moment. Finally, he said, "Men die."

A pause. Then he turned toward the church doors. A dismissal. A warning. An ending. But as he stepped inside, I saw something flicker across his face.

It was doubt. It was unease. And it was fear.

The women pretended not to care. They continued their work as if the doctor's presence was nothing more than a passing wind. But I saw the shift. The way their hands stilled for just a second longer than usual when he passed. The way their gazes moved toward him, sharp and knowing. The way their laughter, once free and unguarded, became more restrained, spoken in lower tones, wrapped in layers of caution.

They knew. They all knew. And yet, no one spoke of it.

It was the way things had always been in Nagyrev. Unspoken agreements, silent understandings. The poison had woven itself into the fabric of the village, into the very breath of the women who lived here.

But now, for the first time, I sensed something else. Not guilt. Not shame. A quiet unease.

Because men, for all their faults, rarely questioned what they could not see.

But doctors knew where to look. And worse, they knew what to find.

That night, I sat by the fire, Zsuzsanna's voice cutting through the quiet as she worked beside me.

"He is not the first to come asking questions," she murmured.

I turned to her. "And the others?"

She met my gaze.

"They did not ask twice."

Her meaning was clear. I swallowed hard and stared into the flames.

The doctor had come looking for answers. But I already knew what happened to men who looked too closely.

32

A CLOSE DEATH

The girl was waiting for us when we arrived.

She sat huddled in a wooden chair near the fire, arms wrapped around her knees, shoulders hunched inward. Her apron was twisted between her fingers, knotted, wrung tight, as though she could squeeze the horror out of herself with her own hands. Her eyes, wide, rimmed with red, darted to the door every few seconds, as if expecting someone to come for her.

The smell of boiled onions clung to the air, mixing with the faint, acrid scent of something that had burned too long in the hearth. The house was unbearably warm with the heat of panic.

She was not like the others. The other women who had come to Zsuzsanna after their husbands' deaths—Kata, Ilona, the quiet-faced widows who never looked back—they had done this with certainty. They had been ready.

This girl no older than seventeen, barely more than a child, was drowning in it. She had done it. And now, it was devouring her.

Zsuzsanna moved first, kneeling by the hearth, tossing dried chamomile into a kettle. The scent drifted through the air, but it did not mask the fear that clung to the girl's skin, to her hair, to the walls of the room itself.

She didn't look at Zsuzsanna. She didn't even look at me. She just stared at the floor, her lips trembling, her fingers still gripping the twisted cloth of her apron like a lifeline.

I hesitated, then stepped forward.

"Tell me," I said softly.

She blinked, her mouth parting slightly, but no words came. I crouched beside her, lowering my voice. "You need to tell me."

Her breath shuddered through her lips.

"He knew."

The words were barely a whisper, but they sliced through me like a knife.

I stiffened. "What do you mean?"

She closed her eyes, her fingers clenching into fists in her lap.

"When he took the first sip, his face ... he looked at me. Right at me."

Her voice trembled, her breath shallow.

"Like he understood. Like he knew."

A shiver crawled down my spine.

"He tried to speak," she continued, her voice barely audible. "But then ..." She let out a broken sound, something between a sob and a laugh. "And then he started choking."

The words hung in the air like smoke. I felt my stomach turn. It wasn't supposed to happen like that.

The poison had always been quiet. A sickness, a slow fading. That was how it worked. But this was violent.

I swallowed. "Tell me everything."

She inhaled sharply, her body trembling. "His throat ... he clutched it. His fingers were digging in, like he was trying to tear something out of himself."

I could see it in my mind, too clearly. His bulging eyes, his hands clawing at his throat, the white foam spilling from his lips.

"He fell," she whispered. "He hit his head against the table. His legs ... they wouldn't stop kicking."

She squeezed her eyes shut, gripping her arms so tightly her nails left half-moon imprints in her flesh.

"They told me it would be peaceful," she choked.

A bitter taste rose in my throat. They had lied.

I turned to Zsuzsanna, expecting something. Some kind of explanation maybe. A flicker of remorse? But she didn't even look at the girl. She simply stirred the tea, her face calm, unreadable.

The girl's voice cracked. "They said it would be like going to sleep. That it wouldn't hurt."

Zsuzsanna let out a slow breath.

"Sometimes it's different."

The girl lifted her head sharply, staring at her with wet, furious eyes.

"You knew," she whispered.

Zsuzsanna finally turned to her. "Would you have done it if I had told you?"

The girl's breath hitched and something shifted in her. The fear did not lessen. But something behind her eyes hardened, as if a door had closed somewhere deep inside her. There was no way back.

The walk back to Zsuzsanna's house was silent. The village lay quiet, wrapped in the last fading light of the afternoon, but I felt it pressing in around me. The whispers. The laughter. The knowing glances exchanged over baskets of grain.

I thought of the way the girl had clutched her apron, the way her voice had broken over the words "he knew."

I thought of the foam on his lips. The way his legs had kicked. The way she had not been relieved but horrified.

That night, I sat at the table, watching Zsuzsanna tie bundles of dried thyme, her hands moving with slow precision.

I cleared my throat. "She wasn't ready."

Zsuzsanna didn't look up. "She is now."

I clenched my jaw. "You don't care."

At that, she did pause. She looked at me, tilting her head slightly, studying me as if I were something fragile, something still waiting to be shaped.

"Does it matter?"

I opened my mouth to say yes, to say of course it mattered, to say that what we were doing was different from what they were doing. But the truth was, it didn't. He was dead. And now, she belonged to us.

I lay awake that night, staring at the ceiling, my thoughts tangled and sharp.

I rolled onto my side, pressing my hands to my face. Janos. Istvan. The girl's husband. One by one, they were falling. And there would be more. So many more.

I had tried to mask it; the creeping doubt that wove itself around my ribs, the unease that settled in my stomach whenever I heard the women speak in low voices, discussing who should be helped next. I moved through the village as I always had, watched, listened, kept my hands steady as I worked. But Zsuzsanna saw through it.

She always saw. She waited until we were alone.

The other women had left for the night, their voices fading into the cold, their footsteps swallowed by the darkness beyond the doorway. The house was quieter now, save for the slow crackling of the fire, the scent of burning wood in the air. Shadows stretched long against the walls, shifting with every movement of the flames.

She stood across from me, arms crossed, her expression unreadable. She did not sit, did not gesture for me to join her by the fire. This was not a conversation.

It was something else.

"You are thinking too much," she said.

The words struck like a stone tossed into still water, sending ripples between us.

I swallowed. "Am I?"

Zsuzsanna tilted her head slightly, studying me. Her gaze was sharp, assessing, as if she were peering into my soul and weighing whatever she found there.

"Do you regret helping them?"

Her voice was quiet, but the meaning behind it was anything but.

I hesitated. "I ..."

Her dark eyes narrowed.

"Do you regret Kata's freedom?" she pressed. "The widowhood of the women in this village? Do you regret the safety they have now?"

I spoke slowly. "No."

That was true. But it was not the whole truth.

Zsuzsanna stepped forward, her movements slow, deliberate. She had always had a way of filling a space, of making her presence feel larger than her body, of drawing you into her words like a moth to a flame.

"You hesitate now," she murmured, "because you are thinking in the way they want you to."

I frowned. "Who?"

Her mouth twitched. Not in amusement, but something colder. Something more knowing.

"Men," she said simply. "Men teach us to bear suffering. To endure. To kneel beneath their hands and call it duty."

Her voice did not rise, did not sharpen, and yet it filled the space between us, pressing against my skin like the heat of the fire.

"They make you believe that justice is theirs to decide," she continued. "That mercy is their gift to give."

She let the words settle before speaking again, softer now, but no less firm.

"But what we do is mercy."

Zsuzsanna reached out, pressing a hand to my shoulder. Her fingers were warm, firm, grounding.

"Do not let men's rules make you weak," she said as the fire crackled softly.

I wanted to believe her. I wanted to let her words smooth the sharp edges inside me, to let her certainty become my own. Because what she said was true. Wasn't it?

I thought of the girl. I thought of the fear in her eyes, the tremble in her hands, the way her voice had cracked over the words: "He knew."

I imagined the froth on her husband's lips, the way his limbs had seized and jerked. I remembered Janos, floating face-down in the river, his bloated body tangled in the reeds. And I knew this was no longer just mercy. It was something else.

It was growing, spreading like a sickness, seeping into the cracks of the village, turning something once righteous into something far more dangerous.

Dropping my gaze to the worn wooden floor as Zsuzsanna's fingers clutched slightly against my shoulder.

"Look at me," she murmured.

I forced myself to lift my eyes to hers. She studied me for a long moment. Then, her grip softened.

"You are afraid," she said.

It was not a question.

I swallowed. "Shouldn't I be?"

She smiled, but there was no kindness in it.

"No," she murmured. "Not unless you betray us."

The words sat between us, suffocating our speech.

I held my breath.

Zsuzsanna released me, turning back toward the fire, reaching for a bundle of dried herbs. She spoke again, but this time, her voice was lighter, as if the conversation had already passed.

"You'll understand in time," she said simply. "You're still learning."

I nodded, because it was what she expected.

But as I watched her work, watched her fingers move with quiet precision, I couldn't shake the feeling that something was terribly, terribly wrong.

And worse I couldn't shake the feeling that it was already too late.

33

A FUTURE NOT TO BE

The first leaves had begun to turn.

The wheat had been harvested, and the fields stood bare, golden stubble stretching across the land like the bones of something long dead. The air smelled of woodsmoke and wet earth, of autumn creeping closer, of change pressing at the edges of the world.

I had not expected to find him there. But Ádám was waiting.

He stood by the river, where the land dipped into reeds and rushes, where the water moved slow and dark beneath the willow trees. He was skimming stones across the surface, his shirt untucked, his boots muddy from the fields.

He looked up when he saw me, his face breaking into a smile that felt easy and warm.

"I was hoping you'd come."

"Why?" I asked, though I already knew.

Because lately, I had been drawn to him like a moth to flame. And the more I tried to stay away, the harder it became.

"Walk with me."

He reached for my hand, and this time I did not pull away.

We walked along the riverbank, the wind cool against my

skin, the rustling of dry leaves accompanying our steps. The grass was tall here, bending at the edges of the path, the ground uneven beneath our steps.

Ádám had the kind of presence that made lack of conversation feel natural. He did not fill the air with unnecessary words, did not demand answers from me that I was not ready to give.

But tonight, something felt different.

"I need to ask you something," he said at last.

His voice was different. Not light. Not playful.

I swallowed. "What is it?"

"Come with me."

I stopped walking.

"What?"

"Leave Nagyrev. Come with me." His eyes were steady, the kind of steady that made my breath catch in my throat. "Be my wife."

The world tilted.

I felt it in my breast, in my stomach, in the sudden, dizzying warmth that spread through me like light spilling through a crack.

Because I wanted this. God, I wanted it.

I wanted to say yes. To let him take in my arms, to let him lead me away from this place, to build something new with him in a village where no one knew me, where the past did not press its fingers around my throat.

I could see it so clearly: a house of our own, the scent of fresh bread, of hay and soil, of a life untouched by secrets. A life where I was not a midwife's apprentice. A life where I was just a woman, a wife, a mother. A life where I belonged to myself.

I opened my mouth, ready to say it. And then I saw her.

Zsuzsanna. Standing on the hill above us, watching.

She was still as a statue, her arms folded across her chest, her dark dress blending into the long shadows of the trees behind her.

She did not move. She did not call my name. She only watched.

And just like that everything collapsed.

The dream, the warmth, the impossible thing that had come to life inside me, it died before I could even name it.

"Eszter?"

Ádám was still waiting. Still watching me. He did not see her. He did not understand.

"I can't," I whispered.

His brow furrowed.

"Why not?"

"Because this is my home."

"No, it isn't," he said fiercely. "You don't belong here. I see it every time you look at me. You want more than this place."

"I can't," I said again, more forcefully this time.

"Eszter—"

"Please don't ask me again."

His hands clenched into fists at his sides. Not in anger, never in anger, but in frustration. In something close to heartbreak.

"You're afraid," he said softly.

"Of what?"

"Of what will happen if you stay," he said. "Or of what will happen if you leave."

I turned away from him because I did not have an answer. Because both were true.

The air felt colder now. The trees loomed taller, the river a dark, endless thing winding toward a world I would never see.

Ádám took a step closer.

"Tell me you don't love me, and I'll let you go."

I felt my breath catch.

"Tell me, Eszter," he said, his voice quieter now, "and I swear I'll never ask again."

I closed my eyes. If I lied, he would believe me. He would leave. He would stop waiting for me beneath willow trees, stop looking at me in the village square, stop giving me hope for a future that could never exist.

If I told the truth, the truth would ruin us both.

I had no place in his world. And he had no place in mine.

"Goodbye, Ádám."

His heart was wounded. I could feel it, the way the air shifted, the way his body tensed as if bracing for a blow.

He did not stop me when I turned to leave. He did not call my name. I did not look back. I did not have to. Because I could still feel Zsuzsanna's eyes on me. Because I could still feel Ádám's heartbreak settling into the space between us.

Because I knew that this was the last time Ádám would ever ask me to go.

34

THE WEIGHT OF SECRETS

Zsuzsanna was waiting for me when I returned. I had known she would be.

The door was left slightly ajar, swaying faintly in the cool evening breeze. Inside, the hearth glowed low, casting shapes against the walls, the air suffused with the mingling scents of drying herbs, moist wood, and the remnants of whatever she had been brewing earlier.

The room felt too warm, too tight, too full of something unsaid.

She sat at the wooden table, her posture straight, her hands placed loosely around a cup of tea. She had not changed out of her work dress; the sleeves still rolled up past her elbows, the dark fabric still dusted with dried lavender and specks of powdered root.

She looked up when I stepped inside, and though her expression remained unreadable, I felt her eyes press into me.

"You were with him."

Not a question. A statement.

I set the water bucket down by the door, feeling the heat creep up my neck.

"I was walking by the river," I said carefully. "He was there."

Zsuzsanna tilted her head slightly, her dark eyes watching me with something close to amusement, or perhaps suspicion.

"And?"

I swallowed.

"And he made advances. But I did not accept."

For a long moment, she said nothing. Then, to my surprise, her mouth curved slightly. Not a smile. Something else. Something almost like curiosity.

"Why not?" she asked.

I hesitated.

"Because I know better."

"Do you?"

"Yes."

Zsuzsanna turned her cup slowly in her hands, the steam blurring the sharp lines of her face. She took a slow sip, her fingers wrapped around the clay as if absorbing its warmth.

"It would be easier to believe that," she said at last, "if you had not stayed so long."

Heat rushed to my face.

"I told him no," I repeated, firmer this time. "I turned him away."

"But you listened to him first."

Her voice was soft. Even. Too even. And that was worse than anger. Because it meant she knew. She knew that I had wanted to listen. She knew that I had wanted to stay.

"Not all men are bad," I said suddenly, before I had time to think.

Zsuzsanna raised an eyebrow, but she did not look surprised.

"No?"

"Some are good," I insisted. "Some are worthy."

"Worthy of what?"

I clenched my fists.

"Of love. Of trust. Of not being poisoned in their sleep."

A shadow passed over her face. She set her cup down carefully, the ceramic making a soft *clink* against the wood. She did not argue. She did not agree.

Instead, she said, "Getting close to a man can be dangerous."

"I know that."

"Good."

"That is why I turned him down."

She studied me again, the soft light catching the lines around her mouth, the faint silver in her hair. I had never thought of her as old but tonight, she looked tired. As if she had already lived through too many stories like this. As if she already knew how it would end.

"He will ask again," she said.

"No. He won't."

"And if he does?"

"I will say no again."

Zsuzsanna nodded.

"Good," she said again.

And just like that, it was settled. Or so I thought.

"I wish things were different."

The words left my mouth before I could stop them. Zsuzsanna did not look at me.

"How?" she asked.

"I wish I could have a normal life."

"And what is normal?"

"A husband. A home. Children."

A sharp breath, barely there. She did not scoff this time. She only stared into her tea, as if something inside the cup might give her an answer.

"Is that what you want?" she stirred her tea.

"It doesn't matter what I want."

"No," she murmured. "It doesn't." She reached for the kettle, pouring more tea into her cup, though she did not drink it. "But you wish it did."

I nodded. "I do."

Her fingers tapped lightly against the table. A thoughtful, rhythmic sound.

"Why?" she asked at last.

I swallowed. "Because I fear I never will."

"And why is that?"

"Because of the burden of the secret I have to carry."

There. I had said it.

I had named it, the thing that had laid in my chest for months now, the thing that had kept me awake at night, that had followed me in the void between conversations.

Zsuzsanna did not react. Not at first.

Then, after a long pause, she said, "We all carry secrets, Eszter. It is what we do with them that matters."

"And what do you do with yours?"

For the first time, she smiled. But it was a smile without warmth.

"I make sure they do not carry me."

The room felt suddenly colder, despite the fire. The significance behind her words settled over me, pressing into my ribs, my throat, my lungs.

I looked at her then, really looked at her. The sharp lines of her jaw, the hands that had delivered dozens of children, and taken away just as many men.

She had no regrets. Not one and yet for the first time, I wondered if she had ever wished for something else.

"You are young," she said suddenly, her voice softer now. "And young women are allowed to dream of things they will never have. But dreams don't change the world, Eszter. We do."

I wanted to argue but I didn't. Because I knew that no matter what I said, she would never see the world the way I did. And perhaps I would never see it the way she did. Not entirely. Not yet.

I sat down across from her at the table, staring at the cup she had poured for herself but had yet to drink.

"Do you think it is possible to love a man and still be free?"

Zsuzsanna's lips parted slightly. Then she closed them again, her gaze turning toward the fire.

"I don't know," she said at last.

It was the first time I had ever heard her admit that there was something she did not know. We sat there, the fire crackling softly, the air thick with unspoken things.

I thought of Ádám. I thought of what I had lost. I thought of what I would never have. And knowing that, whether I had meant to or not, I had already made my choice.

35

THE WRONG MAN

The news spread quietly, slipping between doorways, carried in the whispers of women at the well, in the flicker of glances exchanged across the square. Another death. But this time, it was not the right man.

By the time I heard, the body had already been removed from the house, taken to the churchyard to be washed and prepared for burial. There was no rush of grief, no wailing widow collapsed in the dirt, no neighbors gathering in concern. Only a dull murmur of irritation, as if the death were no more than an inconvenience.

I found Ilona at the market stall, carefully selecting potatoes from a wooden crate. She was speaking in hushed tones with another woman, a sharp edge to her words.

"It was the father-in-law," she muttered, shaking her head.

The other woman sucked her teeth. "Careless."

Ilona nodded. "She meant it for the husband, but the old man ate first."

"She should have been more careful," the woman scoffed, tossing a potato into her basket. "Now there'll be questions."

I stood frozen, fingers tightening around the empty basket in my hands. No one was mourning. No one spoke of the man himself, whether he had been cruel, whether he had deserved it, whether he had wronged the woman who had unwittingly killed him. None of that mattered. What mattered was that he was the wrong one. And that meant trouble.

I made my way to the house where he had died. The door was ajar, the scent of wood smoke and stale sickness clinging to the muggy air inside. I stepped over the threshold, my heart pounding, my skin cold despite the heat of the fire still smoldering in the hearth.

The woman sat at the table, hunched over, her fingers twisting in her lap. She was young, not much older than me, her hair unkempt, a smear of flour still clinging to her sleeve, as if the day had gone on without her. She did not look up when I entered.

I swallowed hard, stepping closer. "I heard what happened."

"He wasn't supposed to drink it," she whispered. Her voice was raw, hollow, scraped clean of anything but disbelief.

I pulled out a chair and sat across from her, watching as her fingers dug into the fabric of her skirt, twisting, untwisting.

"He sat first," she said numbly. "I thought my husband would take the bowl, but the old man, he was always hungry. Always the first to eat."

Her breath hitched.

"And then he ..." She stopped, swallowing hard.

I already knew what came next. The coughing. The retching. The realization. I reached for her hand, but she flinched.

"They told me it would be easy," she murmured.

I stiffened. I had heard those words before. From the girl. From the others.

And they had been lies every time.

By afternoon, the talk in the village had turned from the death itself to what it meant. Not grief. Not regret. Not pity for the woman who had to watch an innocent man choke to death in her own home.

No. They spoke of carelessness. Of mistakes. Of risk.

"It's drawing attention," one woman muttered as we gathered at the well.

"She should have been more careful," another agreed, shaking her head.

A third scoffed. "It was a stupid mistake. If she couldn't do it properly, she shouldn't have done it at all."

I felt something sour rise in my throat.

There was no sadness here. Only irritation. They weren't worried that a man had died who hadn't deserved it. They were worried that it would bring trouble to the rest of them.

I turned away, gripping the handle of the well, forcing myself to breathe.

That night, I sat by the fire, staring into the flames, watching as they twitched, licking hungrily at the blackened wood.

Zsuzsanna sat beside me, her hands steady as she ground herbs into a fine powder, as if nothing had changed.

I spoke carefully. "It was the wrong man."

She did not stop her work. "It happens."

I turned to her sharply. "That's all?"

She met my gaze, her face unreadable. "What else should I say?"

I opened my mouth to say it mattered, that the man had not deserved it, that what we were doing was not supposed to be like this, but I stopped myself. Because I already knew what she would say. He was a man. And to Zsuzsanna, that was enough.

I swallowed hard.

Something was shifting. Something was slipping out of control. And I wasn't sure I could stop it. I wasn't sure anyone could.

The first body was dug up at dawn. No announcement. No warning. Just the sound of shovels breaking into frozen earth.

I hadn't seen it happen, but by the time I arrived at the churchyard, the air was filled with whispers. The women spoke in hushed voices, their hands gripping baskets too tightly, their eyes shifting toward the small group of men gathered near the graves.

The doctor stood among them, his dark coat buttoned high against the cold, his gloved hands tucked neatly behind his back. His face was unreadable, but his posture was stiff, calculated, purposeful.

Something inside me twisted. He wasn't just here to visit the dead. He was here to unbury the truth.

I stayed at a distance, watching as they pried open the coffin. The scent hit first. A sickly-sweet staleness that clung to the air.

The men recoiled slightly, covering their noses with handkerchiefs. The doctor, however, did not move.

He crouched beside the body, pulling on a pair of thin leather gloves. I could not see inside the coffin, but I didn't have to.

I already knew what lay within: a body too well-preserved, the bones too clean, the flesh too strangely intact for a man dead nearly a year. Arsenic did that. It did not just kill. It preserved.

The doctor reached into his bag and removed a vial, a small brush, something made of metal. He scraped gently at the exposed bones, collecting a fine powder. Then, with slow precision, he dropped it into the vial.

Then, he turned to the magistrate. And I saw it. The confirmation in his eyes. He had found what he was looking for.

And then I saw him. Ádám.

We stood locked in time for a moment. He did not smile. He did not frown. The expression on his face was one of pain. Of disgust. He knew. He understood. And he would never forgive me.

I kept my head down as I walked back toward the village, my pulse thrumming beneath my skin.

I needed to tell Zsuzsanna. We had been careful. The poison was quiet, nearly undetectable. Except, it seemed, to men who knew exactly where to look. And this doctor knew.

That afternoon, I overheard them.

The magistrate and the doctor stood just outside the tavern, speaking in low, urgent tones. I kept to the shadows, my back pressed against the rough wooden wall, my breath shallow.

"You're sure?" the magistrate muttered.

The doctor sighed. "I don't need to be sure. The bodies speak for themselves."

"You understand what you're suggesting."

"I understand that men are dying," the doctor hissed. "Too many. Too suddenly. And now I have proof." His voice dropped lower. "This village is hiding something. Someone. And if you don't act, more men will die."

The magistrate hesitated. "And what do you expect me to do?"

The doctor's response was instant.

"Exhume the others."

The words sent a cold shock through me. He wasn't stopping. He wouldn't stop until he uncovered everything. I turned and hurried into the dark that was falling. We needed to act. And we needed to act now.

36

A DISAPPEARANCE

The doctor was gone by morning. No goodbyes. No warnings. Just gone.

The last time I had seen him was the night before, outside the tavern, speaking in urgent, clipped tones with the magistrate. The cold had turned their breath to mist, their voices carrying in the stillness of the evening. The doctor's stance had been rigid, his gloved hands moving as he spoke, his words measured but unmistakably certain.

"This village is hiding something," he had said. "And I intend to find out what."

I had watched from the darkness, my shawl drawn tight around my shoulders, unseen but listening.

He had proof now.

Arsenic, lifted from the bones of the dead. Evidence. And he had no intention of keeping it to himself.

By dawn, the news had spread. The doctor had left town, but he had never arrived at his next destination.

His cart had been found abandoned along the road that led away from Nagyrev, left near the edge of the fields where the trees grew sparse and the land dipped toward the river.

The horse had still been there when a passing farmer had found it, tethered to a post, stamping impatiently at the dirt, its breath showing in the morning air.

His bags, packed for travel, had been in the back of the cart, untouched. His hat had lain in the grass, misty with morning dew. But the doctor himself was missing. And everyone knew what that meant.

The magistrate arrived at the tavern later that afternoon, a deep furrow between his brows. He was a thin man with greying hair and a perpetually weary expression, his coat always buttoned too tightly as though bracing against a chill only he could feel.

I had seen him before, but never like this. Never uncertain.

He sat at the wooden table near the hearth, his fingers drumming idly against the rim of his tankard as the men around him whispered and muttered, throwing uneasy glances toward one another.

"The river took him," one of them said finally, shifting in his chair.

"Aye," another added. "Too much rain upstream. The banks are slick."

Someone else let out a slow breath. "It happens."

I sat at the far end of the room, my hands wrapped around a cup of tea, listening.

"It's strange, though," a younger man murmured, lowering his voice. "The road he was traveling, it doesn't pass the river." He paused. "Not unless he was taken there."

The words sent a chill down my spine. No one spoke after that. Because we all knew what the river meant. The women did not speak of it. They did not whisper by the well, did not exchange nervous glances in the square. They went about their work as they always did. But I could feel it. The shift.

It was in the way their hands moved a little steadier, their voices a little lighter. The way their shoulders sat looser, as if some unseen load had been lifted.

The doctor had been a threat and now, he was not.

I wasn't sure if that made me feel relieved or sick. Maybe both.

~

That night, I sat at the table, staring into the fire, the heat licking at my skin, my thoughts tangled and sharp.

Zsuzsanna sat across from me, tying bundles of dried thyme, her hands steady as ever, her face unreadable.

I had seen her like this before. Silent, careful, anticipating.I exhaled slowly, forcing the words out.

"They killed him."

Zsuzsanna didn't look up. Didn't pause.

"You think so?"

I swallowed hard. "Don't you?"

She exhaled through her nose, shaking her head slightly. "You still don't understand."

Her hands continued their work, methodical, precise.

"The river took him."

I stared at her.

I wanted to argue. I wanted to push, to say what we both knew but were too careful to admit aloud. But I didn't.

Because what was the point?

A lie. A truth. Or maybe, in Nagyrev, they were the same thing.

37

THE WOMAN WHO KNEW TOO MUCH

Her name was Erzsébet.

She had been a widow for nearly a year, ever since her husband had fallen ill and died in his sleep. No one questioned it. No one asked if she had helped him along, if the sickness had truly been natural, if she had measured out careful drops from a glass bottle before setting his supper before him.

No one asked because it no longer mattered.

At first, Erzsébet had been careful, like the others. She had lowered her eyes when men spoke, laughed in the same quiet way all the widows did, lived lightly, free of grief but not so free as to arouse suspicion.

But lately, she had been talking too much.

It started small. Whispers over the bread stall at the market, careless comments at the well. Nothing outright, nothing that could be traced, but enough. Enough for the women to notice.

"I suppose my husband went when it was his time," Erzsébet had said one morning, leaning her hip against the edge of the well, the other women gathered around her. "Funny, though. Some men go sooner than others, don't they?"

The women had stiffened slightly, their hands stilling over their buckets. One of them let out a small, forced laugh.

Erzsébet smiled. "Maybe it's the air here," she mused, shaking her head. "It's good for some, bad for others."

It was the way she said it. Not with fear. Not with caution. But with amusement. She enjoyed it. The power. The knowing. She liked that they all knew what she had done. She liked that she could say it without saying it, that no one would dare speak against her. And that was dangerous.

At first, the others tried to quiet her in small ways.

Kata pulled her aside at the river one afternoon, speaking to her in a hushed, urgent voice, but Erzsébet only laughed. "Oh, don't look so worried," she said, wringing out her washing. "No one would dare touch us now."

Ilona ignored her at the market, refused to meet her eye, refused to acknowledge the way Erzsébet made her little jokes.

But Erzsébet noticed. And instead of stopping, she leaned into it.

At the tavern, she let her fingers linger just a little too long on the rim of her cup as she watched the men drink.

At the well, she let her voice drop, low and knowing, when speaking of which men were ailing, which men had a cough that wouldn't go away.

And worst of all, she started hinting at names.

just the ones already gone. But the ones who might be next. It was no longer just whispers between women. She was playing with it. And the women of Nagyrev did not play.

Zsuzsanna called a gathering at Ilona's house that evening.

Only the trusted ones were there. The ones who had been part of it from the beginning, the ones who did not waver. And I.

The small house was dimly lit, the fire burning low. The air was filled with the scent of drying herbs, the wooden table at the center of the room worn smooth from years of use.

I sat among them, my stomach twisting as the quiet settled over us.

Zsuzsanna stood at the head of the table, arms folded, her face unreadable.

"You've heard her," she said simply. No one had to ask who she meant.

Ilona exhaled sharply, shaking her head. "She's reckless."

"She enjoys it too much," Kata muttered.

"It's bringing attention."

The words sent a shiver through me.

They paused.

"We have to stop her." The words dropped into the room like a stone into water.

No one flinched. No one gasped. No one argued. Because we all agreed. Erzsébet had been useful. Now, she was a threat and in Nagyrev, threats did not last long.

After the meeting, I walked with Zsuzsanna back to her house, the cold night air biting at my skin.

I forced myself to speak. "Are we really going to—"

She cut me off with a sharp look. "Don't ask questions you already know the answer to."

I had to try. "She's one of us."

Zsuzsanna exhaled slowly. "She was."

Her meaning was clear.

I clenched my jaw. "And that's it?"

She turned to me, tilting her head slightly. "You still don't understand, do you?"

I stiffened. Zsuzsanna stepped closer, her voice low.

"She thinks this is a game," she murmured. "She thinks she is untouchable." She let the words settle before continuing: "She is wrong."

The next day, Erzsébet was still laughing. Still making her little comments, still glancing toward the men with that knowing gleam in her eye. But I saw the way the other women moved around her. The way they did not linger near her at the well. The way they did not return her smiles. The way they had already decided.

She did not notice. Or maybe she did, and she thought it did not matter.

The glass bottle felt heavier than it should have.

It was small enough to fit in the palm of my hand, smooth and unassuming, its contents clear as water. But I knew better.

Zsuzsanna had handed it to me that morning, pressing it gently into my palm, moving my fingers around it like a mother guiding a child's hand. She had not spoken a word. She didn't need to. We both knew what she was asking.

She held my gaze for a long moment, her expression calm. Then, she turned back to her work, stripping dried thyme from its stalks, her hands moving with the same steady precision they always did, as if she had not just asked me to take a life. I stood there for a moment, gripping the bottle too tightly, feeling the glass bite into my palm.

I had always known this moment would come. It had come for Kata. For Ilona. For so many others. Now, it had come for me.

The widow's house stood at the edge of the village, a squat little thing with an overgrown garden and shutters that never quite closed properly. The wooden fence that had once surrounded it had fallen into disrepair, slats leaning and rotting from years of neglect.

The door was slightly ajar when I arrived, swaying gently in the breeze, as if it had been left open for me. I hesitated before stepping inside.

A single candle burned on the table, its weak flame barely illuminating the room. The air inside was stale. It smelled of wet wool and something sour, like old sweat and fear.

Erzsébet sat at the table, hunched over, her hands wrapped tightly around a cup. She looked smaller than I remembered.

Not the woman who had laughed at the well, not the woman who had tossed knowing glances over her shoulder, not the woman who had spoken too freely, too carelessly. No. This was a woman who had finally realized what she had done. And what it had cost her.

She lifted her head slowly, her eyes bloodshot, her lips dry and cracked.

"You came," she murmured.

I forced my feet forward. "I brought something to help you sleep."

Her gaze turned to the bottle in my hand. And I knew she knew.

Her fingers tightened around the cup. "I won't say anything," she whispered. "You have to believe me."

The wind rattled the shutters.

She swallowed hard. "I was careless, I know that now. But I would never bring harm to any of you. I ..." Her breath caught. "Please," she whispered. "I don't want to die."

The words sent a shiver down my spine.

I thought of Kata's husband, Janos in the river, the doctor's empty cart. All the others.

I thought of Zsuzsanna's voice, low and steady. "Do not let men's rules make you weak."

I thought of the intensity of her eyes on me as she placed the bottle in my hand. And then I thought of myself. I thought of what it meant to be here, standing in this room, standing on this line that once crossed, could never be uncrossed.

I looked at Erzsébet. She was not a man. She was not cruel. She was not dangerous. She was only afraid. Just like me.

And that was the moment I knew I could not do this.

I turned toward the basin. Uncorked the bottle and tipped it over. The liquid splashed against the worn porcelain, swirling for a moment before vanishing down the drain. I set the bottle down on the counter, empty.

Erzsébet let out a soft, broken sound; something between a sob and a laugh.

"Thank you," she whispered.

I turned and left without another word knowing at last I had done the right thing.

She was found that night. Hanged. The news reached me before dawn, passed in quiet voices, exchanged in quick, knowing glances.

No one questioned it. Only a few women sighed, shaking their heads, murmuring about "foolish mistakes" and "women who do not learn."

But I knew the truth. I had not killed Erzsébet. But someone had. And when I lifted my gaze across the square, Zsuzsanna was watching me. Her expression did not change. She did not need to say anything.

She knew. She knew I had emptied the bottle. She knew I had hesitated. She knew I had failed my test.

I forced myself to keep my face smooth, to keep my hands from shaking.

I had made my choice. But now I had to live with it. And in Nagyrev, living with it might be the hardest thing of all.

38

GOODBYE

The evening was cool, the sky painted in soft strokes of pink and gold. A thin mist moved low over the fields, clinging to the earth like something reluctant to leave. The scent of wet soil and the faint sweetness of dying leaves hung in the air, a quiet reminder that summer had gone.

The village was quiet at this hour.

The women were inside, tending to their evening meals, stoking the last of the fires before the night settled in. Somewhere in the distance, a dog barked once, twice, then fell silent. A horse whinnied from the stables near the square.

Even the trees stood still, their branches drooping low, their leaves barely rustling in the soft wind. And then footsteps. Slow, measured. I heard them before I saw him.

I knew it was him before he spoke.

"Eszter."

His voice was quiet. Steady. But there was something beneath it, something I had never heard before. Finality.

I turned. Ádám stood a few paces away, his hands held in loose fists at his sides. He had cleaned up. His shirt was freshly washed, tucked neatly into his trousers, his boots polished. A small leather bag hung from his shoulder, the strap worn, the edges of the bag fraying from years of use.

His face was calm, but there was something in his eyes; a kind of tiredness that had not been there before.

I felt my stomach sink.

"You're leaving."

"Tomorrow morning."

My throat tightened.

"Where will you go?"

"Anywhere but here."

The words cut through the space between us like a blade, clean and sharp.

I could see the way his jaw tensed, the way he shifted slightly, as if he had been waiting for me to stop him. But I wouldn't. I couldn't.

He exhaled sharply, rubbing the back of his neck. He wasn't angry anymore. That was what made it worse.

"I thought I could make a life here," he admitted. "I thought maybe ..." He hesitated. The words hovered between us, unfinished.

"But you can't."

"No."

The truth of it settled over us. We had known it from the beginning. Nagyrev was not a place for men like him. It was not a place for men at all.

"I wanted to say goodbye," he said.

I swallowed against the ache rising in my throat.

"You didn't have to."

"Yes, I did."

He took a step closer, just enough that I could see the faint lines of exhaustion on his face, the way his skin had darkened from long hours in the fields, the way his curls still held the scent of wheat and river water.

"I wanted you to know something."

The breeze stirred between us, shifting his dark curls. His brown eyes softened as he looked at me, and for a moment, I let myself memorize the way he looked right then; without the burden of expectation, without anger, without the hope that had once burned so bright in him.

"I hope you find what you're looking for," he said.

I opened my mouth to ask him what he thought that was. But I didn't. Because I wasn't sure I wanted the answer.

"I hope one day," he continued, "you allow yourself to be happy."

My breath caught.

"Ádám ..."

"No," he said gently, shaking his head. "Don't say anything you don't mean just because I'm leaving."

I closed my mouth because he was right. Because what could I say? That I wished I could go with him? That I wished I were someone else, living in a world where love was not dangerous? That in another life, maybe I would have chosen him?

"Take care of yourself, Eszter."

He reached for my hand, barely brushing his fingers over mine before pulling away.

And then he turned and he left. And I did not stop him.

The night pressed in around me. The air was colder now, the drizzle creeping through my clothes, clinging to my skin. I stood there for what felt like forever, staring at the spot where he had been, as if somehow he might return, as if the moment could be undone.

But it couldn't.

The wind sighed through the trees, stirring the dry leaves at my feet. A twig snapped behind me. A sharp breath. A slow, uneven inhale. I turned, and my stomach clenched.

Zsuzsanna stood in the doorway, half-shadowed, half-lit by the dim glow of the lantern inside.

She had been there the whole time. She had heard everything. But she was not watching me. Her gaze had followed him. And then a tear slipped down her cheek.

A single tear. She did not wipe it away. She only turned and stepped inside, the door closing softly behind her.

The house swallowed her whole. And I was alone. For a long time, I did not move.

The cold bit at my skin, but I barely felt it. The silence pressed into my ears, into my ribs, into the space inside my chest that had been emptied out by his leaving.

I thought of Ádám's hands. Strong, warm, steady.

I thought of his voice, the way he had said my name, like it was something solid, something real. I thought of what he had said.

"I hope you find what you're looking for."

I closed my eyes unsure if I ever would.

39

THE WOMEN

The balance had shifted. I could feel it in the air, as choking as the smoke coming from the chimneys. Before, there had been an unspoken unity, a shared understanding that bound the women together. We did not speak too freely. We did not act too boldly. We were careful.

But that unity was cracking.

Something had changed after Erzsébet. And now, the fear no longer belonged only to the men.

It belonged to us. It started with whispers.

I heard them at the well, at the marketplace, in the hush of the tavern when the men weren't listening. Women's voices, lower than before, sharper.

"She shouldn't have spoken so openly," Kata murmured one morning, shaking her head as she kneaded dough.

"It was her own fault," Ilona added from her place by the fire, her voice clipped, businesslike. "She knew the rules."

"She was reckless."

The word settled between them like an accusation. No one disagreed. But the worst part, the part that made my stomach knot, was that they weren't just talking about Erzsébet anymore. They were talking about each other.

Two nights later, they held a meeting.

I had seen gatherings before. Hushed meetings in back rooms, women standing in small circles, shoulders angled inward, their voices barely above whispers. But this was different. This time, there was distrust.

Zsuzsanna called it at Ilona's house, just as she had before. But where once the air had been filled with quiet confidence, now it was filled with something else. Unease. Suspicion.

I took my place at the edge of the room, heart pounding, trying not to let my face betray me. They were already arguing.

"It's gotten out of hand," Ilona said sharply, her hands gripping the back of a wooden chair. "Too many men. Too quickly."

"It had to be done," Kata countered. "Would you rather they lived?"

"You think I'm saying we should stop?" Ilona snapped. "I'm saying we need to be more careful. The doctor—"

"The doctor was handled," Zsuzsanna interrupted smoothly.

Handled. The word was soft, but it burned my skin like ice.

Zsuzsanna's voice remained calm as she continued. "We have survived this long because we do not let fear rule us. Because we do not turn on each other."

She let the words settle.

"But mistakes are being made."

The room shifted. Someone cleared their throat.

Ilona exhaled sharply. "Yes. And mistakes bring attention."

Another voice, quieter, more hesitant: "We should be asking who's making those mistakes."

A cold feeling settled in my bones. I knew what this was. This wasn't about the poison anymore. This was about control. Who had it. Who didn't. Who was dangerous.

I forced myself to speak. "You think there's a traitor?"

Zsuzsanna tilted her head slightly. "Not a traitor. But a liability."

The room was silent.

A liability did not mean someone who would go to the authorities. A liability did not mean someone who would betray them. A liability was someone who was weak. And weakness would not be allowed.

Zsuzsanna's eyes swept over the room, taking in every face, pausing for a fraction of a second too long on me.

I forced myself to keep my breathing steady. I had made a mistake. I had let her see me hesitate. And now, I had to convince her I was still one of them.

I walked home alone that night, the cold biting through my shawl. My breath misted in the air, my footsteps the only sound against the frozen dirt path.

The words from the meeting still echoed in my ears. Mistakes are being made. Mistakes bring attention. I had seen what happened to those who made mistakes.

Janos in the river. The doctor's empty cart. Erzsébet hanging in her own home. And now, the women were watching each other.

I reached the door to Zsuzsanna's house and hesitated as a thought struck me then. Sharp, sudden, undeniable.

I was a mistake, too. I had emptied the bottle. I had hesitated. And Zsuzsanna knew.

I shivered, though not from the cold. I wanted to leave. I wanted to run. But I knew better than anyone. There was no way out of Nagyrev.

Sleep did not come easily that night. I lay awake, staring at the wooden beams above me, my thoughts twisting into shapes I couldn't unsee. At some point, I must have dozed, because I woke to the sound of movement outside. Footsteps. Slow. Measured.

I stayed still, my breath shallow, my body stiff beneath the blankets. The footsteps stopped. Then, a soft creak. The door shifted, just slightly. My stomach turned to ice. I didn't move. Didn't breathe. Someone was there.

And then, just as suddenly, the sound retreated. Footsteps fading into the night.

I lay there for a long time after that, until the first light of dawn seeped through the cracks in the wooden walls.

When I finally forced myself to move, my muscles ached from how tense I had been.

I dressed slowly, mechanically, forcing my hands to stay steady. Then, I stepped outside.

The ground was hard with frost, the sky still tinged with the last remnants of night. The village lay still, untouched.

But something was there. Something had changed.

I didn't know who had been at my door. But I knew what it meant. I was being watched and my mind felt unsettled as I drifted off to sleep.

It was warm in the dream. The kind of warmth that wraps around you, soft and golden, pressing against your skin like the touch of something gentle, something good.

The fields stretched wide and endless, the wheat swaying lazily under a sun too bright to be real. A house stood in the distance, small but sturdy, white-washed stone with a red-tiled roof, its windows flung open to let the breeze carry the scent of fresh bread from the kitchen.

Laughter rang through the air. Not just one voice. Two. High, sweet, unburdened by the weight of the world. Children's laughter.

I turned, and they were there. Two small figures running barefoot through the grass, their giggles spilling into the warm afternoon.

A boy and a girl. The boy had dark curls like his father, his skin bronzed from hours in the sun. He was fast, his legs moving with the wild, uncoordinated confidence of youth.

The girl was softer, lighter, her hair catching in the wind, her eyes bright as she ran to me, arms outstretched, her voice calling my name.

"Mama!"

I bent down, scooping her up, pressing my lips to the top of her head. She smelled of sunshine and dirt and wildflowers.

"Look at them," a voice said beside me.

Deep. Steady. Familiar. Ádám.

I turned, and there he was. Standing beside me, his sleeves rolled to his elbows, his shirt slightly wrinkled, his hair sticking to his temples as if he had just finished working in the fields.

He smiled at me, and it was the kind of smile that reached his eyes. The kind of smile that said, *we have built something good here.*

The kind of smile that said, *we are safe.* I smiled back. And for the first time, I felt weightless.

"You're happy here," he said.

"Yes."

"This is what you want?"

"Yes."

He nodded slowly, looking out over the fields, watching our children chase each other through the tall grass. The wind played with his hair, lifting it in soft waves, the way I had always loved.

And then, something changed.

The sun dimmed. The warmth began to slip away. And when I turned back to him, his expression was different. Darker. Distant.

"I cannot stay with someone I cannot trust."

The words punched the air from my lungs.

"What?"

"You knew it all along, Eszter." His voice was calm. "You knew this was never real."

I reached for him, but my fingers passed through nothing. He was already walking away. The fields began to fade.

The sky grew dark with storm clouds, the wind rising, ripping the warmth from the dream in great, howling gusts.

"Ádám!" I cried.

But he did not turn back. He only walked away, his silhouette fading into the distance, dissolving like smoke.

And I was left alone, standing in a field that no longer existed. Holding a child that had never been born. Watching a life that had never been mine disappear into the dark.

I woke gasping. My face was wet with tears. The room was dark, too dark, too cold. The air smelled of damp wood, of herbs drying in the rafters, of a life I had never wanted but had chosen anyway.

I moved onto my side, pressing my hands to my face, willing the dream to fade, willing my heart to quiet. But I could still feel it. The warmth of the sun. The feeling of a child in my arms. Ádám's voice.

"I cannot stay with someone I cannot trust."

I had never told him the truth. And now, I never would.

The dream was gone. The life was gone. And I would never have it back.

~

Morning came slow, creeping over the village in dull streaks of gray. The sky was dark with low clouds, the air ripe with the scent of earth. The world looked the same. But I knew better.

Something had changed in the night. Something I could not yet name. I had barely slept.

Every creak of the wooden beams, every gust of wind against the shutters had felt like footsteps, like someone standing outside my door, listening, waiting. My body was stiff from lying too still, my breath shallow from holding it too long. By the time the first traces of light pushed through the cracks in the walls, I had already known I would not be able to shake this feeling.

Because it was real. And as I stepped outside, I knew it was only getting worse.

The square was quiet when I arrived. The women moved as they always did, fetching water, pulling bread from ovens, shaking out rugs over fence posts. But beneath the surface, something had changed.

I could feel it in the way they watched me. Not directly. Never directly. But I caught it. Quick glances from the corners of their eyes, pauses in their conversations when I passed, the slight stiffening of shoulders when I came too close.

They were waiting. For what, I wasn't sure.

I kept my head down, forced my hands to stay steady as I filled my bucket at the well, listening to the murmurs drifting through the air. The voices of the women blended together, indistinct at first, but then I caught something beneath them.

"Things are different now," Kata was saying to someone.

"They have to be," another voice muttered.

"They have to be," I repeated silently in my head.

The words made my stomach knot.

And then, Ilona stepped in front of me.

She was one of the older women, broad-shouldered, her graying hair twisted tightly beneath her headscarf. She had always been kind to me before, or at least, what passed for kindness in Nagyrev.

But there was no kindness in her face now.

"Walk with me," she said. It was not a request.

She led me away from the square, past the well, past the edge of the village, to the narrow footpath that wound toward the river.

The mud was wet beneath my boots, the wind sharp against my skin. The trees lining the path were bare, their skeletal branches reaching toward the sky like fingers.

"You wouldn't betray us, would you?"

The words landed softly, but they hit like a stone to the ribs.

I swallowed hard. "Of course not."

Ilona kept walking, her boots sinking slightly into the muddy ground. "That's good," she said lightly, as if she were discussing something trivial, something small. "We all have to look out for each other. Especially now."

She glanced at me then, and something in her gaze sent ice through my veins.

I forced a nod. "Of course," I repeated.

She nodded once, satisfied, before turning her eyes back to the path ahead.

"You've been with us long enough to understand," she said. "We take care of each other."

The river was just ahead now, the water dark and sluggish, choked with reeds. A memory flashed through my mind. Janos in the river, his bloated body tangled in the currents.

I felt a shiver twist through me. Ilona followed my gaze.

"But we also take care of problems," she continued, her voice even, measured.

She stopped walking and turned to face me fully. Her

expression had not changed, not really, but something in her face was harder now. Less patient.

I met her gaze, my fingers twisting into my shawl to keep from trembling. She smiled. And I knew. This was a warning. Another test. A final chance to prove myself.

I forced a tight, careful smile.

"Of course," I said.

Her eyes stayed on mine a moment longer, then she nodded.

She turned and started back toward the village, her pace unhurried, as if she had merely gone for a walk.

I stayed where I was. The river whispered at my feet, sluggish, endless. I stared at it, my breath coming too fast, my skin cold despite the warm wool of my coat.

I had always known I was trapped. But now, I knew it for certain.

And I knew this, too. If I made one wrong move, I would not live to see another morning.

40

ANOTHER LIFE

The call came just as the last light of the day slipped below the hills. A pounding at the door. A sharp, urgent voice in the cold.

"She's laboring!"

Zsuzsanna was already moving before I had fully stood, sweeping her shawl over her shoulders, grabbing her leather satchel from the peg on the wall. I followed without thinking.

Outside, the village was cloaked in the deep blue of early night. The stars were just beginning to emerge, scattered pinpricks in the sky.

The woman's house stood near the center of the village, one of the smaller homes, its walls patched with uneven plaster, the door slightly askew on its hinges. A crowd had gathered outside; women, mostly, whispering in tight knots, their faces drawn.

Some of them looked tense, others excited, their breath misting in the cold. I heard fragments of conversation as we passed.

"She's been laboring since midday."

"First baby, it always takes longer." Zsuzsanna said.

Inside, the air was hot. The fire had been stoked high, the

scent of burning tallow mingling with the unmistakable smell of sweat and blood.

The woman, Éva, lay on a straw-stuffed mattress, her shift soaked with sweat, her hair clinging to her face. Her belly was impossibly round, stretched taut, the skin flushed red from exertion.

She was moaning, low and keening, her fingers clawing at the blankets beneath her.

Zsuzsanna knelt beside her without hesitation, rolling up her sleeves. "How long?"

Her mother-in-law, a thin, sharp-faced woman, wrung her hands in the corner. "Since midday," she murmured. "The pains are close now."

Zsuzsanna nodded, pressing her hands gently to Éva's belly, feeling the tightness of the contraction. She was calm, measured, entirely different from the woman who had spoken so coolly about death.

"She's ready," she said simply as she turned to me.

"Boil water. As hot as you can make it."

I nodded and rushed to the hearth, grabbing the kettle, setting it over the flames.

"Where's the knife?" Zsuzsanna asked.

The mother-in-law hurried to a shelf, retrieving a small, curved blade wrapped in a strip of linen.

I swallowed hard. That knife.

I had seen it before. Not in use, but in its place, among Zsuzsanna's things. The blade was slightly rusted, but sharp, honed by years of necessity.

She set it beside her on a wooden stool. "Good."

She turned back to Éva. "It's time."

The next contraction came hard and fast, tearing a ragged cry from Éva's throat.

"Push," Zsuzsanna instructed.

Éva sobbed, her fingers gripping the sheets, her entire body trembling with the force of it.

I hovered near the hearth, unsure, uneasy.

I had seen birth before but this was different. This was raw. Pain and power woven together, the closest thing I had ever seen to both life and death at the same time.

Zsuzsanna moved with ease, placing a moist cloth on Éva's forehead, pressing her hands gently but firmly against the woman's thighs, guiding her.

"You're strong," she murmured. "Stronger than you think. Push again."

Éva gasped, her body straining, the veins in her neck standing out.

And then, a head. Small, slick with blood, emerging slowly.

Zsuzsanna wiped her hands quickly with a clean cloth, then reached down, her fingers careful, practiced. "One more," she urged.

Éva let out a final, shuddering cry.

Then came a wet, gasping sound. A wail. Zsuzsanna lifted the child, turning it slightly, clearing its tiny nose with her fingers.

"A girl," she murmured.

A collective exhale filled the room, the release of so much tension, of fear giving way to relief.

Zsuzsanna wrapped the baby quickly in a linen cloth, holding her close, murmuring soft words that I had never heard from her before.

She was gentle. Tender. I could not reconcile it with the woman I had come to fear.

I stayed after the others had gone, cleaning the bloodied sheets, gathering the discarded rags. Zsuzsanna was sitting beside Éva, watching the child sleep, her face unreadable. I hesitated.

"Did you have children?"

She looked at me, surprised by the question. Then, slowly, she shook her head.

"No," she murmured. "I never had the chance."

Then I asked the question I had always wondered but had never dared say aloud.

"What made you like this?"

She was quiet for a long moment.

"My husband," she said simply.

I swallowed.

"He was not a kind man," she continued, her voice even. "He drank. He took his anger out on me. On others. It was not a special story, just an ordinary one."

I had never heard her speak like this before. I wanted to ask more, but she kept talking.

"And one day," she said, her voice softer now, thoughtful, "I realized I didn't have to take it anymore."

A pause. I already knew what she would say next.

"I gave him arsenic," she murmured. "Just a little. Just enough." She looked at the sleeping baby, her gaze strangely gentle. "And after that, I helped other women do the same."

She exhaled slowly.

"That's all there is to it."

I stared at her. Because it wasn't all there was to it. Not anymore. Not after Janos, after Erzsébet, after the doctor.

What had started as freedom had turned into something else. Something I no longer understood.

And yet here she was, holding a newborn in her arms like she had never taken a life in her own hands.

"Do you regret it?" I asked.

She met my gaze and smiled.

"No."

Her answer came too easily. Too quickly.

I looked at the child in her arms, at the way she cradled her. At the way her fingers, capable of so much destruction, could also bring life into the world.

She was two women at once.

A healer. And a killer.

I did not sleep well again that night.

41

AN EXECUTION

The news came before dawn, whispered from house to house, spreading like smoke through the village.

István Farkas was dead. It had happened too fast. Too suddenly. The details traveled on hushed lips, carried between women at the well, exchanged over baskets of bread in the market.

"Fell ill after supper," someone muttered.

"Vomited blood," another whispered.

"Was dead before the priest could even be summoned."

There was no panic in the village, no alarm. Only the quiet, unspoken understanding that had long settled over Nagyrev. But I felt it. The difference. This was not the careful, deliberate work of the past. This was something else. This was an execution.

István had been one of the most powerful men in the village. Not because he was good. Not because he was wise. But because he was feared. His voice could cut through a crowded tavern like the snap of a whip, and his fists could do far worse.

He had once been a soldier, and he carried war with him wherever he went. The battlefield had never truly left him. It lived inside him, hungry for another fight. And his wife, Margit, had been his battlefield.

By midmorning, the women had gathered in small clusters, their voices low, their hands undertaking their chores with forced normalcy. But there was a straining. I felt it in the way they stood closer together than usual. The way their glances lingered too long before darting away. The way they spoke with care. This death was different.

Kata stood near the well, her shawl pulled tightly around her shoulders, her face drawn. "It was quick," she murmured, not looking at anyone directly. "Fell ill after supper. Gone before midnight."

"Quick," Ilona echoed, frowning.

That was what worried them. Most deaths here were slow, a careful sickness, a gentle decline. But this had been sudden. This had been intentional. And worst of all, people beyond Nagyrev had noticed.

The priest had been summoned, but by the time he arrived, István was already cold. And now, whispers carried beyond the village, reaching the ears of those who did not understand what we did here. Those who would not approve.

I caught Ilona watching me, her dark eyes assessing, her expression unreadable. I forced my face to remain smooth. I could not look uncertain. Not now. Not when doubt had already taken so many.

I found myself outside Margit's house, my feet carrying me there before my mind had decided to go. The door was open, as was custom. A sign of mourning. But inside, there was no mourning.

Margit sat at the wooden table, her hands folded in her lap. She did not weep. She did not wail. She did not shake or rage. She simply sat. There was something unnerving about her composure. I had seen grief before, real grief. This was not it.

"Margit," I said softly.

She lifted her gaze to me. Her face was calm. Peaceful, even. I felt my stomach tighten.

"You must be in shock," I tried.

Her lips twitched. "Why should I be?"

I hesitated. "Because ... because he's dead."

She blinked slowly, as if she had not considered that fact before now.

"Yes," she murmured. "He is."

She tilted her head slightly, her dark hair falling over one shoulder.

"But tell me," she continued, her voice even, "would you be in shock if a wolf fell dead at your feet?"

I did not answer. Because I understood. I had heard the stories. I had seen the bruises she had tried to hide, the way she shrank into herself whenever István's voice turned sharp. I knew the truth, as well as she did.

He was not a husband. He was a wolf. A predator. And now, he was gone.

Margit looked satisfied. And that was when I knew. She had killed him.

I left the house feeling sick. Not because István was dead. He had been a monster, and monsters deserved to die. But because it had been too easy. There had been no struggle. No fear.

Just a quiet meal, a sip of something bitter, a long night, and a still morning. Margit had not needed help. She had not needed saving. She had chosen this. And she had done it without hesitation.

~

That night my thoughts were tangled and dark. Zsuzsanna sat

beside me, slicing dried herbs into thin strips, her hands steady, precise.

"You're quiet," she observed.

I exhaled. "Margit did it."

Zsuzsanna nodded. "Yes."

I turned to her. "You don't seem surprised."

She lifted one shoulder in a slow shrug.

"I'm not."

I frowned. "Why?"

She met my gaze, her expression unreadable.

"Because women learn," she murmured.

A long pause.

"Don't they?"

I did not answer. I was afraid of what my answer would be.

42

THE CONFESSION

The church stood at the highest point in Nagyrev, just beyond the square, where the land sloped gently downward toward the river.

It was small and weathered, the wooden beams darkened with age, the stone steps worn smooth by years of footsteps. It had stood longer than most of the houses in the village, older even than the trees that surrounded it, their bare branches scraping against the roof whenever the wind picked up.

It was a cold evening when I went there, the sky the color of lead, the air holding the promise of coming rain.

I had not intended to go. But something in me—a pull, a quiet dread, a feeling I could not name—had led me up the hill, through the graveyard, toward the large wooden doors.

The doors groaned as I pushed them open, the scent of candle wax and wet stone rising to meet me. Inside, the air was still. The last of the evening light filtered through the high windows, casting faint colors onto the floor.

And at the altar, standing in the half-shadow of the candlelight, was Father Bálint. He had always been an old man, as far as I could remember. His face was carved with deep lines, his thin white hair combed neatly back, his hands always clasped behind his back as he moved through the village.

He had never spoken much to me. But I had watched him. I had seen the way his eyes lingered too long on certain women, the way his voice had sometimes sharpened when he spoke of a woman's duty, a wife's obedience.

He was not cruel, not like some of the men in the village. But he was not kind, either. And yet, as I stood in the doorway of the church, observing him, I realized he looked afraid.

"You should not be here," he said without turning.

His voice was hoarse, quieter than usual.

I hesitated. "I didn't—"

"You should not be here," he repeated.

He exhaled, running a hand over his face before finally turning to me. His eyes, usually sharp, were sunken, shadowed. He looked like a man who had not slept in days.

He stared at me for a long moment, as if weighing something. Then, finally, he spoke.

"I know," he murmured.

A chill shuddered down my spine. I forced myself to keep my voice steady. "Know what?"

His jaw tightened. "Do not insult me, child."

He stepped forward, his boots echoing against the stone floor.

"I have heard the confessions," he said, voice low.

I swallowed hard. Confessions. I felt my pulse quicken. He knew.

I did not know who had spoken, whose guilt had pressed too heavily against their ribs, whose fear had driven them to whisper the truth into the darkness of the confessional. But it did not matter. He knew.

I did not move as he came closer, his gaze fixed on mine, searching. His voice softened, almost pleading. "It must stop."

I opened my mouth, but no words came.

He sighed. "Do you think I do not understand? Do you think I do not see?"

He shook his head, as if speaking more to himself than to me.

"I know what the men of this village have done," he murmured. "I have buried too many women with broken bones, with bruises still blooming on their skin. I have buried too many children who never should have died."

He exhaled slowly.

"But this ... this is not justice. This is ..." He stopped himself. "This is something else."

His words pressed against my skin like a warning, twisting around my ribs, tightening. Because I had thought it, too. I had felt it, creeping beneath my skin, whispering in the back of my mind. This had begun as survival. But now, it was something else. Something darker. Something I no longer recognized.

"I will go to the magistrate," Father Bálint said.

I stiffened. His gaze did not waver.

"I have kept quiet for too long," he murmured. "I have closed my eyes to too much. But no more. It must stop."

The church was too quiet. Outside, the wind had picked up, rattling the trees, whispering through the graveyard. And in that moment, I knew. He would not leave this church alive.

That night, he died in his sleep. I heard the news before dawn, whispered like a prayer through the village.

"Peaceful," someone said.

"A good death," another murmured.

A good death.

I stood in the square, listening, feeling the cold bite into my skin. He had been old. His heart had simply stopped. That was what they said. That was what everyone would say.

But I knew better. And when I turned, Zsuzsanna was watching me.

~

The magistrate arrived at dawn. I heard him before I saw him.

The sound of hooves cut through the morning stillness, their rhythmic pounding sending birds scattering from the rooftops. A carriage, dark and unremarkable, rolled into the village square, its wheels groaning against the frozen dirt.

I watched from the doorway of Zsuzsanna's house, pulling my shawl tighter around my shoulders.

The magistrate stepped down, boots crunching against the frost. I had seen him before, though never this close. Never with his eyes narrowed in suspicion, never with his lips pressed into a thin, knowing line.

He was a tall man, lean and severe, his gray coat buttoned high against the cold. He moved with purpose, not pausing to greet anyone, not offering pleasantries.

He went straight to the priest's house. A chill moved through me. I had known he would return. I just hadn't expected it to be this soon. By midday, the order had been given. The magistrate stood in the square, surrounded by a handful of men; officials from beyond the village, men whose eyes did not yet carry the burden of knowing.

"The bodies must be examined," he said, his voice carrying through the cold air.

A murmur rippled through the gathered villagers.

No one argued. No one protested. But I could feel the fear, creeping like ivy through the crowd.

I found Zsuzsanna in the throng of women. She did not speak. She did not look at me. She only watched, her face smooth, unreadable. But I knew her well enough by now. She was calculating. She was deciding who would be next. The first grave was dug up before sunset. I stood at the edge of the churchyard, my hands buried deep in the folds of my shawl.

The gravediggers worked silently, their shovels slicing into the frozen ground, the scent of the wet earth rising into the air. It took longer than I expected. The ground was hard, reluctant to give up its dead.

The first coffin was lifted from the grave with slow, deliberate movements. The wood was soft, the edges weakened with decay. One of the men pried the lid open. A hush fell over the crowd. Inside, the body lay as it had been buried, wrapped in linen, the contours of the face barely visible beneath the cloth.

But I saw the hands. Even from where I stood, I saw them. The nails, blackened, curled at the edges. Fingers that had stiffened into unnatural shapes, clawed, as if the body had fought something long after the breath had left its lungs. I swallowed hard.

The magistrate stepped forward, peering into the coffin. His face did not change. But I saw it. The way his jaw tightened.

"Another," he said.

They dug up three more before the night was over.

Each one the same. The same blackened nails. The same brittle, yellowed bones. The same quiet proof, whispering from beneath the dirt. Arsenic.

The wind picked up as the last coffin was pried open, howling low through the churchyard, rattling the bare branches of the trees. I pulled my shawl tighter around me, but the cold was inside me now, creeping beneath my skin, settling in my bones.

The magistrate turned to his men.

"Send word to Szolnok," he said. "We need confirmation."

I felt my stomach twist. Szolnok.

The town beyond the river, where the doctors had already begun to suspect what was happening in Nagyrev.

If the bodies were examined there, they would know. They would see the poison, resting in the bones, refusing to fade. And then the women would have nowhere to hide.

I could not sleep that night. I lay on my cot, staring at the wooden beams above me, listening to the wind rattle the shutters.

Zsuzsanna sat at the table, her knife moving slowly over a bundle of dried roots, slicing them into thin, precise strips. She had not spoken since the exhumations. But I could feel her watching me. And I realized something.

The magistrate did not know who had done it.

Not yet. But he would. And when he did, someone would have to answer for it.

Sometime past midnight, I heard footsteps. I wasn't sure if I had been asleep or simply lost in the nothingness of the night, but the sound jolted me awake, my pulse leaping into my throat. Soft, measured steps. Not those belonging to a man. A woman.

I sat up slowly, my breath shallow. The footsteps stopped outside the door. I held still. Then came quiet knock. Not urgent. Not frantic.

My fingers twisted into the thin blanket. I glanced at Zsuzsanna. She had not moved. She did not look at me.

"Go on," she murmured.

Her voice was unreadable.

I swallowed hard and rose to my feet, padding carefully to

the door. I hesitated before opening it. Ilona stood in the moonlight, her shawl pulled tightly around her shoulders, her face pale, unreadable. She exhaled when she saw me.

"They are asking questions," she said quietly.

I nodded.

"Zsuzsanna needs to decide," she continued.

I stiffened. "Decide what?"

Ilona tilted her head slightly.

"You know what."

I did. I had always known.

The magistrate wanted names. He would have them. And the women of Nagyrev would make certain they were the right ones. Ilona reached into her pocket, withdrawing a small glass bottle. She held it out to me.

"For tomorrow," she murmured.

I stared at it. The liquid inside was clear as water. I did not take it.

Ilona sighed, then tucked it into the folds of my skirt herself. She patted it once.

"Don't be foolish," she said.

Then she turned and disappeared into the night. I stood there for a long time, feeling the bottle against my hip. It was light. Lighter than it should have been. But it felt like it had already buried me.

43

LAST WORDS

I knew she had been waiting for me.

She sat at the table, her back straight, hands resting lightly in her lap, a half-empty cup of tea in front of her. The fire had burned low, barely more than glowing embers. The air inside smelled of something faintly bitter. The scent of Zsuzsanna herself, something sharp and unyielding, something that had soaked into the very bones of this house.

She didn't look up when I entered.

"You were gone a long time," she murmured.

I hesitated, closing the door behind me. "Ilona stopped me."

A small pause.

"Of course she did."

Zsuzsanna lifted her cup, took a slow sip. I stayed where I was, standing just inside the doorway, my hands still cold from the night air. I could feel it in the room. The shift in tension, the knowledge settling between us like a stone.

She knew. She had always known. And now, it had finally come.

I forced myself to speak. "The magistrate is looking for names."

Zsuzsanna set her cup down with careful precision.

"They already have names," she said. "They just don't know it yet."

I swallowed. "Who will they take?"

She looked at me then and smiled. The kind of smile a mother gives when she has already decided something for you.

A soft, quiet thing. Final.

She stood and moved past me, reaching for her satchel, her hands as steady as ever. I watched as she pulled out bundles of dried herbs, glass bottles filled with dark liquids, a small knife wrapped in cloth.

Her tools. Her weapons. The things that had made her both feared and revered. The things that had kept the women of Nagyrev safe. And now, they would be used as evidence.

I exhaled slowly. "You should leave."

Zsuzsanna's lips twitched, amused. "And go where?"

I had no answer. She already knew that.

She moved past me again, this time to the fire, stirring the embers absently with a piece of iron.

"If they take me, they will come for you next."

Her voice was calm, measured. Not a warning. Not a threat. A fact.

I gripped the back of a chair, my hands shaking. "Then what do we do?"

She turned to me. And I realized she had no intention of running. She had already accepted it. The end was coming. And she would not fight it. I sat down slowly across from her, my legs unsteady.

"You knew this would happen," I said.

She inclined her head slightly. "Of course."

The fire crackled between us, throwing gold light against her face, illuminating the deep lines around her mouth, the shadows beneath her eyes. She looked tired. She looked old.

"You could still leave," I pressed. "We could go before they come back."

She smiled again. A patient smile, a teacher's smile.

"And do what?" she asked. "Live in another village, another house, another life? You think I can simply stop being who I am?"

I had no answer. She reached for her cup again, took another sip.

"I have never feared death."

Her voice was softer now, almost thoughtful.

I stared at her. "Why not?"

She met my gaze.

"Because I chose my own life," she said simply. "And that means I choose my own end, too." I exhaled shakily, my fingers pressing into my lap. I wanted to say something, anything. But what could I say?

She was already gone. The wind shifted outside, rattling the shutters against the walls. Zsuzsanna glanced toward the sound, then back at me.

"They will come at dawn," she said.

I stiffened. "How do you know?"

A faint smile ghosted her lips. "Because that is what men do. They take what they do not understand, what they cannot control."

She pushed back her chair and stood, moving to the shelf above the hearth. She reached for a small wooden box, the lid smooth from years of use, and placed it on the table between us.

I stared at it.

She sighed slowly. "You should be ready."

I frowned. "For what?"

She met my gaze. "For the choice."

I did not ask what she meant. Because I already knew. Run, and betray her. Stay, and be taken with her.

“I could have had children. A family. Love.” I didn’t speak his name. She knew what I was saying. I swallowed hard, my throat dry. "What are you going to do?"

She tilted her head slightly, studying me.

"I am going to sleep."

And with that, she turned away, as if the conversation had never happened. As if tomorrow was just another day. As if she had not just accepted her own death.

I sat there long after she had gone, staring at the fire, my hands clenched in my lap. Because for the first time, I did not know what I was going to do.

~

It began with the sound of horses. Distant at first, a dull rhythm against the frozen dirt, barely audible beneath the whisper of wind through the trees. But then it grew. Hoofbeats multiplying, pounding, steady, relentless.

I was already awake when I heard them. I had not slept. I had sat by the dying fire, listening to Zsuzsanna’s slow, measured breathing from the cot across the room; her last words pressing against my ribs.

"If they take me, they will come for you next."

The shutters rattled as the wind shifted. The air inside was filled with the scent of burnt wood and something herbal. The remnants of whatever Zsuzsanna had been brewing the night before.

The horses were close now. Then came shouting. Voices, deep and urgent, cutting through the early morning stillness.

A sharp bang against a door. Not ours, somewhere else in the village.

I shot to my feet. Zsuzsanna stirred, exhaling slowly before opening her eyes. She didn’t look afraid. She didn’t even look surprised. She only looked at me, and in that moment, I knew she had been waiting for this.

She sat up, stretching her arms over her head as if it were an ordinary morning, as if the shouts outside were nothing more than birdsong.

Then, calmly, she said, "You should stay inside."

She stood, reaching for her shawl, draping it loosely over her shoulders.

I swallowed hard. "What are you going to do?"

She glanced at me, her expression unreadable.

"I am going to greet them."

By the time I reached the door, the soldiers were already in the square. There were at least a dozen of them, their coats buttoned high against the cold, rifles slung over their shoulders. Behind them, the magistrate stood tall, his face grim, unreadable.

I saw Kata first, her long braid tangled, her face twisted in fury as two men dragged her forward.

"Let me go!" she spat, her voice hoarse. "I have done nothing wrong!"

A sharp crack, one of the soldiers striking her across the face. She stumbled but did not fall. Blood dripped from her lip. She spit at the ground.

"Nothing wrong?" the magistrate repeated, his voice cold. "Then explain the bodies."

No one moved. No one spoke. A harsh gust of wind whipped through the square, stirring dust from the frozen ground.

I stood at the threshold of Zsuzsanna's house, hidden in the shadow of the doorway, my breath caught in my throat. And then I saw her. Zsuzsanna.

She walked toward the square with slow, measured steps, her shawl drawn loosely around her shoulders. She looked almost regal. The soldiers stiffened as she approached, gripping their rifles a little tighter. She stopped in front of the magistrate. Held his gaze.

"Zsuzsanna," he said, tilting his head slightly. "I imagine you know why we're here."

She smiled. Not kindly. Not warmly. A small, knowing thing.

"Of course," she murmured.

The magistrate's eyes moved over her, searching.

"You will come with us," he said.

A pause.

"Will I?"

A ripple of unease moved through the gathered soldiers. I could see it in their faces. They had expected resistance. A fight. They had not expected her calm.

She yawned slowly, casting a glance around the square, her gaze lingering on the faces of the women who stood frozen in their doorways. Then, without another word, she held out her hands. The magistrate hesitated. With a slight nod, one of the soldiers stepped forward, binding her wrists with strong rope.

Zsuzsanna did not flinch. I gripped the edge of the doorframe. She was not afraid. I could see it in her face, in the way her shoulders remained straight, in the way her chin remained high. And suddenly, I wanted to run. Not to save her. Not to stop what was already happening. But because I did not want to be next.

They took five women that morning. Kata. Ilona. Two others I did not know well. And Zsuzsanna.

They were pulled from their homes, marched through the square with their hands bound, their heads held high. No one fought. No one begged.

They disappeared beyond the trees, swallowed by the path that led toward the river. I stood in the doorway long after they had gone, my breath shallow, my body stiff. No one had come for me. Not yet.

But I knew the truth. Zsuzsanna's last words echoed in my head, settling into my bones.

"If they take me, they will come for you next."

I exhaled shakily, closing my eyes. I did not know how much time I had. But I knew one thing for certain. I was not safe.

44

THE DARK ROOM

The prison sat on the outskirts of Szolnok, built from black stone, crumbling with age. A place meant for men. A place never meant for women. It loomed against the gray sky, its iron gate coated with rust, but still strong enough to hold its prisoners. The walls rose high, lined with frost, the windows too small to let in any real light.

I did not want to go inside. But I had no choice.

The guards led me down a narrow corridor, the air filled with the stench of unwashed bodies and rotting straw. The floor beneath my feet was uneven, the stones worn from years of boots dragging men to their fate.

We passed several cells, each one filled with shadows. Thin, broken figures hunched against the walls, their faces lost in the gloom.

Then we stopped. The guard beside me pounded his fist against the bars.

"Wake up, witch."

I flinched at the word. But the figure inside did not move. Not at first. Then, slowly, a stirring.

The woman shifted in the darkness, unfolding herself from

where she had been sitting. She stepped forward, her face emerging from the shadows. My breath caught in my throat. Zsuzsanna had always been strong.

Her face, weathered by years of work, had held the kind of beauty that came from knowing one's own power. Her skin, once golden from the sun, had always carried the scent of dried herbs, of earth, of something alive.

But the woman standing before me was not the Zsuzsanna I knew. She was gaunt, hollowed out, shrunken. Her cheekbones jutted sharp beneath her skin, her lips cracked, her hair tangled, unwashed.

Bruises bloomed along her jawline, yellowing, fading, replaced with fresh ones. A dark smudge beneath one eye, a cut at the corner of her mouth, a line of dried blood where her lower lip had split.

Her hands, once steady, once capable of bringing both life and death, trembled as she gripped the bars.

I swallowed hard. "Zsuzsanna."

Her lips curved. A ghost of her old smile.

"Well," she rasped. "You're still free, I see."

I opened my mouth, but no words came.

The guard beside me shifted, impatient. "Five minutes."

Then he turned and walked back down the hall, boots echoing.

Zsuzsanna tilted her head slightly. "Brave of them, leaving you alone with me. Aren't they afraid I'll poison you through the bars?"

Her voice was hoarse, a ruin of what it had been.

I swallowed hard. "What have they done to you?"

She exhaled slowly, leaning her forehead against the rusted iron. "What haven't they done?"

She told me in fragments. The first night, they had not let them sleep. The guards had kept the torches burning, pacing outside the cells, shouting their names, calling them witches, murderers, whores.

"They think if you are tired enough," she murmured, "you'll tell them anything. And some do."

Her fingers clutched tightly at the bars.

"They beat Ilona first," she said. "One of them held her arms back while another struck her. Open palm, at first. Then fists."

A muscle tightened in her jaw.

"She didn't scream," she whispered.

Her eyes turned toward the cell across the corridor, where Ilona was lying on the floor, her back turned to us.

"They will hang her first," Zsuzsanna said softly.

I inhaled sharply. "You don't know that—"

She lifted a hand. I stopped.

"I do," she murmured.

And I believed her. They had used other tactics, too. They had tied their wrists too tightly, until the rope burned through skin. They had thrown water on them in the middle of the night, soaking them through, letting the cold gnaw at their bones.

"They like to watch you shiver," Zsuzsanna said. "It makes them feel strong."

They had not given them real food in days. Only stale bread, coated in something bitter, something that made them ill if they ate too much.

"They want us to be weak," she said simply.

And then, the worst part. She hesitated before she spoke.

"Kata told them everything."

My stomach twisted.

"She didn't mean to," Zsuzsanna said. "She thought they would let her go if she did." She shook her head. "They won't."

A pause.

"They will take me next."

I reached for her hand before I could stop myself. Our fingers touched through the bars, her skin ice against mine.

"You don't know that," I whispered.

She smiled. A slow, knowing thing.

"You still don't understand, do you?" she murmured.

I swallowed. "Then help me understand."

She studied me for a long moment.

"I was never meant to leave this place." She tilted her head. "But you ..."

Her grip tightened, a flicker of strength still left in her.

"You still have time."

I stiffened. "To do what?"

Her eyes moved past me, toward the door.

"Run."

I exhaled slowly. "I can't."

"Yes, you can."

Her fingers pressed into mine. "If you stay, they will break you." She paused. "Do you want to end up like me?"

I pulled back as the guard's footsteps returned. Zsuzsanna straightened, her expression smoothing into something unreadable.

The key rattled in the lock.

"Time's up," the guard muttered.

I swallowed hard. Zsuzsanna's eyes did not leave mine.

"Run."

I turned. I did not look back. Because I knew if I did, I would never be able to leave.

45

THE VILLAGE WATCHES

They brought the women back just after sunrise. The sky was a dull, leaden gray, the kind of sky that swallowed the sun whole and never let it return. There was no warmth, no light; just the creeping moisture in the air, the promise of rain that never quite came. The kind of cold that sank into your bones and stayed there.

It was a miserable day for a funeral. Or an execution. I hadn't wanted to come, but somehow, deep inside me, I had known I would.

The village square had been made ready for them. Someone had hammered a wooden post into the frozen earth. Not a gallows, not yet, but a place to tie them, a place to keep them still while the magistrate decided their fate. Nearby, the magistrate's men stood in a loose half-circle, their rifles slung lazily over their shoulders, their expressions unreadable.

The ground beneath my feet was frozen solid, rutted with deep lines from the cartwheels that had passed through earlier that morning. The air smelled of of burning tallow from the torches lining the square and of something acrid and metallic. Blood. Though I did not know where it had come from.

The houses surrounding the square loomed silent, their doors shut tight, their windows dark. But the village had gathered.

They stood in clusters, wrapped in woolen shawls and heavy coats, their breath misting in the cold air. They did not speak. They only waited. And then the cart came.

It rolled into the square slowly, deliberately; its wheels groaning against the dirt, the horse straining against the burden it carried.

The women sat in the back, their wrists bound in front of them, their ankles shackled to the wooden boards beneath them. The iron cuffs were too tight, biting into flesh, leaving raw, red marks.

They had been in the prison for two weeks. And now, they barely looked human. The first woman was pulled down roughly. Ilona. She staggered as her feet hit the ground, the sharp shove of a soldier sending her forward. She caught herself before she fell, her shoulders squared, her chin lifted.

Her hair had come undone from its usual braid, wild strands tangled over her shoulders, dirty, knotted, stiff with old sweat.

Her skin was pale beneath the grime, her lips cracked and bleeding, her eyes sunken and rimmed with dark bruises.

Her hands trembled, but she held her head high. She would not let them see her break.

Behind her, Kata. She looked worse than the others. Her face was hollow, her cheeks sharp, her bones pressing too close to the surface of her skin. Her hands twisted in front of her, fidgeting, restless. She was shaking so hard I could see it from where I stood.

She would beg, if given the chance. And for that, the other women did not look at her.

Then, Zsuzsanna.

She moved slower than the rest, not because she had been

dragged, but because she refused to be rushed. She stepped down with careful, deliberate movements, as if she were not a prisoner but a queen.

She was thinner than the last time I had seen her, her skin stretched tight over sharp cheekbones, her lips bloodless, her eyes sunken, dark hollows beneath them.

But she did not stumble. She did not waver. She held herself with the same quiet certainty she always had, even as the chains rattled against her ankles, even as the magistrate's men flanked her on either side.

Her eyes swept over the crowd and then they met mine. She did not smile. But she did not look away.

The village men stood in tight clusters along the edge of the square. They did not move. They did not speak. They only watched. Their faces were unreadable, their expressions carved from stone but I saw it.

For the first time, I saw the doubt. The uncertainty. The creeping, unspoken question in their eyes. Some of them had lost wives, fathers, brothers. Some of them had been cruel. Some of them had not.

And now some of them were wondering. Had their wives ever looked at them the way these women looked at the magistrate now? Had they ever been close to drinking from the wrong cup? Had death ever brushed their shoulders without them knowing? I could see it in their faces. The guilt. The fear.

And for the first time, something else. Shame. Then, I felt it. The slow, steady realization that their eyes had turned toward me. It was subtle at first. A flicker of recognition, a quiet questioning. But then it grew.

I could feel them watching me, their gazes pressing against my skin.

Because I was one of them. I had lived beside them my entire life. I had fetched water from the same well, walked the same dirt paths, prayed in the same church.

But now they were wondering. How much had I known? How much had I seen? And how much had I done?

I gripped my shawl tightly, my nails digging into the fabric. For the first time, I thought of the road beyond the village. The road I had never taken. And for the first time, I thought maybe I should.

Zsuzsanna was still watching me. I forced myself to hold her gaze, even as my hands trembled, even as my heart slammed against my ribs.

The village square was silent. The magistrate stepped forward, unrolling a sheet of parchment, his voice calm, even.

"The women standing before you have been accused of crimes against God and man."

The sky darkened. A sharp gust of wind stirred the dust from the ground. The magistrate's voice carried over the square.

"They will be judged accordingly."

I swallowed hard. I already knew what the verdict would be. I had always known. Zsuzsanna had, too.

She had never been afraid of death. She had told me that once.

"I chose my own life. And that means I choose my own end, too."

46

THE TRIAL BEGINS

I stayed. I could have run. That night, after the women were marched back to the prison, after the magistrate had read his accusations aloud in the village square, I could have gone.

There was still time. The roads beyond Nagyrev stretched in all directions. Paths I had never taken, places I had never seen. I could have disappeared. But I didn't.

I told myself I stayed because it was too late to run now, anyway. Because the magistrate's men were watching, and leaving would have only called more attention to me.

But the truth was that I owed Zsuzsanna this much. She had walked toward her death with her head high. And I would not let her die alone.

The trial began at sunrise. The courtroom was a cramped and airless space, no bigger than the village tavern, its wooden beams blackened with age, its floor warped from years of mould. The smell of tallow candles mixed with sweat and mildew, clinging to the low ceiling like smoke. There were no grand wooden benches like in the cities, no rows of powdered wigs and robed men. Just a room, a raised platform for the magistrate, and a handful of wooden chairs meant for the accused.

They had dragged the women to the town hall, a narrow stone building that smelled of dank wood and old sweat. The courtroom was nothing more than a large, cold room. Wooden benches lined against the walls, a raised platform at the front where the magistrate and the prosecutor sat, their black coats stiff with starch.

There was no jury. There would be no deliberation. This was not a trial. It was a sentence, already decided, waiting to be spoken aloud. I slipped in through the back, taking a seat near the door. The air held scent of unwashed bodies, of burning tallow, of fear.

And then they brought them in. Zsuzsanna entered first. She walked slowly, deliberately, her wrists bound, her dress hanging loose over her thin frame.

The prison had taken its toll on her. Her face had thinned, her skin stretched tight over her sharp cheekbones, the hollows beneath her eyes dark with exhaustion. Her lips, usually firm, were chapped, cracked at the edges where she had been struck. A bruise bloomed just below her left eye, fading from deep purple to sickly yellow.

But her eyes were still sharp. She did not look at the magistrate. She did not look at the prosecutor. She only looked at me.

And in that moment, I felt it. The significance behind her actions. It was not defeat. It was something else. Something stronger, deeper.

Ilona came next. She looked worse than Zsuzsanna, her once strong frame now thin and frail, her hands trembling slightly as she was forced into her seat. Her dark hair, usually braided neatly over her shoulder, hung in tangled clumps, streaked with filth, with blood where she had been struck.

She had always been the quietest of them. But today, she was seething. Her hands curled into fists, her nails digging into her palms, her gaze burning with something close to fury.

Then, Kata. She was shaking. Not from cold. Her lips trembled around words she did not dare say. Her dress was torn at the hem, her bare feet peeking out beneath the fabric, purple with bruises. Her once plump face was now gaunt, her skin too pale, her eyes darting between the guards like a rabbit cornered by wolves. She would beg, if given the chance. And for that, the other women did not look at her.

Behind her, the others. Women whose names I barely knew but whose hands had mixed poison into tea, whose fingers had pressed arsenic into paper.

They had all killed. And now, they would all die.

They turned on each other before the trial had even begun. The moment they were placed before the magistrate, Kata broke. She fell to her knees, hands clasped, her voice hoarse from screaming.

"I didn't do anything!" she sobbed. "I swear it! It was them, they made me do it! I was never part of it!"

She turned to the other women, her body shaking.

"You know the truth! Tell them! Tell them I was innocent!"

No one spoke. Ilona's lips twitched.

"You were innocent?" she whispered. "Didn't seem that way when you were asking for more poison."

Kata's face crumpled.

"I didn't know what it was!" she cried. "I—"

"Enough!" the magistrate snapped.

Kata flinched but the women had already begun turning on each other, the air cracking with whispered accusations.

"It wasn't me, it was her—"

"I only did what I was told—"

"They're lying—"

The prosecutor sighed. He did not care who was guilty. They were all guilty. And they would all hang.

Only one woman did not speak. Zsuzsanna.

She stood in silence as the others fought, her face unreadable, her hands still bound in front of her. She did not argue. She did not beg. She only watched.

She had always been the strongest among them, but now, I saw it. This was the first time she had truly accepted her fate. I felt something uneasy settle in my chest.

The prosecutor turned to the magistrate.

"The punishment must fit the crime," he said simply.

His voice was calm. Even. Unshaken by the women's cries, by the accusations, by the truth tangled in their words.

"We ask for the death penalty."

The courtroom was silent. I knew the magistrate's next words before he even spoke to them. It was already decided. It had always been decided.

And still hearing it aloud made my stomach turn.

"They will be hanged," the magistrate said.

A final sentence. A death sentence. Zsuzsanna inhaled deeply, then exhaled. And then, finally she smiled. Not at the magistrate. Not at the prosecutor. At me.

In that moment, I knew she had never needed saving. She had known how this would end from the very beginning. And she had never been afraid.

47

THE MIDWIFE'S WORDS

I didn't want to go. When the guard arrived at Zsuzsanna's request, I almost refused. But refusing would have been just as damning as going. So, I followed him through the prison corridors, keeping my hands folded inside my shawl, my head low.

The walls were slick with moisture, the stones beneath my feet uneven and crumbling. The air was filled with the smell of rot, stale sweat and old blood.

I could hear them before I saw them. Women, muttering in the dark, their voices moving like smoke through the narrow hallway. Some whispered prayers. Some did not speak at all.

I passed cells where thin shadows pressed against the walls, where bodies twisted into themselves, bones sharp beneath skin, faces unrecognizable beneath bruises and filth. I did not look too closely. I was afraid of what I might see.

The guard stopped in front of a large wooden door and pulled a rusted key from his belt.

"She asked for you," he muttered.

There was something in his voice. Not quite amusement, not quite disgust. I did not respond. The lock groaned as he turned the key, and then the door swung open. And I stepped inside.

Zsuzsanna was sitting on the floor when I entered. They had taken everything from her. Her chair, her cot, even the thin blanket she had been given. She had nothing left but the shift she wore and the rusted chains around her wrists.

The prison had hollowed her out. Her face, once sun-darkened and lined with quiet strength, was pale, gaunt, her cheekbones jutting out too sharply, her lips cracked, bloodless.

The bruises had not faded. One darkened the edge of her jaw, a sickly yellow stain beneath her left eye. Her wrists were raw where the irons had bitten into them, her fingers trembling slightly as she shifted. But her eyes were still sharp. Still watching. Still waiting.

"You came," she murmured.

Her voice was quieter than I remembered. Hoarse. As if it had been worn down to the bone. I hesitated.

"I didn't have a choice."

Her lips contorted into something like a smile.

"None of us do," she said softly. "Not anymore."

The door slammed shut behind me. I flinched. She didn't. For a long moment, neither of us spoke. The room was too still. There was no sound except the slow dripping of water from the ceiling, a steady rhythm against the stone.

I took a slow step forward.

"Why did you call for me?"

Zsuzsanna exhaled. Her fingers twitched slightly, the chains rattling with the movement.

"Because you still don't know what you are."

I stiffened.

"What does that mean?"

She studied me, tilting her head slightly.

"If you betray me, you will never be free."

A pause.

"If you don't, you will die."

The words hung between us, heavier than the walls of this prison. I opened my mouth, but no sound came. She waited.

"That's not true," I whispered.

Zsuzsanna smiled again. Slow. Sad. Knowing.

"You think they won't take you?" she murmured. "You think the magistrate doesn't already suspect?"

I swallowed hard.

"They will come for you," she continued. "Maybe not today. Maybe not tomorrow."

She leaned forward slightly, her eyes dark, unreadable.

"But one day, you will wake up, and the guards will be at your door."

Her voice was steady. Matter-of-fact. Like she had already seen it happen. Like she had already accepted it.

"Do you want to live?" she asked simply.

I did not answer. Because I did not know. I did not know if I wanted to live like this. With the pressure of it pressing down on me every day, the fear of it clenching around my ribs, waiting to take me. I swallowed hard.

"I never wanted this," I whispered.

Zsuzsanna closed her eyes briefly, then opened them again.

"I know," she murmured. She exhaled slowly. "You should go."

I hesitated. There was something final in the way she said it. As if we both knew this would be the last time. I turned toward the door. Her voice, softer now.

"Do you regret it?"

I stopped. A long pause. Then, without turning back,

"I don't know."

She sighed. Neither did she.

The guard unlocked the door. The cold air rushed in. I

stepped out. And I did not look back. I walked down the corridor, my steps slow, careful. The walls seemed to press in on me, the knowledge of what had just happened settling over my shoulders like a wool cloak. Outside the cell, the guard smirked at me.

"You look pale," he muttered.

I did not answer. Because I was pale. Because something inside me had just cracked, and I did not know if I could put it back together again.

The air outside was sharp and cold, burning against my skin as I stepped into the open courtyard. The village square was just beyond. The gallows had already been built.

48

THE COURTROOM

I was not the first to take the stand. I had sat in the back of the courtroom for what felt like hours, hands holding the folds of my skirt, back pressed stiffly against the wooden bench. The air inside was close, the scent of burning tallow clinging to the walls like old grief. Outside, the wind howled through the cracks in the stone, rattling the shutters against the building as if even the elements wished to bear witness to what was happening inside.

The magistrate had called witness after witness. First, the men. They had been the most eager to speak.

Some stood with their shoulders squared, speaking of the sickness that had gripped the village, the unnatural deaths that had claimed so many of their fathers, their brothers, their sons.

Others shifted where they stood, their hands wringing their hats, their eyes darting toward their wives in the crowd, uncertain now whether to mourn the men they had lost or to fear the women who had survived them.

"It was them," one of the older men, Janos Boros, declared, his voice hoarse with age and old resentment. "They spoke in whispers. They met in corners. They never mourned."

He spat onto the stone floor.

"I never saw my son get sick. Not once. Then one morning, he is dead in his bed. And his wife ..." He turned, leveling a shaking finger toward the women sitting in their shackles. "She did not cry. She barely seemed surprised."

The prosecutor nodded solemnly, scribbling something onto the parchment in front of him. I did not look at the women. I could feel them without seeing them. Still. Silent. Waiting.

Then came the wives. Some of them cried as they spoke, clutching their shawls tightly around their shoulders, speaking in voices dripping with guilt and shame.

"I never wanted him dead," one woman sobbed, pressing a handkerchief to her mouth. "I never thought ... I never imagined ..."

She broke off. She did not finish her sentence. Because the truth was she had imagined it. They all had. At least once. At least in the quiet corners of their minds, where no one could see, where no one could know.

The prosecutor said nothing for a brief time before nodding, as if he understood. He did not.

And then they called me. I did not expect them to say my name. Not truly.

I had thought I might slip through the cracks, a shadow at the back of the courtroom, nothing more than another pair of eyes watching the inevitable unfold.

But when the magistrate turned toward me, his expression blank, and spoke my name, I knew. I had never been invisible. And I never would be again.

The wooden bench beneath me creaked as I rose, the sound unnaturally loud in the still air. My legs felt stiff, my knees locked, refusing to bend properly as I walked toward the raised platform. I could feel their eyes. The prosecutor. The magistrate. The villagers. And worst of all, the women.

Their gazes pressed against me from where they sat, bound

and waiting, their faces drawn, their eyes sunken with exhaustion and something far worse. Resignation.

I did not dare look at Zsuzsanna. I knew if I did, I would not be able to breathe.

The chair they had placed for me was hard, uncomfortable, its legs uneven against the stone floor. The magistrate watched me carefully, his quill poised over the parchment before him.

"You have lived in Nagyrev your whole life," he said.

Not a question. A statement. I nodded, my throat too dry for words.

The prosecutor stepped forward. A thin man, his hair slicked back, his face pinched in permanent disapproval. He clasped his hands behind his back, tilting his head slightly.

"You were the midwife's apprentice," he said.

Again, not a question. I gripped the edges of my skirt.

"Yes," I whispered.

His lips twitched.

"Then you must have known what she was doing."

The words landed like stones in water. I swallowed hard. This was it. The moment everything had led to. The moment where I could save myself or condemn myself.

"She is guilty," the prosecutor continued, pacing slowly before me. "We have more than enough evidence of that."

He paused, turning toward me.

"But the question is, how many others were involved?"

The quiet that followed was suffocating. The crowd behind me shifted.

I could hear the wooden benches creak, the scrape of boots against stone. Everyone was waiting. Waiting for me to say it. To confirm what they already suspected. To give them another name to carve into the execution list.

I opened my mouth and my heart slammed against my ribs.

I could tell them what they wanted to hear. I could say

Zsuzsanna had worked alone, that I had known nothing, that I was innocent. Or I could tell the truth.

I could tell them how the women of Nagyrev had met in kitchens and back rooms, how they had whispered names in the dark, how they had passed small glass bottles between them like sacred relics.

I could tell them how some had wept as they poured the poison, and how others had smiled. I could tell them everything. But if I did, If I spoke the truth, I would not leave this room alive.

The prosecutor's gaze sharpened.

"Well?" he prompted.

I glanced toward the accused. Toward Ilona, whose lips were pressed into a thin, bitter line. Toward Kata, whose body trembled, whose hands twisted in her lap. And finally, toward Zsuzsanna.

She was not watching the magistrate. She was not watching the prosecutor. She was watching me. Her expression was unreadable. But I knew what she was thinking.

"If you betray me, you will never be free. If you don't, you will die."

My hands trembled against my lap. The prosecutor exhaled sharply.

"Did you know about the murders?" he asked again, slower this time, his voice edged with impatience.

Another shift in the crowd. Another creak of wood. I felt the world closing in around me. And then I opened my mouth to speak. The room waited.

The magistrate's quill hovered over the parchment. The prosecutor's eyes narrowed, expectant. The women stared, unmoving. Somewhere outside, the wind shifted, rattling the windowpanes, a warning, a whisper, a breath of something final.

I took a deep breath. And then I spoke.

49

THE BETRAYAL

I did not know what I was going to say until the words left my mouth. It was not a decision. It was a release.

A breath I had been holding since the first body was exhumed, since the magistrate's men arrived in Nagyrev, since I first watched a woman pour arsenic into her husband's soup and say nothing.

The room was deathly still. The prosecutor's face was tight with expectation, his quill hovering above the parchment, waiting to scratch my words into the record.

I glanced once more at the women. At Ilona, her hands bound in her lap, her eyes hollow but alive. At Kata, trembling. At the others, their faces sunken and pale, but not lost. Then at her.

Zsuzsanna sat perfectly still, her hands resting lightly in her lap, her bruised wrists barely moving as she breathed. Her expression did not change. She had known what I would say before I did. She had known it long before this day, long before this moment.

I felt her eyes upon me; I sensed the quiet urging, the silent lesson that she had been teaching me all along. And so, I did what she had prepared me for. I betrayed her.

"It was Zsuzsanna."

The words felt strange as they left my tongue. Thin, fragile, like glass that had yet to shatter.

I gripped my skirt tighter in my hands. I did not say more. I did not add unnecessary words. I did not explain, did not expand. I did not speak of Ilona, or Kata, or the others.

I did not speak of how the women met in the dark, whispering names over boiling pots, how the bottles of arsenic passed from hand to hand like holy relics, how some wept as they poured, and how others did not.

I did not say how many of them had been desperate. Or how many had enjoyed it. I only gave them her.

For a single heartbeat, nothing happened. Then the room erupted. A roar of voices, overlapping, colliding, shaking the walls of the courthouse with the force of it.

"HANG HER!"

"MURDERER!"

"WITCH!"

The word *witch* cut through the others, repeated again and again, growing louder, carried by the mob like the crackle of fire through dry fields.

"Witch! Witch. Witch!"

It was not just hatred. It was fear. I turned toward the crowd, my breath catching in my throat.

The men who had once been silent in their grief, now furious in their loss. The women who had once been accomplices in whispers, now desperate to separate themselves from the condemned. They all wanted blood. And I had just given them a name to carve into the noose.

I forced myself to look at Zsuzsanna. She had not moved. The cries of the crowd did not touch her, did not reach her. She sat perfectly still, her posture straight, her hands calm against the wooden table before her.

But at the corners of her mouth, a smile. Small. Barely there. But real. A knowing thing. I had done what she wanted. I had learned. Zsuzsanna had always known how this would end. But now, she had made sure that I would survive it. Even if she did not.

The magistrate rapped his hand against the wood.

"Enough!" he bellowed.

The room quieted. The prosecutor turned toward Zsuzsanna.

"Do you deny it?" he asked.

The entire courtroom held its breath.

Zsuzsanna tilted her head slightly, her dark eyes flashing as she regarded him, the look of a woman who had already won, even as the noose waited for her neck. She smiled.

"I have nothing to say," she murmured.

The courtroom roared again. I closed my eyes. I had made my choice. And I did not know if I would ever forgive myself for it. The courtroom was sweltering, though the air outside was cold.

The walls, built of stone, should have kept the heat out, but instead, the room was suffocating. Too many bodies packed together, too many breaths clouding the air, too many emotions —fear, fury, curiosity—saturating the space like a sickness. The light was poor.

Dusty shafts of pale morning sun slanted through the high, narrow windows, illuminating the motes of dust that hung in the air. Shadows stretched long across the wooden benches, where villagers sat pressed together, their shoulders hunched, their faces pinched with expectation. They had come to see justice. Or vengeance. It was impossible to tell the difference.

The magistrate sat in his high-backed chair, stiff as an executioner's blade. His face was angular, sharp, lined with deep creases that made him look as though he had been carved from old, knotted wood. He was an older man, his thinning hair hidden beneath his powdered wig, his mouth a thin, unmoving line.

He looked at Zsuzsanna the way one might look at a wild animal caught in a trap, with something between satisfaction and disdain.

He had been waiting for this moment. We all had.

The prosecutor sat beside him, quill poised, his lips pursed in silent judgment.

I had watched him throughout the trial, had seen the way his small, darting eyes lingered on the accused, lingering longest on the ones who looked the most afraid.

He had a way of twitching his lip just slightly whenever he read a piece of testimony, as if the words themselves disgusted him. A man who enjoyed his work too much.

And now he unrolled a sheet of parchment, its edges curling, yellowed with age. A formal sentence. One that had been written long before this moment.

He cleared his throat and began.

"For the crime of murder," he announced, "for the crime of conspiring to poison the men of this village, and for the crime of bringing shame upon the land of Nagyrev—"

He paused, glancing at the women, his lip twitching. There was no mercy in his face. None at all.

"—you are all sentenced to death by hanging."

The women sat in their chairs like ghosts.

Ilona sobbed first. It was not a scream, not a wail. Just a broken sound, something that had been held back for too long, something that cracked open inside of her and could not be put back together. She covered her face with her bound hands, her shoulders shaking.

Kata followed, shaking so violently she nearly slipped from her chair. She had been terrified from the moment she had been arrested, but now the terror had become something worse. Something final.

The other women did not cry. Not yet. But I could see it in their faces. The realization sinking in, the air becoming suffocating.

There would be no more bargaining. No more denials. This was the end.

The magistrate lifted a second sheet of parchment. His voice was colder this time.

"And as for the midwife, Zsuzsanna Sárkány."

I did not breathe. Zsuzsanna sat motionless, her hands resting lightly in her lap, her bruises standing out like ink against her skin. She did not blink. She did not flinch. She was waiting.

The magistrate studied her, as if deciding whether she was even worth addressing.

Then, with a slow, deliberate breath, he said, "You will hang last."

The room held its breath. Kata made a strangled noise, something that might have been a protest but collapsed into a whimper.

The magistrate continued.

"You will watch each of the others die first. And when it is done"--he leaned forward slightly--"when they are dead, and you have had your fill of what you have done, then we will take you to the gallows."

A cruel sentence. But a calculated one.

The men wanted her to suffer. To see it. To feel it. They wanted her to break. She did not. Zsuzsanna turned, slow, measured, and then smiled. Not a wild, unhinged smile. Not a smirk of defiance. Just—acceptance.

"Is that all?" she asked, her voice smooth, even.

The magistrate's face darkened. The prosecutor's quill

scraped furiously against the parchment. The courtroom erupted into murmurs, gasps, another round of whispers.

"She's a devil."

"She's not even afraid."

"A demon wearing a woman's skin."

Zsuzsanna ignored them.

She turned her head, slowly, deliberately and looked at me. I had been spared. I knew it before the magistrate spoke, before the words were even formed. But I did not feel relief. I felt empty. I felt cold.

And when the magistrate turned to me, his voice an afterthought, dismissing me in only a few clipped words: "You are free to go."

I felt nothing. Because the truth was, I had already been sentenced, too. I would carry this day with me until the end of my life. And I did not know if I would ever live again.

50

SOMETHING IN THE AIR

The village was different now. It was quieter. Emptier.

Not in the way of houses abandoned or fields left to grow wild, but something deeper, something that could not be seen, only felt. The hush that hung over the streets was not a peaceful one. It was unnatural, like the pause between thunder and lightning. A silence born not of absence but of something taken, something buried.

There were no more whispers in doorways, no more quiet gatherings at the well, no more women who met each other's eyes with knowing looks, with the faintest flicker of understanding. The well-worn paths between homes, once softened by the tread of secret steps, seemed sharper now, more exposed. Even the trees lining the outskirts of the village stood differently, their skeletal branches twisted and reaching as if to grasp at something unseen.

Secrets had been the breath of Nagyrev. Now, the village was suffocating.

They had built the gallows just beyond the churchyard. Not inside the village square. No, that would have been too close, too real. Instead, it was placed at the edge of the fields, where the river could still be seen in the distance, its slow-moving current reflecting the dull winter sky. It stood stark and black against the pale horizon, the rough-hewn wood still fresh, splintered in places where the executioner's saw had worked too hastily. The structure loomed like an omen, a terrible punctuation mark at the end of a sentence that had already been written.

The judge stood beneath it, dressed in his finest black coat, his hands gloved in kid leather. He was a tall man, narrow-faced, with a mouth that barely moved when he spoke. His eyes were small and black, set too deep into his face, as if he had been carved from something lifeless. He did not blink as he surveyed the gathered crowd, nor did he acknowledge the condemned. His presence was cold, clinical, the slow tap of his fingers against his sleeve the only sign of life within him.

He enjoyed this. Not justice, not order, this.

He liked the spectacle of it, the way the village gathered in clusters, shoulders hunched, expressions tight with dread and grim satisfaction. He liked the waiting. The way the condemned were paraded through the cold, thin and trembling, but still alive, for now. The way quiet fell just before the final moment, that breath before the drop, the hush of inevitability.

I stood at the back of the crowd, wrapped in my shawl, the wind biting at my cheeks. I did not want to be here. But I had to be. I had made this happen. And I would not look away.

The village square was full, a great, heaving mass of people standing shoulder to shoulder, packed so tightly that the air itself felt thick with breath, with heat, with anticipation. The scaffold loomed high above us, its wooden beams dark with mould, the ropes swaying slightly in the breeze.

The sky was gray, the sun struggling behind the clouds, its light pale and thin. There was no warmth here. No softness.

The women were led to the platform one by one. I knew them all.

Had grown up beside some of them, had fetched water with them, had whispered with them at the well. Had watched them shed tears and shed blood, had seen the bruises they had hidden, had felt the burden of their secrets because I carried them too.

But now, their faces were pale and drawn, their wrists bound in front of them, their dresses neat, as if someone had tried to make them presentable before their deaths.

Some walked with pride, heads high, their gazes defiant. Some walked like ghosts, already gone, already emptied of whatever had made them real. Some wept. Some whispered prayers.

And then there was Zsuzsanna. She did not cry. She did not beg. She only lifted her chin as she walked, her dark eyes scanning the crowd, searching for something. For someone.

I wanted to believe she was looking for me. I wanted to believe she was saying goodbye. But maybe she was just looking for the sky. Maybe she just wanted to see something beautiful before the end.

The priest muttered his last rites. The magistrate stood stiffly at the edge of the scaffold, his expression hard, unmoved, like a man who had long since grown accustomed to death.

And then, I felt it.

A gaze. A presence. Not from the scaffold. From the crowd. I turned and there he was. Ádám.

I had not expected him to be here. But maybe I should have.

His coat was damp at the shoulders, his boots caked with mud, as if he had traveled far to stand in this place. His face was thinner than I remembered, his jaw more defined, his dark curls unruly as if he had barely slept.

But his eyes were the same. Deep, dark, unchanged, and they were fixed on me.

He did not move. He did not speak. But his presence was

louder than the murmurs of the crowd, louder than the priest's prayer, louder than the restless shifting of boots against muddy earth.

Why are you here? I wanted to ask.

But I already knew. He had not come for revenge. He had not come for justice. He had come because he needed to see it for himself. The truth of it. The end of it.

And as we stood there, the space between us teeming with everything we had never said, I realized something. This was the last time I would ever see him. The last time our paths would ever cross. And we both knew it.

The scaffold groaned beneath their feet. A hush fell over the crowd. I turned back, forcing myself to watch. Forcing myself to see. The ropes were tightened.

Ilona went first. She was pale, but she did not fight. She did not struggle as the rope was tightened around her neck, as the executioner—a man from Szolnok, not one of our own, for who would have taken that job?—pulled the knot firm, as her hands were bound at her sides. Her lips trembled, her mouth shaping a prayer.

The judge watched her closely, his gloved hands folded in front of him, his head tilted ever so slightly, as if admiring a painting. The executioner adjusted the rope, pulling it taut, his hands practiced, indifferent. Ilona's chest rose and fell in rapid succession, but she did not resist. She exhaled once, as if she had been waiting for this moment all along.

Then the lever was pulled. A short drop. A snap. And then, stillness.

The sound of the body settling was somehow worse than the drop itself. The sudden slackness, the limp sway of limbs, the absence of anything human. The crowd did not cheer. They only watched. Faces like stone. Some of the men whispered amongst themselves, but no one moved. A dog barked somewhere in the distance, high and sharp, its sound cutting through the silence like a blade.

The others followed. One by one.

Kata screamed. She begged. She fought so hard that two guards had to hold her still as the noose was placed around her neck, as her feet scraped against the wooden planks. She writhed, twisting against the bonds that held her, her breath coming in ragged gasps.

"I didn't do it!" she shrieked. "I didn't do it!"

No one answered her.

The judge raised his hand. The executioner nodded.

When the lever was pulled, her legs kicked violently, her body jerking, her last moments messy, desperate, ugly. The strangled sound she made in those final seconds did not seem real. A noise that should never come from a human throat. And the judge, he smiled. Just slightly. A curl at the corner of his mouth. He was enjoying this.

When I turned back, Ádám was gone.

There was only an empty space where he had been. An empty space that would remain. Forever. I did not know if he had left before Kata had taken her last breath. I did not know if he had turned away in grief, or if he had watched until the very end. But I did know this, I would never see him again. And somehow, that hurt worse than all the rest.

Zsuzsanna had been forced to watch them all die. She had been brought out last, her hands still bound, her expression unreadable. She was made to stand beneath the gallows, the hems of her skirts brushing against the bodies that swayed above the dirt. The others had sobbed, had pleaded, had cursed. But she did not flinch. She did not look away. Not when Ilona fell. Not when Kata kicked and fought. Not when the last woman went limp, the wind swaying their bodies like rotten fruit hanging from a tree.

She only breathed. And then she turned her head, slowly, toward the judge. And she smiled.

I went to the prison that night. I asked to see her. The guard barely looked up from his seat by the fire, his boots stretched out, a tin cup of brandy in his hand.

"She doesn't want to see you," he said simply.

The words hit harder than I expected. Hadn't she wanted this? Hadn't she taught me to do it? Hadn't she prepared me for this very moment? And yet she would not even look at me.

I turned away. And that night, I did not sleep well. The first nightmare came as soon as I closed my eyes. I was back at the gallows. But the village was empty.

The bodies still swayed, but there was no one to watch them, no judge, no crowd, only me.

I stepped closer. The ropes creaked as the wind shifted. And then they turned their heads.

Their faces, blackened, swollen, turned toward me, their eyes bulging, lips parting, as if they still wanted to speak.

Then Zsuzsanna stepped forward. She was not hanged. She was alive. She stood beneath the gallows, looking up, watching the bodies sway.

And then she turned to me.

"You made your choice," she murmured.

I tried to speak. I could not. She smiled. And then the rope fell around my throat.

I woke gasping for air, my hands clawing at my own neck, my skin soaked with sweat. The room was too quiet. The village was too quiet. It would never be the same again. And neither would I.

51

THE LETTER

The letter arrived in the early morning, slipped beneath my door like something shameful, like something that had crawled through the night unseen. I did not hear footsteps. Whoever had delivered it had been careful, silent. They had not knocked, had not lingered.

The faint rustle of paper against wood. At first, I thought I had imagined it.

I had spent the night in half-waking, twisting in my sheets, trapped between nightmares and the cold echo of the house. My body ached, not from illness, but from exhaustion, from lying still for too long.

I had not left my bed since the executions began. I had barely moved, barely eaten, barely existed. My world had shrunk to the four walls of my home, the stiff sheets against my skin, the candle burned to a stub beside my bed.

The air was stale, permeated by the scent of wax and sweat. The hearth had gone cold. The shutters were drawn, but through the thin slats, the morning light seeped in; pale, watery, the color of old bone. The sky beyond was overcast, the kind of dull, swollen gray that promised rain but never delivered it.

I had long since stopped listening for voices outside. The village no longer whispered with the murmur of conversation, with the quiet conspiracies of women exchanging glances at the well, with the clatter of hooves on the road. There was nothing left to whisper about.

Nagyrev had been hollowed out. And yet here it was. A letter. A last breath from the condemned.

It was folded neatly, the edges crisp despite its journey. The paper was thin, coarse beneath my fingers, the ink darker than it should have been, as if the words had been written in the dim glow of a prison cell.

My hands shook as I reached for it. The seal was unbroken. A plain, wax-stamped fold, the color a faded, murky red.

It felt heavy, though it could not have weighed more than a few ounces. A thing like this should have been heavy.

I hesitated. Then I broke the seal. And she spoke to me for the last time.

You did as I asked.

No greeting. No softness. Just the plain truth, unadorned, unyielding.

I traced the words with my fingertips, feeling the indentations where the pen had pressed too hard against the paper, as if she had carved the words into the page rather than written them.

The ink had bled slightly, as if moisture had touched it before it had dried.

Had her hands trembled as she wrote it? Had she pressed her fingers against the ink, smearing it in places?

I could see her so clearly, sitting on the hard stone floor of her cell, her back straight, her hair tangled, her wrists bruised from the shackles.

She had never been one for despair. She would not have wept as she wrote this. She would not have hesitated. She would have written as she had always spoken, with certainty.

I have always known how this would end. I knew it before they dragged us from our homes, before they built the gallows, before you opened your mouth in the courtroom. I knew it the day I put arsenic into my husband's tea.

I closed my eyes. I had not wanted to think about her husband, about the man whose death had set everything into motion. I had never known his name. She had never spoken it to me. She had never asked for pity. Not when she killed him. Not now.

They think I fear death.

They think they have won.

They are fools.

My breath caught.

I could hear her voice in my head, calm, almost amused, the way she had looked at the judge beneath the gallows, the way she had watched the other women fall one by one and had not looked away.

Men have always thought they could control us with their laws. With their rules. With their nooses. But we have always found ways to live beyond them, haven't we?

We chose our own lives.

And now, we choose our own deaths.

There was no regret in her words. No grief. Only the truth as she saw it. I gripped the paper so tightly it crumpled beneath my fingers.

There was a smear of ink where my thumb had pressed too hard against the last lines, as if I could erase them, as if I could take them back. But the words would not change. Nothing would change.

I will not see you in this life again.

The sentence was stark. Final. My hands trembled. I had done what she asked. I had betrayed her because she wanted me to. Because she had taught me how to survive.

But why, then, did it feel so wrong? Why did it sit in my stomach like poison, spreading, filling my lungs until I could not breathe?

You were a good apprentice. I hope you will not be a fool.

Then:

Live, young one. If you can.

. . .

She did not sign her name. She did not need to.

I let the letter slip from my fingers. It fluttered to the wooden floor, landing near the dying embers of the hearth. The fire had gone out overnight, but the coals still held a whisper of heat, a faint glow in the ashes.

For a brief, absurd moment, I thought about throwing the letter into the flames. Watching it curl, blacken, disappear into nothing. But I didn't.

Because even as I sat there, staring at the broken seal, at the words written in a careful, steady hand, I realized I could not let them go. I could not unwrite them. I could not unlive them. I could not forget them. Because they were not just her last words.

They were a warning. And I did not know if I would ever be able to do as she asked.

Winter had melted into spring. Spring had dried into summer. Summer had transitioned into autumn, and still, Zsuzsanna lived.

A full year had passed since the women were hanged, since the nooses swung heavy with the weight of their crimes, since the village had gathered to watch the poisoners put to death.

But not her. Not the midwife. The judge had sentenced her to something worse. She would wait. She would rot in the prison, knowing that every breath she took was stolen, that every sunrise was one she was never meant to see. And the village village waited with her.

I had not seen her since the day she refused me. I had not gone back to the prison. I had not asked again. I had told myself that she was already gone, that she was as good as dead, that the waiting did not matter. But the waiting did matter. I thought about it more than I wanted to.

I thought about the cell where she sat; dark, her body wasting away in the filth, her breath misting in the cold air, her bones sharp beneath thin, rotting fabric.

I thought about her wrists, raw from the iron shackles, the way her fingers must have been clenched to keep her hands from shaking.

I imagined the hunger, the endless gnawing, the way the prison must have smelled. Of piss, of sweat, of despair.

I pictured the rats, their small, yellow teeth flashing as they scurried between the stones. The guards, their faces hard, their hands rough and cruel.

Did they beat her? Did they mock her, spit at her, call her the names the villagers had screamed? Did she still smile that strange, knowing smile? Did she still hold onto whatever strength she had left? Or had they broken her at last?

I woke up that morning with a suffocating feeling.

The village had grown too quiet. There was no life in it anymore. Not the kind that had once kept it turning. The secrets, the whispers, the quiet nods passed between women in the marketplace. Now, everything felt stretched thin, brittle. People spoke less.

Men, once loud in the tavern, now sat hunched over their drinks, staring into the dregs as if the answers to their suspicions might float to the surface. The women did not meet each other's eyes. Their heads were bowed, their steps quick, as if their very existence was something to apologize for.

The streets felt colder. Even when the sun burned hot in the sky, there was something lifeless in the way the air settled over the rooftops.

It was as if the gallows had taken something more than the women's lives. Something unseen. Something vital. I could not stand it any longer. And so, I went to the graves.

The graveyard sat at the edge of the village, beyond the last row of houses, where the trees began to fill out, the earth sloping toward the river.

It was old. Older than the village itself, perhaps. Some of the headstones had long since crumbled, nothing but jagged stumps of stone jutting from the earth.

Others remained, standing crooked and half-sunk into the dirt, their carved names softened by wind and rain, unreadable except to those who had once known them.

I stepped carefully between the rows, the ground uneven beneath my boots. The leaves had begun to turn, dry and brittle, like the last remnants of something long dead.

The graves were at the back, hidden away from the rest. Not forgotten. Just unwanted. There had been no markers, no headstones. Just five shallow mounds of earth. The soil had begun to settle, sinking slightly where the bodies had been placed.

There were no flowers. No offerings. Nothing to suggest that anyone had mourned them. I stood at the edge of Ilona's grave.

I tried to remember the sound of her voice, but all I could hear was the way she had sobbed when the noose tightened.

I looked at Kata's grave and thought of how her body had kicked, how her fingers had clawed at the rope in those last, desperate moments.

And the others, their names already fading from my mind, as if the village itself had swallowed them whole.

Had they expected this? To be erased? To be buried beneath dirt that no one would tend? Had they known that this was always the end?

I felt it then, the presence of Zsuzsanna's letter in my pocket.

I had carried it with me every day since it arrived, folded neatly, worn soft at the edges where my fingers had traced the creases over and over again. I had memorized her words, though I did not want to.

She had told me to live. But what kind of life was this? A life of waiting? Of watching the village rot from the inside out? Of knowing that very soon she, too, would be placed in the dirt?

I closed my eyes and listened. The trees whispered above me, their brittle leaves shivering in the wind. The river murmured in the distance, its slow, steady breath snaking through the reeds.

I opened my mouth. But I said nothing. Because there was nothing left to say.

52

THE WEIGHT OF SILENCE

Winter came again, dragging its cold fingers through the streets of Nagyrev, settling into the spaces where voices once lived. The village was quieter than ever, its silence no longer expectant but final.

I still dreamed of the poison.

It came in different forms; dripping from my fingers like honey, swirling in cups of tea, soaking into the cracks of the floor like spilled milk. Sometimes it was colorless, odorless, invisible as breath. Sometimes it was dark, staining my hands until no amount of scrubbing could wash it away.

In the worst of the dreams, I was not the one mixing it. I was the one drinking.

The dream was always the same. I sat at a wooden table, my hands resting in my lap, my throat dry, my stomach turning. Across from me sat Zsuzsanna, watching. Her eyes were dark and endless, the corners of her mouth twisted in that faint, knowing smile.

"Drink."

Her voice was soft. Kind.

I reached for the cup. The porcelain was cool against my

palms, the rim pressing lightly against my lips. The liquid inside was clear, clean, no different from water.

I could feel her watching me.

"Go on."

I swallowed. A warmth spread through my body first, pleasant, almost soothing. Then came the burn.

It crawled up my throat, eating me from the inside out. My breath came fast, uneven. The cup slipped from my fingers, shattering on the floor, the liquid seeping into the cracks.

Zsuzsanna did not move. She only watched.

"Now you understand," she whispered.

I always woke with the taste of it on my tongue, metallic, bitter. My body drenched in sweat, my mouth dry as dust. I would sit upright in my bed, staring into the darkness, my hands gripping the sheets as if I still had a choice.

But I knew the truth. There was no escaping it. The poison had seeped into the bones of this village. And into mine. The village never fully recovered.

It changed in small ways first. The well where the women used to gather fell silent. The market became a place of necessity, not conversation. The church pews, once filled with whispered prayers and exchanged glances, sat empty more often than not. The roads, once worn smooth by the shuffle of feet and the turning of carts, seemed rougher, untouched for days at a time.

Some of the men left, disappearing into other towns, remarrying elsewhere, pretending they had never lived among us. The ones who stayed became quieter, duller, hunched with suspicion. They watched their wives too closely now, flinching at the meals set before them, sniffing the water in their cups as if they expected the past to rise up and choke them. And the women became shadows.

They moved differently now, their backs bowed, their heads

low, their voices softer. They did not linger in the marketplace, did not whisper at the wells. Their laughter was gone. There were no more secrets. But there was no freedom in that. Only absence. A hollow where something had once been.

I could feel it pressing against my ribs whenever I walked through the village, whenever I stepped outside and caught the scent of wet earth, of cold wind blowing through the fields. The kind of silence that meant something had been taken, and there was no one left to mourn it.

Nagyrev had been carved open, its insides laid bare, and now we all lived inside its emptiness.

The men who remained tried to move forward. They told themselves that the village was safe again, that the danger had been rooted out, that the women they had killed had been the rot in the foundation. But the rot was still there. It had only gone deeper, eating into the walls, settling into the earth, waiting for the right moment to rise again.

I had become the midwife now.

The first time a woman came to me, knocking softly at my door, it had been just after the last snowfall, when the earth was still frozen and the trees stood naked against the sky. She was young, barely more than a girl, her hands clutched over the swell of her belly, her face drawn with fear.

I had not answered at first. I had stood at the window, watching her shift from foot to foot, her breath curling in the cold air. Then, I let her in.

I boiled the water. I gathered the linens. I heard Zsuzsanna's voice in my head, steady and clear, telling me what to do. And when the child was born, red-faced and wailing, slick with life, something inside me twisted.

I had done this before, but never alone. Never without her hands guiding mine, without her presence at my back.

The mother looked up at me, eyes shining with relief, with

something close to gratitude. And for a moment, I thought about the other women who had come to Zsuzsanna before her.

The ones who had sat in that same chair. The ones who had clutched at their stomachs, not with life, but with bruises. With fear.

The ones who had left with small bottles pressed into their palms, glass catching the light like a promise.

I sent the girl home with her child. I did not think about how easily things could have been different. How, in another time, under different circumstances, I might have placed something else in her hands.

More women came. Not many. But enough. Enough to keep me busy, to keep me distracted, to keep the memories from creeping in at night when the house was quiet and the candle burned low.

I did not speak of the past. Neither did they. There were no questions. Only careful glances.

Only the quiet understanding that some things had changed, but some things would always remain.

I still walked past the prison sometimes. I did not stop. I did not ask.

But I knew she was still there. I knew she was still waiting. And I did not know what it would mean when that waiting was finally over.

53

THE LAST LESSON

The gallows had stood waiting for her for a year.

It had been there through the seasons. Through winter's first ice, through spring's hesitant thaw, through summer's suffocating heat. It had remained standing as the leaves fell from the trees, as the river's edge hardened with frost, as the village learned to breathe again in its hushed, fractured way.

It had waited for her longer than it had waited for any of the others.

And now so had I. I had dreamed of this day.

Sometimes, in the restless haze of sleep, I saw her walk to the gallows and turn away from me at the last moment. Sometimes, the rope tightened, the lever was pulled, and she did not fall. She only stood there, smile at the edges of her lips as if she had always been one step ahead, as if she had never needed saving.

But the morning of her execution was not a dream. It was bitterly real.

The sky was dull and overcast, the clouds stretched thin and pale like washed-out linen, the wind sharp against my face as I pulled my shawl tighter around my shoulders. The village had gathered again, though not in the way it had for the others. There was no frenzy this time. No hissing whispers passing between lips, no shouts of "Witch! Murderer!" ringing through the air.

Instead, there was quiet. The kind that filled the spaces between ribs, that settled in the hollow of a throat, that felt like something foreshadowing an ending, a reckoning. For her.

The judge was there again, standing beneath the gallows, his black coat buttoned to his throat, his gloved hands folded before him, his expression as impassive as ever. His polished boots barely disturbed the frostbitten ground, his stance too precise, too careful, like a man posing for an artist's rendering of justice.

If he felt any satisfaction in this final act, he did not show it. Perhaps it was not enough to him, this last hanging, this final breath stolen from a woman who had refused to break.

Perhaps he had hoped she would have withered in her cell, that time itself would have done what his verdict could not.

But Zsuzsanna was still standing. Still strong. Even now, as they brought her forward, her wrists bound, her steps slow but steady, she did not stumble. She climbed the steps as if they had been built for her alone.

The rope was waiting. And so was I.

The air felt cloying, the cold pressing in, weighing against my skin as I watched her ascend.

She did not look at the judge. She did not look at the executioner, who stood waiting beside her, his face a blank slate, his hands practiced in the art of taking life. She did not look at the crowd, at the men who had once feared her, at the women who had once come to her in the dead of night, whispering their husbands' names like prayers, pressing silver coins into her palm.

She looked at me. Her eyes found mine. They were dark, sharp, endless. The same way they had been the first time I had met her, when I was little more than a girl, awkward in my movements, naive to the ways of the world.

The same way they had been when she placed a bundle of herbs in my hands and told me, "Watch closely."

The same way they had been when she whispered, "Some of us are born knowing how we will die."

And now, she knew. She had always known. And she smiled. Not a smirk, not a grimace, not a mask for fear. A real, quiet smile. The kind meant only for me. Her last lesson.

The executioner tightened the noose around her throat. The coarse rope pressed into her skin, marking her, cutting into the delicate hollow of her collarbone, framing her jaw like the hands of a lover.

The fibers, darkened from years of use, wrapped tightly, firm against her throat, yet she did not flinch. She only let out a slow, measured breath, the kind that comes before sleep, or death, or something in between.

The wind stilled. The world held its breath. I held mine. And the lever was pulled.

She fell.

The rope jerked, snapping her back, her body suspended in midair.

A single, brief struggle. Her feet twitching once, twice, the last remnants of life still clinging.

And then, nothing. Stillness. A life ending in the space of a breath.

I did not move. I did not look away. Because she had not looked away from me.

I do not know how long I stood there.

The village had begun to move again; men dispersing, boots scuffing against the frozen ground, women glancing at one another but saying nothing. The judge had already turned away, his coat snapping in the wind as he strode back toward the village square, his duty fulfilled.

But I stayed. I watched as her body was lowered, as the executioner's knife sliced through the rope, as she crumpled to the frozen dirt with the finality of a felled tree.

A shudder ran through me.

Not from the cold. Not from fear. From the realization that she had never been afraid at all.

When I finally stepped forward, the executioner was already cutting her down. I almost told him to stop. To leave her there a little longer. To let the wind rock her gently, to let the village hold her in its grip just a moment more.

But the blade sliced through the rope. And she collapsed. And just like that, she was gone.

I walked home alone. The wind had picked up again, whispering through the trees, twisting through the narrow streets of Nagyrev, lifting the dead leaves in quiet spirals along the dirt roads.

I could hear it in my ears, in my lungs, in the space where words should have been. I wanted to say something. To speak her name. To let her exist in the air one last time.

But my throat was tight. And I had no words left. So, I let the silence have her. Let it take her into the bones of the village, into the soil beneath my feet, into the sky above the gallows.

And when I reached my house, stepping inside, staring at the wooden chair she had once sat in, at the fire that no longer burned, at the shadows stretching long across the floor.

I whispered into the emptiness.

"We thought we were angels."

The wind howled against the windowpane, sighing. The sky, pale and endless, did not answer.

I swallowed, closing my eyes. "We were not."

EPILOGUE

I am dead.

I was dead the moment the rope tightened.

There was no pain, only pressure. A sharp, brief jolt as the world lurched, as the trapdoor beneath my feet gave way, as my body fought for a breath that would never come. Then nothing.

I did not struggle. I did not beg. I did not disgrace myself.

I had seen men and women hang before, their bodies twitching, their faces turning shades no living flesh should be. I had seen their legs kick, their fingers claw uselessly at the air.

I did not kick. I did not claw. I simply let the world take what it had always intended to take.

I had long since made my peace with death. I had known from the moment the first husband died that it would come for me eventually. The men would not stand for it forever.

They had not stood for it at all, not really. They had been blind. They had been stupid. That was what had saved us for so long. Not secrecy, not caution, but simple stupidity.

For years, they buried their fathers, their brothers, their sons, and they never thought to question why.

A bad stomach. A sickness of the lungs. A weak heart, a curse, the will of God.

They believed every word of it. Because men like to believe that death is natural. That it comes when it is meant to. That they are not so easily undone.

And so, we let them believe it. And one by one, we led them to their graves.

There is no use regretting it now. What's done is done. They died. We lived. That is all history will remember, if history remembers anything at all. There is no justice. No fairness. No grand meaning behind any of it. Only this: they had power and we took it.

I watch the village now. Nothing has changed. Not truly.

The men still work the fields. The women still tend the homes. The river still moves in its slow, winding path, carrying reeds and fish and bones toward places no one here will ever see.

If the ground remembers us, it does not say so. If the trees still whisper our names, no one listens. Even the graveyard does not mourn us.

The crosses are thin and rotting, the names carved into the wood already softening, fading under rain and wind and time.

We are not legend. We are not even warning. We are nothing.

I watch my apprentice. She is older now. Her hair is streaked with gray. Her shoulders are not as straight as they once were. She is alone.

She does not carry a husband's name. She does not carry a child on her hip. She carries only herself and the burden of things she cannot speak. She still tends to the sick. She still walks the village roads at dawn and at dusk, a basket on her arm, her eyes lowered, her step quiet. She does not speak of me. But sometimes, when she is alone, she turns her head suddenly, as if expecting to see a figure in the corner of her eye.

She never does. But I am there. Always. I do not pray. But if I did, I would pray for this:

That she never meets a man like my husband.

That she never learns what I learned.

That she never has to place her hands on a bottle and wonder if she is strong enough to use it.

I would pray that she never hears the sound of a body hitting the floor.

That she never learns how easy it is.

That she never learns how quickly it becomes easier.

I would pray that she sleeps at night.

I would pray that when her time comes, it is gentle. That she goes in her bed, with warm blankets and the scent of dried lavender, with a hand holding hers, with someone whispering that she was loved.

Not like me. Not with a noose. Not with a crowd watching. I do not regret what we did, what I did.

Not the first death. Not the last. Not a single one in between.

There is no use regretting survival. We took what was never meant to be ours, and for a long, sweet time, we won. That should be enough. It has to be enough. And yet, I do not want to be forgotten.

I do not want my name to rot in the earth. I do not want our work to fade into dust. I do not want the stories to stop. I do not want the world to move on. I do not want to wonder if it was all for nothing. And I think for the first time, in death, in nothingness, I am afraid. I will forever be afraid that my name will be forgotten.

So, when you close your eyes at night, and you tuck your children into their beds, and your husbands return home from work, whisper my name.

Remember that abuse is not to be tolerated.

Remember you are not alone. I am here. I have always been here. I am you. And I remain. Watching.

The End

ACKNOWLEDGEMENT

The Angel Makers of Nagyrév were a group of women in early 20th-century Hungary who engaged in a series of poisonings, leading to the deaths of numerous men in their village.

In the village of Nagyrév, starting around 1911, midwife Zsuzsanna Fazekas began providing women with arsenic derived from boiling flypaper. This poison was used to kill husbands and other male relatives, especially those who were abusive or unwanted. The isolated nature of the village and the complicity of local officials allowed these activities to continue undetected for years.

Estimates of the number of victims vary. Some sources suggest around 40 deaths were confirmed, while others claim the number could be as high as 300. The true figure remains uncertain due to the secretive nature of the crimes and limited documentation.

The poisonings came to light in 1929 after an anonymous letter prompted authorities to investigate. Exhumations of several bodies revealed lethal doses of arsenic. Subsequently, 51 women were arrested, and several were tried and convicted. Fazekas, the midwife who facilitated the poisonings, reportedly committed suicide before she could be arrested.

The events in Nagyrév have been the subject of various cultural works, including the documentary film *The Angelmakers* (2005), which explores the motivations and societal conditions that led to the poisonings.

The women of Nagyrev, Hungary, who were convicted of

poisoning their husbands and other men in the early 20th century, were executed by hanging in 1929. However, there is little detailed information on what happened to their bodies after execution.

While many were arrested, only a few were sentenced to death, and others received prison terms. Some of the accused, including Fazekas herself, committed suicide before they could be arrested or tried.

No one knows for certain what inspired this group of women to do what they did. The motives remain a mystery, but one thing is know for sure, they will forever be known as The Angel Makers of Nagyrev.

Printed in Dunstable, United Kingdom

84576525R00170